deep in death
A SHELBY NICHOLS ADVENTURE

Colleen Helme

Book Cover Art by Damonza.com Copyright © 2014 by Colleen Helme
Book Layout ©2013 BookDesignTemplates.com

Deep In Death/ Colleen Helme. -- 1st ed.
ISBN 978-1500367220
ISBN 1500367222

Dedication

To Mom and Dad
With love

ACKNOWLEDGMENTS

Once again, I would like to thank my wonderful family for all of your support and enthusiasm! A huge thanks to Melissa Gamble for being my alpha-reader and all around idea bouncer. I couldn't do this without you and your wonderful insights! Another big thanks to Kristin Monson for your fantastic edits and attention to detail. You make this a better book. Thanks to Damonza.com for the fabulous book cover! Last, but not least, thanks to all of my special fans whose words of encouragement keep me writing, I hope you enjoy this next adventure!

Shelby Nichols Adventures

Carrots
Fast Money
Lie or Die
Secrets that Kill
Trapped by Revenge
Deep in Death
Crossing Danger
Devious Minds
Hidden Deception
Laced in Lies
Deadly Escape
Marked for Murder
Ghostly Serenade

Devil in a Black Suit ~ A Ramos Story
A Midsummer Night's Murder ~ A Shelby Nichols
Novella

Contents

Chapter 1

A twinge of pain burned through my arm, and I gently rubbed the spot where I'd been shot nearly three weeks ago. Getting a shot in the arm may sound like a simple thing for most people, but when it's done by a bullet, it's a whole different story. At least it was healing nicely, and the scar wasn't too big, but every once in a while my arm ached like it had happened yesterday, probably because I was overdoing it again. After a few seconds the pain subsided, and I finished pulling on my shirt and got dressed.

Today was my first day back at work since the shooting, and I was ready to take on a new project. This time the job was a client from my consulting agency, which suited me just fine. My last job for Uncle Joey, the local mob-boss, had gotten me both arrested for murder and shot by a bullet in the arm, so I was a little nervous about doing anything for him again.

A few months ago I had to tell Uncle Joey my secret that I could read minds so he wouldn't kill me. We'd worked out a compromise, and over the course of our association, we'd even become close. Crazy as it sounded, I'd started to think of him as my real uncle, even though he wasn't. Since most of his errands seemed to get me into trouble, he'd also saved my life a few times. Well, to be honest, it was his hit-man, Ramos, doing most of the saving. But it was Uncle Joey who'd told him to watch out for me.

I sighed every time I thought of Ramos. He had a troubled past which only I knew about, and I'd helped him come to terms with it. Besides saving my life several times, there was also a physical attraction that I only dared admit out loud to my best friend, Holly. Of course after seeing him, she had a crush on him too, and since we were both happily married, I had to think it was all right. But with all of that going on, I had to wonder about myself. I mean, Uncle Joey was a big, bad mob-boss who had threatened to do me bodily harm, and Ramos was his hit-man. They were the bad guys and I had a soft spot in my heart for them. Was something wrong with me?

My husband, Chris, had no qualms about severing all ties with Uncle Joey, and it put me in a hard spot trying to please them both. But since the last job, things had changed. After I got shot, Chris had a long talk with Uncle Joey, and I hadn't heard from him in three weeks. In some ways it was a relief, but in others, I kind of missed him...and Ramos...well...mostly Ramos. Still, I wasn't about to call and offer my services. Not considering what had happened last time. Nope. I wasn't ready to get shot again. In fact, I would be pretty happy if I never saw another gun in my life.

I took a deep cleansing breath and checked the time. I had an appointment with my client at ten this morning, and it was time to go. Her name was Tiffany and this was her senior year of college. Since I didn't have a real office, I'd told her we could meet at the campus library in-between her classes, and with her busy schedule, meeting on campus worked out great for both of us.

I drove through town with my windows down and breathed in the crisp fall air. It was the first part of October and the sky was the perfect color of blue. The trees were just beginning to change into brilliant autumn colors, and framed against the blue sky, the pure beauty and serenity lifted my spirits. With everything I'd gone through lately, I knew I was lucky to be alive.

I parked at the visitor parking meters near the library and headed toward the front of the building. It had been several years since I'd been there last, and a wave of nostalgia washed over me. I'd only been to one year of college before I'd talked Chris into marrying me. It was love at first sight for me, but it had taken some gentle persuading on my part to help Chris see how perfect we were together. Right after our marriage, we'd gone off to law school in another state. Josh had been born exactly nine months later followed by Savannah two years after that. There were times when I regretted not finishing college back then, but I wouldn't trade the life I had now for anything.

I loved my family and, as it turned out, I had a pretty good career without a degree, and I was proud of what I'd accomplished. Of course, if I hadn't gotten shot in the head during a bank robbery, which left me with the ability to read minds, it might be a different story.

It was still hard for me to believe how my life had turned upside down simply because I'd stopped at the grocery store for some carrots. Who would have thought? Now I had my own consulting agency where I could get paid for helping people, and most of the time, all I had to do was read their minds. Not that it was always that easy, but after getting shot, I'd take some simple cases for a while.

A young woman sat on a bench near the fountain where we'd planned to meet. Her gaze caught mine and her eyes widened slightly before she recognized me. As I approached, she smiled and gave me a quick wave. She had long blond hair and a sweet face, but her somber eyes seemed out of place for someone her age, like she'd gone through some hard times.

Since she was a college student, I was a little nervous that she couldn't afford my one-hundred-and-fifty-dollar-an-hour fee. But we'd talked about that before I had agreed to meet her, and she'd seemed fine with it then. She stood to greet me.

"Shelby Nichols? Hi. I'm Tiffany Shaw. Thanks for meeting me."

"Hi Tiffany, nice to meet you in person," I answered.

"I know this is kind of informal, but it's such a beautiful day. Do you mind staying out here in the sunshine?"

"I think that's a great idea."

"Good." She resumed her seat on the bench and I sat beside her. She was thinking that she wasn't sure how to start. What she needed might not even be possible, but she'd read about me in the paper and figured if anyone could help her, it was me. She'd been saving up for years to hire a private investigator and wanted the best. After a little digging, she'd heard rumors that I had premonitions. It didn't faze her in the least. In fact, after all this time, she thought it might be the only thing that would solve the case. She just had to make sure her dad didn't find out, since he was the over-protective sort. He'd tell her she was throwing away her money, and probably accuse me of taking advantage of her.

That certainly put a lot of pressure on me, and my stomach tightened with dread that her father would disapprove. But since she was thinking about not telling him, maybe he'd never need to find out. Considering her age and circumstances, I had hoped she'd hired me for something easy, like finding out if her roommate was after her boyfriend. But no, she was thinking about her mother, and that she was probably dead, and I knew nothing was ever as easy as I wished.

"I'd like to hire you to find my mother." Her lips tightened and pain flashed through her eyes. "You see...I'm getting married in a few weeks and I really want her to be there." She didn't add 'if she's still alive' like she was thinking.

She'd always imagined her mother would be at her wedding, and now that it was actually happening, she couldn't stop wondering where her mom was and what had happened to her. The day her mother had gone missing was the worst day of her life, and thinking about it brought all the horror back, but she knew she would never move on unless she had some answers.

"Tell me what happened," I said gently.

She took a deep breath. "It's been nearly six years, and I know that's a long time, but just hear me out before you decide if you can take the job or not."

"Okay." I encouraged her with a smile. "Go on."

"Like I said...it will be six years on the twenty-eighth of October since she went missing. That night, she drove to the office where she worked to drop something off and never came back. They found her car parked in the parking structure with the keys in the ignition. Her purse was on the passenger seat. Nothing was taken, and there was no sign of a struggle. It was like she just disappeared off the face of the earth."

"What did the police tell you?"

"Well...they dusted for prints, checked her office, put out a missing person's report, questioned her colleagues at work, and brought my father in for questioning." She hated that they had suspected him. He was innocent. He had nothing to do with it. He loved her mom. It still made her angry. It was part of what had made the day so bad. She not only lost her mother, but her father was never the same after that.

"What happened to your father? Did they charge him with anything?"

Tiffany shook her head. "No. They had no evidence that he was involved, but the police always suspect the husband first. So it was bad enough that my mom disappeared, but the fact that they thought my dad had something to do with it made it ten times worse."

She sighed, wondering for the thousandth time what kind of person she would be right now if she still had her mom. She'd probably be a lot happier, that was for sure. "My dad's doing better now. He even got married a couple of months ago."

"That's good," I said.

"Yeah." She was glad he had finally moved on, and wished it was something she could do. But the ache just wouldn't go away, especially with her upcoming wedding. This was the most important day of her life, and her mother should be there. So where was she? What had happened? Who had taken her? Why hadn't she come home?

In her heart, she knew her mother never would have left unless she was forced into it. Speculation from the police and others of affairs, with her mom running off with another man, only deepened the wound, and she wouldn't believe any of it. That's why a small part of her had to believe her mom was dead, but what if she wasn't? What if someone was holding her captive? It could happen, and she just couldn't give up until she knew for sure.

"What did the police decide about the case?" I asked.

"Officially, she's missing and presumed dead. At least that's what they declared so my dad could re-marry. I don't know what happened to the case files. But I'm hoping you can dig them up and maybe find something that got passed over. I know it's a long shot, but I've never had the resources to hire a private investigator until now. Do you think you could look into it for me?"

I bit my bottom lip. The chances of finding out what happened at this point were pretty slim. My mind-reading ability wouldn't be of much use, although I could still question her dad. Even though she didn't think it was him, I'd learned that some people were really good at keeping secrets, and I wasn't about to rule him out. I could probably get my hands on the police file and talk to the detectives who handled the case, but beyond that, I didn't have much hope.

She was thinking that I was going to say no and she was starting to feel stupid that she'd even asked. No one in their right mind would think they could solve the case after six years. But even if she was throwing away her hard-earned money, she still had to try.

"It's okay if you don't find her," Tiffany said. "I just want someone to take one more look at the case. Maybe there's something you'll see that they missed. Don't worry about the money. I'll still pay you, even if you don't find anything new. Just...please say you'll take it. I have to do this one last thing before the wedding. Maybe then I'll know I've done everything I could and I can finally let her go."

"It sounds like you've thought this through," I began. "So you know the chances of finding anything are pretty slim?" She nodded, and I continued, "My rates are negotiable in certain cases, but I still need to be paid for my time."

"I've got five thousand dollars. Is that enough?"

I glanced at her and raised my brows. "How about we take it an hour at a time? I'll get the police files, talk to a few people, and let you know what I've found. That shouldn't take long. We can decide after that if it's worth pursuing."

Her expression cleared. I was really going to do it. "Yeah...okay. That sounds good." She grabbed her backpack from the bench and unzipped it, pulling out a manila folder crammed with papers. "I saved everything. There's newspaper clippings, notes, a copy of the police report they gave us, and a picture of my mom. That should help you get started with dates and things."

"This is great," I said. I took the folder and slid it into my bag. "I'll get started right away."

"Wait, you'll need this." She opened her purse and pulled out a wad of cash. "How much do you need up front?"

"Oh...I'll just take a retainer for now. Say...five hundred dollars? Once it's gone we'll talk again."

"Are you sure?" She had brought eight hundred, and was thinking she didn't want me to do a crappy job since five hundred would only cover a few hours.

I tried not to be insulted, but couldn't help raising a brow. "You'd be surprised at how much I can get done in an hour or two."

Her eyes widened. "Oh...well...good." She quickly counted out five hundred dollars and handed it over.

I tucked it into my purse and stood. "I always keep a detailed summary of my time which I'll give you when we meet next, along with a receipt for the money."

She shrugged. "Okay." Her hopes soared, bringing a smile to her lips. "Thanks so much. You don't know how much better I feel about all this."

"You're welcome," I replied. "I hope we find something...but to be honest...it'll be a longshot."

"That's okay. At least we're doing something."

"I'll be in touch." I smiled and turned to leave, knowing she was watching my every step. She was thinking I was

cool, and the fact that I was a real private investigator filled
her with awe. I also hadn't told her I felt sorry for her, or
treated her like a kid, and that went a long way. It was just
the sort of thing she needed, and if I could find out what
had really happened to her mom, she'd gladly fork over
every penny of that money.

Dang. That put a lot of pressure on me. I held my head
high until I was out of sight. Rounding the corner, I heaved
a sigh and my shoulders sagged. I had little hope that I'd
find her mom, and guilt that I was taking her hard-earned
money churned my stomach. At least I could fudge on the
hours. There was no way I could take one hundred fifty
bucks an hour from a kid who'd not only lost her mother,
but was getting married.

Maybe taking her on as a client wasn't the smartest thing
to do, but I could hardly turn her down when it was
something she needed in order to move on with her life.
The fact that she was getting married made it even more
important. I just hoped she could handle the
disappointment in case it was bad news.

I drove straight to the police station. I hadn't been there
since I'd been arrested, but I was finally ready to return and
face them. My favorite detective, Harris, a.k.a. Dimples, was
sure to be surprised, but I hoped in a good way. Besides, he
still had my honorary ID badge and I wanted it back.

I parked and opened the file Tiffany had given me. I
didn't recognize the name of the detective assigned to her
mother's case, but I hoped Dimples would know who he
was. I slid the file back into my bag and got out of the car.

Holding my head high, I swallowed my trepidation and
marched to the door. As I pulled it open, a few people
glanced my way, but most ignored me. It wasn't until I
walked into the detectives' offices that I heard any thoughts
directed my way. I nodded and smiled at everyone who

looked at me, and most were genuinely happy to see me back.

Dimples glanced up and did a double-take, then jumped up from his seat to greet me. "Shelby! What a pleasant surprise. How are you? How's your arm?"

"Pretty good. How about you? Keeping busy?"

"Yes. There's always something going on around here. Come on over and sit down." He ushered me to the chair beside his desk where I usually sat. "So what brings you here?" He was hoping I was coming to offer my services. He could sure use my help... right now in fact. "Looking for something to do?"

"Depends," I answered. "Are you asking?"

"You bet." He smiled and his dimples spun around in his cheeks. I chuckled just to see them, and suddenly, I was happy I'd come. "I was hoping you'd stop by," he admitted. "But after your arrest and all, I wasn't sure you'd ever want to step foot in this building again."

"Hey, I couldn't have made it through that mess without your help. We're friends. That's what friends do. I'd be happy to help, as long as you give me back my ID badge to make it official."

"Oh...yeah...that. I've got it here somewhere." He made a big show of looking through his desk drawers to find my badge, although he knew right where it was. He didn't want it to look like it meant so much to him. But deep down, he was excited to give it back. "Here you go." He hesitated, thinking he could put it over my head like a medal or something, but since that might seem like over-kill, he just handed it to me.

"Thanks." I smiled to let him know I appreciated the sentiment and slipped it on. I was about to tell Dimples my reason for being there when someone's scornful thoughts crashed into my mind. He was wondering what the hell I was doing there, and thought I had a lot of nerve to show my face in the police station again. I knew immediately who it was and turned to give Detective Bates the evil eye. His gaze caught mine and he flushed before sauntering over.

"I never thought I'd see you here," he said.

"Why not?" I asked. "I am innocent you know."

"Did you clear this with the captain?" Bates asked Dimples, obviously ignoring me. "I know she used to work here, but are you sure he's okay with that?"

Dimples stood to face him, his features drawn tight and eyes blazing. He clenched his fists and Bates took an involuntary step back. Before Dimples could speak, the captain came out of his office. He took in the situation with a quick glance and pursed his lips, then focused on me.

"Shelby! Good to see you. How's the arm?"

"Um...lots better," I answered.

"Good." He glanced at Bates. "You have a problem?"

"Uh...no sir," Bates said.

"Good." He turned his gaze to me and noticed my badge. His face broke into a broad smile. "It's nice to have you back, Shelby. I'm sure we can use your help around here." At that he sent one more glare at Bates and strode back into his office.

"That answer your question?" Dimples asked.

"Whatever." Bates frowned and hurried back to his desk. He was thinking he'd probably over-reacted, but his pride had been hurt. Besides, he knew that even though he'd been wrong about me being a murderer, there was still something I was hiding, so I couldn't be trusted.

Dimples sat back down. "Sorry about that. I had no idea he'd be such an ass."

"It's okay. He's just embarrassed that he was wrong and too proud to admit it." That was the truth, and saying it out loud felt pretty good.

"You got that right," Dimples agreed. "Well..." he rubbed his hands together. "Now that we've got that out of the way, when would you like to start?"

"Um...I'm actually here for a job of my own. But I'm sure I can help you too."

"Oh? What job is that?"

"I'm investigating a missing person's report." I pulled out my file and opened it up. "Her name's Darcy Shaw, and she went missing about six years ago. Do you think I could look at your files and see if there's anything I could use?"

Dimples frowned. "From that long ago, it's probably downstairs in the dead files room. Come on, I'll show you where they are."

"Thanks."

I followed him to the hall and down two flights of stairs to the basement. He opened the door to a room and flipped on the light. Wall-to-wall filing cabinets filled the room, and a stale, musty odor permeated the air. From the smell, I'd guess no one had come down here in a long time, kind of how I imagined it would smell visiting a mausoleum. It seemed colder than normal too, and I realized that all of the files belonged to real people who had disappeared and were probably dead, and no one knew why or how.

"Go ahead and take a look," Dimples said. "They're filed alphabetically."

"Um...yeah, okay." I hesitated, not wanting to venture further into the room. It was so cold and dank that it kind of gave me the creeps. But I only needed one file. That wouldn't take long.

"When you're done, come on back up and I'll fill you in on a case I could use your help with." Dimples was anxious to leave me to it, not because he had a lot to do upstairs, but because the room had kind of a weird vibe that he didn't like.

"You're leaving me here alone?" I blurted.

"What? You're not scared are you?" He scoffed. "It's just a room with files in it. There aren't even any guns or crazy killers down here."

"Oh fine," I said, still hesitating in the doorway and wishing I hadn't heard that part about the weird vibe.

"You want me to stay?" He folded his arms and raised his brow in challenge.

"Of course not," I said. "Like you said, I'll be fine."

"Good. Hey...if one of those files attacks you...I'm right upstairs if you need me."

"Ha, ha."

He chuckled and left. I shook my head and hurried over to the cabinets. As I found the cabinet with "S through T" on it, the door clicked shut behind Dimples, sealing me in. It was deathly quiet. The only sounds in the room came from me. My breathing and the shift of my feet echoed from the walls, magnifying each tiny breath and movement I made.

An unexplained sense of urgency rolled over me. I was alone in an enclosed space that seemed to get smaller the longer I stood there. A sudden stab of dread tightened my stomach, and my hands shook a little. It was mostly thoughts of the lights going out and leaving me in total darkness that did it. If Bates knew I was here, I wouldn't put it past him to do that to me, and I wanted out of this creepy place as fast as I could.

With renewed effort, I scanned the labels until I came to the right drawer and yanked it open. I quickly leafed through the folders and caught my breath to actually find the file. I swallowed with relief and pulled the bulky file out. Pursing my lips together, I set it on top of the other folders and opened it up checking to make sure it was the right one.

A larger version of the same picture I'd received from Tiffany stared back at me. Her eyes held a haunting mixture of sadness and foreboding, and goose bumps broke out along my arms. A sudden chill ran up my spine and my heart picked up speed. All at once, it felt like I wasn't alone, and someone was standing right there beside me. I froze. I didn't believe in ghosts, but I didn't dare look either.

My mouth went dry and I hardly dared to take a breath. Glancing back down at the picture, I felt something cold and feather-like brush against my cheek. I inhaled sharply. It came a second time and I jerked my face away, hunching my shoulders to my neck with fear. "I...I'll try and find out what happened to you," I croaked. The chill intensified, then suddenly fell away in a cool breeze, leaving the scent of flowers behind, which I recognized as the distinct smell of gardenias.

With my heart racing, I grabbed the file and slammed the drawer shut, then raced out of the room as fast as I could. In my haste, I left the light on, but I was too scared to go back and turn it off. The smell of gardenias stayed with me all the way up the stairs, but disappeared as I entered the office. With my chest heaving, I hurried over to Dimples' desk and sat down, rubbing my cold arms.

"Whoa. Are you okay? You look like you've seen a ghost," Dimples said with a teasing smile. I tried to smile back, but I couldn't seem to form a coherent response. "Did you find the file?" he asked, drawing his brows together in concern.

I nodded and took a deep breath which seemed to break the fear holding me hostage. "Yeah...I...did. It was kind of creepy down there. Have you ever noticed that?"

He sat back in his chair and studied me, thinking I was a little paler than normal. "Honestly... yeah...I have. I guess I should have warned you about that. Since the room is in the basement, it's kind of cold down there, and since it's called 'the dead files' it's easy to get spooked. It happens to a lot of people, so don't feel too bad about it."

"Oh...right...that must be it." I wasn't about to tell him what had really happened. "Is it okay if I borrow this file for a while? I'll bring it back."

"Sure, that's fine."

"Do you know the lead detective that handled the case? I might want to ask him a few questions."

Dimples took the file from me and glanced through it, feeling a bit sorry he'd left me alone in that room, especially after all the ghost stories he'd heard. "Yeah, I know him. He's retired now, but I can give you his phone number. Just let him know I sent you and he'll tell you everything he remembers about the case."

"Great. Thanks."

Dimples brought up the directory on his computer, then wrote the name and number down on a piece of paper and handed it to me. "There you go."

I took it with wobbly fingers, surprised I was still so shook up.

"Are you sure nothing happened down there?" he asked. He was thinking I probably wouldn't tell him even if it did. But what if having premonitions also made me susceptible to seeing dead people? His eyes widened. Now that would really be weird. It would also explain why I was so spooked. Had I seen something?

"No...no...it was just a little weird and I got spooked, that's all." I realized I'd just answered what he was thinking, but hoped it was close enough to his spoken question that it didn't matter. "So...what have you got for me to work on?"

He knew I was stonewalling him, but wisely let it go. "There was a homicide day before yesterday that's got us all stumped. All the usual suspects have an alibi, and without any leads, I don't know what to do next."

He went on to tell me about a woman who'd been killed by burglars in a possible break-in. She'd been stabbed and bled to death on the living room floor. Her husband had left earlier in the evening because of a fight they'd had and didn't come back until the next morning. That's when he'd found her lying there dead.

"He seems like the prime suspect, but his alibi checks out for time of death. The other thing that doesn't make sense is that if this was a burglary, then why was nothing of value taken? A few things were smashed up, and the door was broken in, but computers, the TV, her cell phone...it was all still there. It also seemed more personal. I mean...she was stabbed over twenty times...so that indicates a crime of passion to me."

"Hmm...yeah it does. What do you want me to do?" I asked.

He frowned, wondering why I was asking that, but chalked it up to my traumatic experience in the basement since I still looked a little pale. "Um...you still have premonitions don't you? I was thinking you could go to the crime scene with me...see if you can pick up anything?"

"Oh yeah...of course." I chuckled to cover my blunder, realizing I'd zoned out while he was talking because I was still in shock from getting scared. "That might work, only...blood makes me a bit queasy. Why don't we talk to the husband again? I think that would be better. I mean...I get better reads off people than objects."

"Really? Hmm...okay. If you're sure." He could tell I was still rattled and wondered again if something had happened in the basement. Then he wondered if getting shot in the arm had gotten to me and I had post-traumatic stress syndrome. Maybe that was why I had over-reacted in the basement. He wouldn't be surprised with all the close calls I'd had in the last few months, but if that was the case I should probably go see someone about it so I could get back to my normal upbeat self. He hated seeing me so upset that even my hands shook.

What? He was serious, and I knew I'd better pull my act together. I stiffened my spine and looked him straight in the eyes. "Of course I'm sure. And there's nothing wrong with me." What did he mean I wasn't upbeat? Getting shot made me more cautious, but it would do that to anyone. I certainly didn't need to talk to someone about it, and I didn't have a syndrome.

"All right," he said, realizing he'd struck a nerve with me but had no idea how he'd done it. "I'll have to make up something to get him here. Can you stay a little longer?"

"Of course." I nodded pleasantly, eager to move on. "Why don't you tell him we have a new lead on the case and we need him to come in to answer a few questions?"

"Uh...yeah, that's a great idea," he answered. "I was just thinking that."

"Great minds think alike," I said, tapping my finger to my head.

He nodded and picked up his phone to make the call.

With his focus off me, I slumped back in my chair. Always knowing what people thought of me was stressful, and I wondered if maybe I should have taken a little more time off to recover. I also had a bad habit of answering unspoken thoughts, and the last thing I needed was for Dimples to figure out I could read minds.

My cell phone rang, and since Dimples was busy, I hurried to a quiet corner where I could talk in private. The caller ID said Thrasher Development, and my heart skipped a beat. I wasn't sure I was ready to go back to work for Uncle Joey, but at the same time, I was happy to hear from him. Did that mean I really did need some kind of counseling like Dimples thought? At least around Uncle Joey I didn't have to pretend I couldn't hear his thoughts.

"Shelby!" Uncle Joey said. "How are you doing? How's the arm?"

"Getting better," I replied. "How are you?"

"I'm all right...but I find myself in a bit of a quandary. Could you come to the office? I could use your help right now."

"Um...are there any dead bodies involved?" I asked.

He chuckled. "No...nothing like that. I just need your special 'touch' to solve a minor problem. How soon will you be done at the police station?"

I gasped. "How...How did you...? Oh...never mind. It might be about an hour before I can get there, depending on how soon things happen here."

"That will be fine," he assured me. "See you soon."

He disconnected and I sighed. Getting mixed up with Uncle Joey was never a good thing. I should have told him I was busy, but part of me looked forward to seeing him. I really was nuts. It also bothered me that my first day back at work was turning into a lot more than I bargained for. Besides helping the police, I didn't mind helping Uncle Joey where I could, as long as it wasn't too bad. But I really should be concentrating on my client and her missing mother. Although from that creepy feeling in the dead files room, I had a pretty good idea she wasn't just missing, she was dead.

A chill ran up my spine. I'd never experienced anything like that before, and I was pretty sure I didn't want to again. Maybe it was just my imagination getting carried away. After all, the room was pretty creepy and cold to begin with. I'd probably just imagined the brush of coldness on my cheek and the smell of flowers.

My stomach clenched. As comforting as that sounded, I had a feeling it wasn't the last time something like that would happen with this case, and just thinking about it gave me the shivers.

Chapter 2

I put my phone away and caught Dimples' curious glance. He'd finished talking a few minutes before me and waited politely for me to finish. I smiled and joined him, hoping he didn't catch the guilty flush on my face since I'd just finished talking with Joey "The Knife" Manetto.

"We're in luck," he began. "The guy isn't far from here and should arrive in about ten minutes."

"Oh...that's great. Did he seem surprised?"

"Actually, yes he did. But he also sounded a little relieved and more than willing to cooperate."

"Huh," I said, narrowing my eyes. "That's interesting."

"Wait...you think it's him? It can't be him. You know that, right? His alibi checks out."

"I'm not jumping to conclusions. I have no idea, but if what you said is true, who else could it be? Maybe he paid someone to do it. You never know."

Dimples' brows drew together and he pursed his lips.

"Don't worry," I assured him. "If it's him...I'll know...trust me."

He was thinking that I hadn't let him down yet, so he might as well go for it. I smiled and nodded at him. He narrowed his eyes, thinking that I'd reacted as if I'd heard his thoughts, just like I'd done earlier with the whole "new lead" explanation. It bothered him a little, but he had to remember that working with me and my premonitions was like that and he just needed to go with the flow and not worry about it.

His gaze met mine and I raised my brows. "Are you okay? You seem a little tense."

"Nah...I'm fine," he said. But his eyes narrowed and he thought that if I really could read minds, I'd know what he was thinking right now. "So...what kinds of questions do you want me to ask him?"

"Just the usual," I answered, a little flustered. "Like, what he argued with his wife about, where he went after he left her, where he stayed the rest of the night... basically anything that will get him focused on his wife." After I said all that, I realized it was exactly what Dimples was thinking.

He nodded, thinking we were either totally thinking alike, or I was reading his mind. He was going to watch me close and see if it happened again. Then he'd know. He was a detective after all. He should be able to figure it out. Of course, if I really did read minds, it probably wasn't something I'd want anyone to know. Saying I had premonitions had worked out pretty well for me.

Then another thought hit him like a bolt of lightning. Was that why I worked for Joey "The Knife" Manetto? Did he know my secret and used that leverage to get me to do stuff for him? Reading minds made a lot more sense than the premonition thing. In fact, that was about the only reason he thought I would keep working for a slime-ball like him.

I kept my gaze lowered, but a sudden impulse to defend Uncle Joey raised my ire. I hadn't thought of him as a slime-ball for a long time, and it kind of got my dander up. Of course, he wasn't exactly a stellar citizen either. Still, I made up my mind that if Dimples ever figured it out, I'd just have to tell him he was crazy. No way was he ever going to know my secret. Calling my mind-reading abilities premonitions had worked well enough so far, and I wasn't about to let that change.

"Do you still do any work for Manetto?" he asked.

I huffed out a breath like that was a silly question. "What? Are you kidding? After getting shot in the arm, I've learned my lesson."

"Good to hear." Dimples smiled with relief.

"I'm going to get me a soda. Do you want one?" I asked.

"Um...no, I'm good."

I left him with a fake smile plastered on my lips, and took my time at the drinks machine. Right now I didn't want to worry that I'd just lied to Dimples, or that I'd say something stupid and give away my secret. More than a little flustered, I mostly wished he'd quit thinking so hard about me and concentrate on the case.

By the time I got back to the office, the husband had already arrived and I found Dimples waiting for me outside the interrogation room. To my chagrin, word had spread that I was going to question him. Bates and a few others had already gathered to listen in on the other side of the two-way mirror. If that wasn't enough, the police chief joined them. My stomach churned. Now, besides trying solve the murder, I'd also have to make it look like I wasn't reading the man's mind or Dimples would figure it out. Talk about pressure!

I picked up that Bates was glad he'd been keeping tabs on me. Finding out the husband was coming in so I could question him was the perfect excuse to tell everyone to come and watch the show. He was hoping I'd fail miserably and get kicked out of my so-called 'consulting' job. When the chief joined them, he glanced at me with a triumphant grin, and my face flushed with anger.

As Dimples opened the door, I took a quick breath and tried to block my nasty thoughts of kicking that man where it hurt the most, and turned my attention to the husband. If this was going to have a happy ending, I needed to calm down and concentrate.

"Spencer," Dimples said. "I'd like to introduce you to Shelby Nichols. She's helping us out on the case."

Spencer stood and shook my hand with a friendly smile, quickly sizing me up. He was of average height and nice looking with thinning brown hair and an easy smile. He came to the conclusion that I was harmless, mostly because I looked too darn nice to be a threat. But why was I there? Did it have something to do with what the police had found? "Are you a detective?" he asked.

"I have my own consulting agency, and I help the police from time to time," I replied, mostly for Bates' benefit.

Spencer's lips turned down, and he wondered what a consulting agency had to do with a murder investigation. Something seemed a little off, and nervous sweat popped out on his upper lip.

My spidey-senses tingled. He was definitely hiding something. Of course, his face only showed mild curiosity, and if I didn't know better, I'd think he was a nice, easy-going guy.

"Thanks for coming in so quickly," Dimples said. He could tell Spencer was a little confused by my presence, and he didn't want him to close up before I could question him. "We just need to clarify a few things so we can build the case against our suspect."

"You have a suspect? Wow, that's great," he said. Right after the words left his mouth, he realized that he might have sounded a little too happy about that, and tried to convey a more somber mood with his next words. "This has been a nightmare for me. I miss Stacy every minute of the day. Whoever did this needs to be caught. What I've gone through is... horrible... I'd hate for someone else to go through what I have."

Dimples nodded. "Let's go over the events of the day. It will help us know if our suspect could have been there at the right time to actually commit the murder."

"Of course," he responded. He relaxed just a little, thinking we didn't know anything.

"Maybe you could fill Shelby in? Just tell her what happened from the time you got home from work until the time you left your house later that night."

Spencer took a deep breath and began his carefully rehearsed story. He told it with such passion that he was starting to believe it himself, although he still couldn't keep the image of placing Stacy's bloody, lifeless body in the freezer. He'd left shortly after that and checked into a hotel, making sure he was seen at the bar. In the early morning hours, he'd sneaked back home and put her partially frozen body back where it was when he'd killed her. Then he'd broken a few things to make it look like a robbery.

All of these thoughts came through during his narrative, and I had to work hard to keep my jaw from dropping open. He'd certainly gone to a lot of work to cover up his crime, and I had a hard time believing that this kind-faced man could do something so terrible. What had she ever done to deserve that?

"Did you love your wife?" I asked.

"Very much." His razor-sharp gaze focused on me, instantly suspicious of why I would ask that.

"What did you argue about?"

"I don't even remember," he said. His gaze dropped to his clenched hands. "All I know is that I left her there and now it's my fault she's dead. If I hadn't left, maybe I could have stopped the killer, and she'd still be alive."

"What did she say that made you so angry?" I asked.

His thoughts went to her confession that she didn't love him anymore, and she'd found someone else who could take care of her like she deserved. How he was a worthless husband and horrible in bed and she never should have married him in the first place. He ran his fingers through his hair, thinking that if he hadn't been cutting up vegetables with that knife in his hand, it might not have happened. He still couldn't believe what he'd done to her.

"You didn't mean to do it, did you?" I asked. "If that knife hadn't been in your hand, it never would have happened."

His gaze jerked to mine and his eyes widened. "How did you..." he realized what he'd said and his breath caught. "I don't know what you're talking about."

"Yes you do," I answered softly. "She told you she didn't love you anymore and there was someone else she'd rather be with. You knew things were bad, but you never expected her to betray you so effortlessly. You just... lost it, and with the knife already in your hand, it was easy to plunge it into her neck. Tell me Spencer... what will the police find when they open your freezer?"

His face paled and he leaned back in his chair as if to put as much distance between us as possible.

"Even if you've cleaned it out with bleach, there will still be traces of her blood inside." I leaned forward, invading his space. "You can't hide what you've done, Spencer. It's time to come clean and tell us what really happened. Even though she was planning to leave you for another man, I know you didn't mean to kill her. It was an accident."

All the bravado left him, and he crumpled, dropping his face into his hands with a wrenching sob. "You're right! I didn't mean to kill her." He sobbed even harder. "It was an accident, I swear. I didn't mean it...all those things she said...it just happened...I loved her. I don't know what came over me. But I didn't mean it!"

Dimples' surprised gaze jerked to mine. He could hardly believe how fast he'd confessed. Both of us watched as Spencer sobbed with remorse and grief. Finally, Dimples stood and gently pulled Spencer's arms back to cuff him. Dimples read him his rights, and then led him out of the room where a uniformed officer took him away for processing. He came back inside the room with awe in his eyes. "That was...amazing."

I shrugged like it wasn't a big deal and stood. "You could tell he was nervous, right? So it only made sense that he was hiding something. You'll want to check his freezer though, just to make sure. I guess that's how he fooled everyone with the time-of-death part."

"Yeah, right," he answered, still gazing at me like I was from another planet.

The police chief pushed his way past the other detectives and burst into the room. "I don't know how you do it, but nice work." He shook my hand like I was a celebrity.

"Thanks," I answered. "Glad to help."

"Make sure you turn in your hours. We don't want to forget to pay you." With a satisfied smile, he left the room. In the doorway, he shooed the other detectives away with his gruff voice. "Don't you have work to do?"

I couldn't help the sly grin I sent to Bates, who turned away with a shake of his head. He thought what I'd done was brilliant... and a little creepy...maybe it was best if he stayed away from me. He didn't want any bad juju coming his way.

Juju?? Did he think I was a witch or something? That was a first.

"Thanks for your help," Dimples said, drawing my attention. His eyes held a new respect for me. He didn't know how I did it, but he didn't really care when the results were this great. "I don't know if we would have ever figured it out without you."

"Oh... you probably would have. He might have given himself away at some point."

Dimples shrugged. "Maybe, but I doubt it."

"Well...I'd better get going. Thanks for the file. I need to get to work."

"Yeah...call me if you need anything else. I think after what you did today, you can pretty much get whatever you want from us."

"Even Bates?" I asked.

Dimples smiled. "Um...maybe not him." He glanced in Bates' direction. "If that guy was smart, he'd try to get on your good side."

I snorted. "Oh well, you can't please everyone." Wanting to change the subject I asked, "So, how's it going with Billie? You guys still seeing each other?" Billie Jo Payne was the news reporter who had the hots for Dimples. I knew they were together, but I didn't want Dimples to get any more nervous around me.

His eyes lit up. "Yes."

I waited for him to elaborate, but he didn't and I tried not to roll my eyes. "That's good. She told me to call her once I was back on the job. Do you know what she's working on now?"

"Well, she's still covering the homicide cases for the paper, so that keeps her busy."

He was thinking she was also doing some snooping into something else, but had kept it from him. Since she wouldn't tell him what it was, he knew it was dangerous and that made him uneasy. He glanced at me, thinking that maybe I could talk to her and figure out what it was and then tell him, so he could talk her out of it.

"I guess now that you've solved this case," he said. "She'll want to know we've made an arrest. Is it okay if I tell her you helped us with this? She might want to interview you for the paper or something."

"Um...sure. Tell her to give me a call."

"Great. I will. Let me know how it goes. Uh...there is something else. I'm a little worried about her...she's following a lead on something and won't tell me what it is. Makes me think it's not exactly legal, you know? Maybe you could talk to her about it?"

"Okay, I'll see what's up."

"Thanks Shelby," he said, smiling with relief. "And thanks for helping with the case. That was...remarkable."

I smiled and said goodbye, then made my way out of the precinct before he asked me to do anything else. As much as I'd liked helping him out, I was glad to leave. Sure, I'd solved the case, but seeing the images in Spencer's mind of killing that poor girl sickened me.

Now I had to worry about what Billie was into, but I knew she was a big girl and could take care of herself. So what she was involved with probably wasn't too bad. After all, she was a martial arts expert. In fact, as soon as my arm was better she was going to help me learn Aikido, so Dimples was probably just a little over-protective, and it wasn't anything to worry about. I hoped.

I took a deep breath and got into my car. As I drove to Thrasher Development, I wondered what Uncle Joey wanted from me. It didn't sound like it would be too unpleasant, and now that I was on my way there, I put everything else from my mind.

A rush of eagerness to see him and Ramos flowed over me, making me doubt my sanity. Maybe I really should go see a shrink and get some help...or...just go to lunch with Holly. Yes, talking to her was what I needed. That would be a lot more helpful, and definitely more fun.

That settled, I pulled into the parking garage and walked to the elevators, grateful no one was trying to kill me today, and that I didn't have to look over my shoulder like a few of the other times I'd been there. I emerged on the twenty-sixth floor and grinned to see the familiar suite of offices with Thrasher Development in big letters across the top.

Jackie sat at her desk, and a big smile popped over her face when she caught sight of me. "Shelby! How are you doing? How's the arm?" She was Uncle Joey's secretary...and his main squeeze.

"Hi Jackie. I'm fine...the arm's healing and I'm ready to get back to work." Did I really say that out loud? I'd better see if Holly was free for lunch tomorrow.

"Great! I know Joe will be happy to see you." She was thinking Ramos would be happy too. Especially today, with the big fiasco he'd unwittingly brought down on them. She felt kind of sorry for him and was glad none of it was her fault.

My elation turned to concern for Ramos. How could he be in trouble? If he was, then I certainly hoped I could help him out.

"Hang on a minute and I'll let him know you're here." She picked up the phone and told Uncle Joey I had arrived, then replaced the receiver. "He said to send you on back."

"Okay." I headed down the hall to his office, grateful I'd picked up who else was in the office from Jackie's mind before going inside. At least now I'd be prepared to see my former nemesis. I was also grateful I looked good in my black leggings and tall boots, with a three-quarter-inch sleeved lace-print tunic. I even had the necklace and earrings on that matched.

I knocked, and then opened the door to go inside. Yup. There was Kate. She'd been after my husband at one point, and it was all her fault I was now involved with Uncle Joey. She was also one of the few people who knew my secret. I don't know why, but just seeing her made something primal in me wake up, and I knew if I was a cat, I'd be hissing and baring my teeth right now.

Our gazes met, and I kept a neutral expression on my face. At least that's what I thought until I heard Ramos thinking I looked like I wanted to bite her head off. So much for trying to look composed. I scowled at him and he just smiled back, thinking he was sure glad to see me, and it couldn't have come at a better time.

"Shelby." Uncle Joey stood. "Glad you could make it. Come on in and have a seat." He motioned to the chair next to Kate, and I sat beside her even though it was the last thing I wanted to do.

"Hi Kate," I said. "What brings you here?" I wanted her to know she was on my turf.

She glanced at Uncle Joey, hating that she had to ask me for a favor, but she'd run out of options. "I need your help." It came out a bit stilted, as if she'd just taken a bite out of a lemon wedge.

Hmm...I smiled. Maybe this wouldn't be so bad after all. I caught Uncle Joey's mental reprimand of *play nice now*, and it kind of spoiled the moment. But then I picked up that he'd already said the same thing to Kate, so it wasn't so bad.

Ramos settled back in his chair and glanced between us, thinking this could be highly entertaining, and that he hoped for a good show. But he was also grateful for anything that might get the attention off his involvement in this mess. I turned my smile to Kate. "What's going on?"

She pursed her lips, unhappy that I hadn't agreed to help her right off the bat. She didn't want me to think she would grovel, so she put on a nice smile, but it suddenly faltered when she realized I knew exactly what she was thinking and there was no way she could fool me. She mentally cursed, and my jaw dropped at the blast of four letter words flowing from her mind.

"Whoa," I said under my breath.

She caught that remark and her face got all blotchy with embarrassment and frustration. Taking a deep breath, she managed to calm down. Still hoping Uncle Joey might step in, she sent a quick glance his way, but his raised brow and pursed lips let her know she was on her own.

"Here's the deal," she began. "I run the shipping company Uncle Joey and I "inherited" from Eddie Sullivan after his death."

I remembered Eddie Sullivan well, since he'd tried to kill me. Lucky for me, Uncle Joey killed him first. Uncle Joey then sent Kate to Seattle to take over what she could of Eddie's businesses. "You got a shipping company out of it. That's good," I said, mostly because it kept her in Seattle and out of my life. "How's it going?"

"Really well," Kate said, preening a little. "I've got a great manager who's taught me the ropes, and things are running smoothly. My problem is with another shipping company. We've been competing for many of the same contracts, and they approached me about a merger between our businesses. It would be great for us, but I'm not sure we can trust them. I was hoping you could tell me if the man I'm working with has ulterior motives." She was really thinking that it was Uncle Joey who didn't trust him, but that was Ramos' fault. If Ramos hadn't stuck his nose in where it didn't belong, she wouldn't be here right now trying to defend her position.

I picked up a strong impression of the man in question, and if he looked anything like she was thinking he looked, there was a lot more to their relationship than she let on. Of course, Uncle Joey already knew that. He was thinking Kate had a problem where men were concerned and that's why he'd sent Ramos in the first place. It was just too bad Ramos had been discovered before he could get to the root of the problem. He was supposed to be better than that.

I glanced at Ramos, and he shrugged, but deep down he wasn't sorry Kate had found him out and waylaid his plans. Even if it put him in a hot spot, he figured Manetto should give Kate the opportunity to fix the problem herself. Sometimes Manetto was a little too heavy-handed where she was concerned. That's probably what drove her to side against Manetto in the first place with Walter, a man now dead, who had tried to take over Uncle Joey's organization a few months ago.

"Okay," I said, more intrigued than anything. "I'll help. Just so you know...my going rate is five hundred dollars an hour." I quoted a sum higher than my normal fees, but she was desperate, and I'd learned from the best how to take advantage of that. I glanced at Uncle Joey for his approval. He hid a smile, but was thinking she probably would have paid more if I would have started a little higher.

"Great," she said, relieved I hadn't asked for more. "I thought maybe you could meet us for lunch tomorrow? Around one? He has an appointment at two, so once he leaves, you can tell me what you picked up and we'll be done." She was thinking that even if it took a little longer than an hour she wasn't about to pay me more. Oops, did I hear that? Her gaze caught mine and she shrugged, hoping I wouldn't be offended.

"That should work. How about we meet at The Cheesecake Factory and you pay for lunch?" Since that was one of my favorite restaurants, I figured if she paid, it wouldn't matter if we went over the hour.

"All right, I'll see you there at one." She glanced at Uncle Joey. "And if you don't mind, I can do whatever I need to from there. Without your involvement." She included Ramos in her statement, then stood and haughtily sauntered out of the room.

We all breathed a sigh of relief to have her gone, and I glanced at Uncle Joey. "She's not too happy with you. Maybe you should just leave her alone from now on."

Uncle Joey's lips twisted. "Not a chance. I've invested heavily in the business, and I'm not about to let her ruin it because of some man she's attracted to."

I couldn't fault him for that. "Hmm...you've got a point there."

He nodded, agreeing with me wholeheartedly. "Now...tell me how you've been. We've kind of missed you around here."

I smiled that he would admit to missing me. It made me feel warm inside. "To be honest, I've been a little bored." At his raised brows, I continued. "Not that I miss getting shot at or anything. That part's been great. It's just that I've kind of gotten used to doing stuff for you. So tell me...Chris made it sound like you wouldn't be calling me so much. Is that right?"

"I told Chris what he wanted to hear," he began. "I knew you needed time to heal and I know he doesn't like that you work for me. But don't ever forget that you and I have an arrangement, and it's not up to your husband how I do business."

His steely-eyed gaze caught mine, sending the message loud and clear that he wasn't about to take orders from Chris. "However," he continued. "I understand his concern for your safety. I have no desire to see you get hurt, so for now, I'll try to keep things simple. Things like meeting with Kate, or coming here for special appointments." He was thinking that sending me on errands hadn't turned out so well, so he was willing to compromise. If I used my abilities where he could keep an eye on me, I should be safe. "If your husband can't handle that, then I suggest you don't tell him."

His meaning was perfectly clear to me. I also picked up a certain amount of satisfaction when he thought of Chris, but I couldn't understand why. "I'm sure that won't be a problem."

"Good. I'm glad that's settled." He let down his guard and I picked up that he tried not to get attached to most people, but I was like family now, and he'd do what he could to keep me safe.

"Thanks," I said. "I appreciate that." He pursed his lips, realizing once again how he couldn't keep much from me.

Maybe now was a good time to leave since I didn't want to make him mad. "Well, I guess I'll go." I stood, and both Uncle Joey and Ramos stood as well.

Uncle Joey glanced at Ramos. "I guess you're off the hook for this fiasco with Kate. Do you think Shelby will be safe meeting with Kate tomorrow, or do you think she'll get shot at?"

Ramos chuckled. "Who knows...it is Shelby we're talking about. Maybe I should go too, just to make sure." He liked teasing me, but behind his words he was thinking how easy it was for me to get into trouble without even trying.

"Hey...I'm touched and all, but I'm sure I'll be fine. It's just lunch. What could go wrong?" I heard both of them thinking that where I was concerned...anything could happen. Especially considering how much Kate and I hated each other. "Come on guys, unless you think Kate's going to try to kill me...which I know you don't, I'll be fine."

"You sure?" Ramos asked, stepping close enough to invade my private space, and gazing deep into my eyes.

"Yeah." Having him this close made my heart flutter, and I knew I wouldn't mind having Ramos along, not for his protection, but because I liked the eye-candy part of being with him. That probably made me a bad wife...dang. "Yeah..." I repeated, stepping away. "You shouldn't come...I mean...you don't have to come. I'll be fine. I've got my stun flashlight, so I can take care of myself."

His eyes narrowed with a mischievous glint. "Hmm...okay. I certainly don't want to make you nervous."

"I'm not nervous. I just think...I mean...I'm sure you've got better things to do, right?"

He was thinking *nope*, but was saved from answering by the ringing of Uncle Joey's phone. "Yes?" Uncle Joey asked. "Ah...yes we're done. Send him on back." He set the phone down on the receiver and glanced at Ramos. "It looks like Shelby will be fine without you." To me he continued, "Just don't forget to let me know what you find out about Kate tomorrow."

"Sure. No problem. See you later." I opened the door, eager to leave, and nearly collided with a man entering Uncle Joey's office. "Oh...excuse me." I stopped short, but we were so close I could smell his aftershave. Our gazes caught and I couldn't help the shiver of danger that passed over me. He had the classic Italian features of olive skin, a straight nose, and black wavy hair. His keen, dark eyes glanced over me in appreciation, and his nostrils flared.

"Please, excuse me," he answered, with a slight accent. "I didn't know such a lovely woman was here or I would have waited before I barged in."

"Oh...it's all right," I said, my voice breathless. My pulse raced and it was hard to keep from fanning my face. I ended up putting a hand over my heart instead. "I was just leaving."

"Yes...I see that," he answered. An amused smile lit his face. "I am Giovanni Passini, at your service." He held out his hand for me to shake, but as soon as I placed my hand in his, he lifted it to his lips and placed a kiss on my knuckles.

If I was rattled before, now I was speechless. I couldn't even remember my name. "Uh...nice to meet you. I'm...uh...Shelby Nichols." I pulled my hand out of his grasp and took a step back. "I guess I'll be going now." I glanced around Giovanni and waved. "Bye Uncle Joey, Ramos."

I hurried out the door, pulling it behind me, but on impulse, left it slightly ajar so I could eavesdrop. That guy was something else, and I wanted to know what he was up to. Giovanni spoke without even a hint of an accent. "What a charming niece you have, Manetto. Where did you get her?"

"That's none of your concern," Uncle Joey said, his voice hard. "And I suggest you walk carefully. You're in my domain and I'm not happy you're here."

"Of course... I apologize," he answered. He was thinking that he enjoyed hitting a nerve with Manetto, even though it was probably a stupid thing to do. "As you know, my father has died. I want to work out a better arrangement for both of us now that he's gone."

I stayed by the door until I heard the squeak of Jackie's chair. Knowing she was probably coming to see what was keeping me, I quickly pulled away and walked down the hall, grateful for the carpet that kept my passage quiet.

She rounded the corner and stopped. "Oh...there you are," she said. Her shoulders relaxed and she smiled, wondering what had kept me so long. Knowing how Joe felt about Jon Passini, she didn't think it was a good idea for me to be involved. If he was anything like his father, he was going to make trouble for them and Joe wouldn't like it one bit. "Did you get everything taken care of?"

"Yes. I'm all set. See you later." I smiled at Jackie with a confidence I didn't feel and hurried to the elevators. My heart was still pounding as I rode down to the parking level, but by the time I got in my car, I could finally breathe normally again.

This Giovanni or Jon person was bad news. No matter how charming he was, he definitely wasn't a friend of the family like he tried to portray. More than that, I picked up deep resentment and anger. He had an agenda to fulfill...and the person he had the biggest plans for was Uncle Joey.

Chapter 3

I drove home determined to get started on my missing person case, and not worry so much about Uncle Joey, but I still couldn't stop thinking about the mess he was in. I pulled into my garage and hurried inside. It was almost three in the afternoon and I was hungry, so I rummaged through my refrigerator for something to eat. Nothing looked good, but it was mostly due to my anxiety about Uncle Joey. In desperation, I whipped out my phone and pushed number seven on my speed dial. He answered on the third ring.

"Shelby? I didn't think I'd be hearing from you until tomorrow. Is something wrong?"

"Yes. Is that Giovanni person still there?" I asked.

"Um...no. He just left."

"Good. There's something you should know about him."

"Okay...what?" he asked.

"I wasn't able to pick up a whole lot, but he's...a bad person." It hit me that I could have been describing Uncle Joey, and my palms got a little sweaty, so I hurried on to explain. "What I mean is, he's just full of resentment and anger and he's got big plans for you, as in...bad-for-you-plans."

"Hmm...do you know what those plans are?" he asked.

"No, I wasn't able to pick up on that."

"Okay. Anything else?"

"Um...yes." I hesitated, not sure how to proceed, but hearing Uncle Joey sigh, I decided I might as well put in my two-bits-worth. "I think you should call off whatever's going on with him, and if you don't, then at least let me listen to him so you know what his plans are."

"Thanks Shelby," he said. "I'm touched that you care so much, but I'm afraid it's too late to call anything off." He was silent for a minute, so I figured he was trying to decide how to best use my abilities in his nefarious schemes. "I know you're worried about this situation, but to be honest, I'm not sure I want you involved in this."

"What?" I squeaked. "Are you crazy? Don't you want to know what his plans are?" This was like a dream come true for me, but for some reason, it didn't make me happy like it should.

He chuckled, and I could visualize him shaking his head. "It's not that. It's just that the last few times I've sent you on simple errands, you've nearly gotten killed. They weren't dangerous errands either. I know this is a delicate matter, so I'm not sure I should involve you. Besides, there are some things about my business that you would be better off not knowing."

"Oh...well...I suppose you're right about that." Did he think I would double-cross him? Or was it more like I was a liability?

"Listen...if I get in a bind and I can see a way for you to help me out without getting you killed, I'll let you know. This situation I'm in has been going on for quite some time now, years in fact, and recently, things have changed. After that meeting I just had, I realize it's time to resolve it...no matter how dangerous...and it could get a little dicey. And by that I mean life-and- death dicey."

"Oh. Okay." What did he mean by that? Did he think he might have to kill someone? Or that he might die? If that was the case, I definitely did not want to get involved.

"I'll let you know if you can help, and I'll expect to hear from you tomorrow after your lunch with Kate." The line went dead, and I sat there in shock. Who would have thought Uncle Joey wouldn't want my help? It was so far from how he normally behaved that I could hardly believe it. What the heck was going on?

He even made it sound like he might not make it out alive. That probably applied to Ramos too, and pain tightened my chest. I realized that just this morning I was thinking that something was wrong with me for liking a mob-boss and his hit-man, and now that he didn't want my help in a dangerous situation, I was relieved, but...what if he died? Would I feel like it was my fault?

I blew out a breath. I'd have to take Uncle Joey at his word and trust that if he needed my help, he would ask. Other than that, it was something he'd have to take care of himself. Chris would certainly be happy about this turn of events, so why was I still worried? Ugh! Maybe I really did need to see a shrink, especially since I couldn't go to lunch tomorrow with Holly now that I had to meet up with Kate.

My cell phone rang. Glad for the distraction, I quickly picked it up. "Hello?"

"Hi Shelby! It's Billie. How are you doing? How's the arm?"

"Oh, hi Billie. Doing better thanks."

"Good," she answered. "Hey...I just got off the phone with Drew. He told me you solved the case he was working on. Single-handedly. He was pretty impressed. I guess everyone was. It made me wish I could have been there."

I let out a soft laugh, a little embarrassed by all the praise. "Oh, yeah...well, you know me and my premonitions."

"Yeah. I think you've certainly made a name for yourself with the police department. Anyway, he told me to give you a call, said you were working on a dead file case."

"That's right," I said. "I'm just getting started on it now. How about you? Got anything interesting you're working on?"

"Well...I'm keeping pretty busy covering the homicides for the paper. If I could interview you about this latest case, that might be good. I know it's late, but have you had lunch yet today? Maybe we could grab a bite to eat...say in about fifteen minutes?" I didn't answer right away, so of course, she plunged in. "There's that Paradise Bakery real close to you... how does that sound?"

"Hmm...well, I've got a lot of work to do, but I haven't had lunch yet and I am hungry..."

"I'll buy," she said, pushy as ever. "And don't forget about the cookie they give you. Those are really good."

"Okay, I'll meet you there." It wasn't lunch with Holly, but maybe this diversion would be good for me, and I looked forward to seeing Billie again. It was also good for Dimples, since meeting in person was the best way to find out what kind of secrets she might be keeping.

When I arrived, Billie was waiting for me and waved me over. I hadn't seen her since she'd helped me beat a murder rap, and for that, I would always be grateful. After a quick hug, we got in line and soon had our sandwiches and cookies in hand.

"So tell me what happened at the precinct," she began. "How did you know Spencer was guilty?"

I told her that I had a premonition of him with a bloody knife in his hand. "He kind of broke down when I told him he didn't mean to do it. That's when he confessed."

"My goodness, you're really good at interrogating people. Those types of leading questions are mostly just guesses. Usually when you do that, you're wrong more times than you are right. But I guess with your premonitions, you've got the upper hand." She'd seen me in action, and it amazed her every time. She also thought it could come in handy with what she was looking into right now. "Hey...I have a couple of projects I've got some leads on, and I'm not really sure which one has the most promise. Do you think you could help me? Do your little voodoo thing?" Her eyes sparkled with mirth.

I smiled. "It depends on what I'd have to do. I'm trying to stay away from the bad guys for a while."

"Oh yeah." She chuckled. "But the thing is...I don't know if they're bad or not. That's where you'd come in. All you'd have to do is go with me when I interview them for a story. You wouldn't even have to say anything. If you got any kind of bad premonitions about them, then I'd know if it was worth pursuing."

Wow. That sounded a lot like Uncle Joey. "That sounds fair. Who did you have in mind?"

"Well the first person is the Attorney General, Grayson Sharp," she began. "You've probably heard in the news that he's been allegedly taking money for his campaign to ensure certain people won't get prosecuted, right? I think one of them might be Joe Manetto, and if I could tie those two together, it would be quite the story, don't you think?"

My breath caught and I started choking on my sandwich. With watering eyes, I spit the food out of my mouth onto my plate and grabbed my drink. Billie jumped up and started pounding me on the back, making it ten times worse. Taking deep breaths, I finally managed to whisper, "I'm okay...I'm okay."

"Are you sure?" she asked. "Do you need me to do the Heimlich maneuver or anything?"

"No! I'm fine now." I took a few more swallows of soda and caught my breath. Billie watched me with anxious eyes until the episode passed. She was thinking my reaction was probably due to what she'd said. She knew Manetto was the reason that judge had shot me in the arm, and she wondered if I knew more about him than I'd said. If so, she needed to know what it was.

"Look Billie," I said. "You should leave Manetto alone. I'm serious."

Now she was more curious than ever. "What do you know about him?"

"No...that's not what I mean. You've heard of his reputation. He's got resources you couldn't even dream of. He's untouchable. Believe me...you don't want to get on his radar." Her brows lifted with speculation. Everything I'd said just made her more interested. My heart sank. I was totally botching this up. "Someday...I'll explain why, but as a personal favor to me, will you just leave it alone?"

Her shoulders dropped and she sat back in her chair. "I guess so."

"Good. I'll be happy to help with Grayson Sharp. In fact, I think I picked up on something about him." I lied.

She straightened, her eyes wide and alert. "What was it?"

Since I wanted to keep her mind off Manetto, I had to make something up and hope it made sense. "I'm not exactly sure. I just got a lot of images of the Attorney General's office door and someone holding a bag of cash. I didn't see a face, so it could be anyone who works there. Anyway, whoever it was placed the bag full of cash on a conveyor belt, like those you see at the airport, and it disappeared into a tunnel."

Billie stared at me, wondering if I was making this up or if it was real.

"A lot of times my premonitions are symbolic...like clues, and I have to figure them out," I explained. "So in this case, I think it's pretty evident that Grayson Sharp is getting cash from somewhere and it's disappearing. That tells me you should concentrate on him and his cash flow."

"All right. I'll concentrate on Grayson Sharp and see if I can get an interview with him or someone from his office. Do you think you could come with me if I do?"

"Sure. In fact, talking with someone would really help me out."

"Great." She checked her watch. "Well, I'd better get going."

"Yeah, me too, and thanks for understanding about Manetto."

She twisted her lips and nodded. "I look forward to hearing your story."

"It's not a story...it's just something I've heard."

This time she smiled, thinking that was a vague answer, but it didn't deter her. Nope. She knew a story was behind it, and since she was good at finding things out, she knew she'd get it out of me at some point. "Fine," she said. I'll keep in touch."

"Okay." I grabbed my cookie and walked out the door with her. After another wave, I got in my car and sighed. Why had I thought eating lunch with her would be good for me? If anything, I felt even worse. How had I promised I'd explain what I knew about Uncle Joey? This was terrible. But at least now I had time to figure out a story to tell her, so maybe it wasn't so bad. Frustrated, I leaned my forehead against the steering wheel and sighed. My first day back on the job had turned into a doozy, and right now I wished I'd stayed in bed.

When I got home I decided to forget about Billie, Uncle Joey, and Kate, and concentrate on my case. I changed into comfy clothes and grabbed a diet soda, then took Darcy Shaw's file into the den and borrowed one of Chris' legal pads to write down anything that might help me keep my facts straight.

The photo of her happy smiling face and the realization of how closely she resembled her daughter opened a flood of determination in me. I wanted...no...needed to solve this case. Someone had kidnapped this woman, and I felt in my heart she was dead. It wasn't right. Someone needed to speak for Darcy, and if I didn't do it, who would?

I spent the next hour jotting down facts about the case, and the more I learned, the closer I felt to this woman. It sent a little shock through me to realize she was only a few years older than me on the day she disappeared. She had blond hair and blue eyes just like me, and at the time of her disappearance, had a couple of teenage kids at home. Her husband, though not a lawyer, was a respected architect with a great firm.

She had just started a new job too, working for a financial investment company. That's where the similarities stopped. She was a wiz at math and that was one of the reasons she'd been hired. The company made investments and drew up portfolios as financial planners for their customers. She'd only worked there for two months before she disappeared.

I looked up the company on the Internet and breathed a sigh of relief to find them still going strong. I didn't know if working there had anything to do with her disappearance, but something told me it was a good place to start. From the notes in the file, I found out the name of her boss, and called the company to make an appointment with him. Lucky for me, he still worked there.

With a little maneuvering, I managed to talk his secretary into letting me take five minutes of his time first thing in the morning. I told her I was a private investigator hired by the police to look into Darcy Shaw's death. It was the truth, though not exactly for this case. But since it was for a good cause, I only felt a little guilty.

I also found the phone number of the detective assigned to the case. His name was Geoff Parker and he'd just retired last year. He answered his phone, and I quickly explained who I was. "Oh yeah," he said. "I remember that case. I always felt bad that we never figured out what happened to her, especially when she had those two kids, you know?"

"Yeah, I'll bet. Is there a time I could meet with you and we could go over the case?"

"I'm not sure there's much more I can tell you, but we can meet."

"Great. How about tomorrow morning? Say around nine or nine-thirty?"

"Hmm...yeah," he said. "That should be fine. The wife and I are canning tomatoes tomorrow, but you can come over and talk while we work...if that's okay with you."

"You bet." He gave me his address and we disconnected.

If I did this right, by the time I talked to him, I'd have more information about the financial company where she worked. After talking to her boss, I also planned on visiting anyone else there who may have worked with her.

Including Darcy's co-workers and Geoff Parker, the next person on my list was Tiffany's father. I wasn't real comfortable calling him since I knew Tiffany wasn't sure she wanted him to know she'd hired me, but if I was going to do this investigation right, I had to talk to him. Maybe if Tiffany called him to break the news first, it wouldn't be so bad. I quickly called her and explained that I needed to interview her father.

"Yeah," she said. "I figured you would, so I called him right after you left and told him all about it."

"How did he react to the news?"

"Um...a little surprised at first, but then he was fine with it. Why?"

From her defensive tone, I got the impression she was worried I thought he did it, so I hurried to explain. "I just wondered if he would be okay talking to me, that's all."

"Oh...I'm sure he'll be fine. Let me give you his cell number. You can call him right now if you like." She rattled off his phone number and, after thanking me again, disconnected.

I put the call through and waited for him to pick up. "Hello Mr. Shaw? This is Shelby Nichols. Your daughter hired me to look into her mother's disappearance and I wondered if I could come by for a chat."

He hesitated before answering. "Um...okay, I guess that would be fine. I'm just...Tiffany just told me about this today so I'm a little surprised. I had no idea she was even thinking of hiring someone, but I guess that's my fault. We haven't talked much lately...at least since I got married and she moved out. She told you I remarried, didn't she?"

"Yes, she did."

He sighed. "There are some things she doesn't know, and I'd like to keep it that way if I can. You see, I hired a private investigator myself after the police came up empty-handed. I never told the kids because I didn't want to get their hopes up. You're welcome to the files he gave me, but I don't think there's a lot more you can do, and I'd appreciate it if you'd drop the case after that. I hate to see Tiffany waste her hard-earned money chasing smoke. She needs to concentrate on something happy...like her upcoming wedding. Believe me, I did everything I could to find Darcy, and after all this time, I don't think it's worth the time or money to go digging into this. There's nothing to find. If there was, I would have found it."

"I understand, Mr. Shaw, and I don't plan on dragging this out. When can I meet you?"

"I've kept the files here at my office. You can stop by anytime tomorrow if you'd like."

He gave me the address and my breath caught. "That's the same building complex where Darcy worked. I've got an appointment tomorrow morning to meet with her boss."

"Yeah...well, we thought it was perfect too, since we could drive to work together. You don't know how many times I wished she'd never taken that job."

"I'm sure...well then...I'll stop by sometime in the morning, probably between eight-thirty and nine."

I set the phone down and wondered what I'd gotten into. There was always more to the story, and it looked like I was about to find out what it was. I sure hoped it would lead me to the truth. I glanced at Darcy's picture once more, then closed the file and put it back in my bag.

As I left the room to get dinner started and talk to my kids about their day, I caught a faint whiff of gardenias. I glanced over my shoulder, but the scent had disappeared, and I wondered if it had been there for real, or if it was just a figment of my imagination.

Later that night, I told Chris about my day while we were getting ready for bed. He was interested in the missing person's case, mostly because he didn't think it was dangerous, and after telling him all about it, I didn't know if I should let on that I'd been to see Uncle Joey. I knew Chris would be happy Uncle Joey didn't want me involved in his latest case, and since it was risky, it was probably best not to tell him anything, especially since I might still help Uncle Joey out, and I didn't want Chris to wonder about my sanity.

I told him about my visit to the police station instead, and the fact that I'd solved a murder right off the bat brought a burst of pride from him. "Wow. That's awesome! I'll bet Bates didn't like that much. What did he do?" I related the story, and after I got done, Chris pulled me to his side and we snuggled together. He was thinking this sure beat hearing about my escapades with Manetto, and he was grateful he'd had that chat with him. And as long as he kept his end of the bargain, I was out of Manetto's grasp.

"What?" I asked, pulling away. "What do you mean by that? What did you and Uncle Joey agree to?"

Chris inwardly cursed that he'd let his guard down and I'd caught him. That wasn't supposed to happen. He tried to cover it with a short response. "I already told you."

"Apparently not everything. Come on...spit it out."

He rose up on one elbow and caught my gaze with narrowed eyes, thinking I might be sorry I asked.

"Why would I be sorry? What did you do? Did you make a deal with him?"

Chris kept his mind blank, but I still picked up the underlying alarm that I wasn't supposed to know anything about it. "Of course not," he ground out, but I knew a lie when I saw one.

"You did too." How had this happened? How did I not know about it? "What was the deal?"

He flopped back down on his back and let out a sigh. "I'm not at liberty to say."

"Oh come on! You have to tell me," I begged. Chris didn't respond and his thoughts closed up tight, so I pulled out the big guns. "Uncle Joey called me and I went to see him today."

"What?" He jerked upright. "He called you? He's not supposed to do that."

"Yeah, well...I guess you're wrong about that. So what did you promise him? You might as well tell me now."

He huffed out a breath and pursed his lips in anger. "I told him I'd personally see to the cases he has with our firm...basically that I'd take Kate's intended spot and represent his 'clients.' In return for that, he was supposed leave you alone. I can't believe he reneged on that." He called Uncle Joey all kinds of names in his mind, which kind of defeated the purpose since I could hear him. Finally running out of steam, he banged his head against the backboard a couple of times. "What did he want?"

"Um...well, now that I think about it, his call wasn't really for him. It was for Kate."

"Huh? Kate's in Seattle, isn't she?"

"So maybe he kept his word after all."

"Shelby..." he growled. "What's going on?"

"Okay...okay." I scooted up in bed to sit beside him. Now that I knew Uncle Joey had Chris working for him, I could understand the satisfaction I'd picked up from his mind earlier. "Uncle Joey asked me to come into the office, and when I got there, Kate was there. She's having some kind of trouble with a partner or something, and she needs me to listen to him so she'll know if he's lying. I told her I'd do it for five hundred dollars...and she agreed. So, tomorrow I'm going to lunch with her and her partner. See? So Uncle Joey hasn't reneged at all."

Chris couldn't believe I was defending Manetto. What about him and everything he'd done for me? Defending Manetto's clients wasn't a picnic, even though it had only been one so far, but still. He quickly shuttered his thoughts and closed his eyes not wanting to get into more trouble, but not before I picked up his frustration with me and my damn mind-reading ability. The underlying conflict that I could read his thoughts had never gone away. It was the source of most of our frustration with each other, and tonight was worse than it had been in a long while.

"I wish I'd known about your bargain," I said, equally upset with him.

"Yeah, well...I probably should have told you."

"Yes." I sighed and tried to look at it from his point of view. "But you were afraid I'd get upset, and you were probably right. Look, I'm sorry you had to do that." I leaned against him with my head on his shoulder to let him know I wasn't too mad, and he wrapped his arms around me, pulling me in tight. "Thanks for trying to keep me safe, honey. That was really sweet."

He was thinking, *Trying? Sweet? I'm working for Manetto and that's the best you can do?*

"Okay... keeping me safe. That's so...macho. Is that better?"

Exasperated, he let out a groan and pulled me down to lie flat underneath him. He was ready to strangle me, but instead began to nuzzle my neck and then my ear before trailing kisses across my cheek to my lips. Kissing me deeply, his frustration turned into passion which fed my own, and soon the only thought in my mind was that if this was how all our arguments ended, I didn't mind in the least.

The next morning I woke up happy, the warm glow of knowing my man had gone out on a limb for me filled me with contentment. Taking on Uncle Joey's clients was no small act on Chris' part, and even though I wasn't sure he should have done that, I knew he'd done it for me, and I felt cherished and loved. I also knew I'd have to confront Uncle Joey and tell him to back off, or at least work out a compromise of some kind. Of course, now that he didn't want me involved in his current situation, maybe I should just leave it alone.

Since everyone in the house had to leave home about the same time, it was a mad rush to get out the door. My kids knew I was working on a new case, but I'd told them it was about someone who'd been missing for six years and presumed dead.

That made both of them feel better. Savannah was especially glad, since she didn't quite trust that I could stay out of trouble. She could never understand how that happened since I had 'premonitions' and should know if something bad might happen to me. I could see what she meant, and I couldn't help the twinge of guilt that twisted my stomach for what I'd put my kids through.

Getting shot...for the second time if I counted the grocery store, had that effect. Someday, I might have to tell her the truth about reading minds, but every time I thought about it, I knew I couldn't do it. I mean...seriously? If I knew my mom could read my mind?? I'd want to die. So there was no way I could tell my kids. I'd just have to keep it at premonitions and hope for the best.

I made it to the financial office just after eight and hurried inside. I introduced myself to the secretary and asked her a few questions before my appointment with her boss. "So, were you here when Darcy Shaw went missing?"

"Oh my...yes," she said. "That was one of the worst things that ever happened here. I'd only been here a few months myself when she disappeared, and I can't tell you how scared I was that it could happen to me. That's when they hired extra security to make sure if anyone stayed late they got to their cars okay."

"Did it happen often that people stayed late?"

"Oh yes, all the time," she said. "Most of our clients come at the end of the day so there's usually someone here until at least seven at night."

"That's interesting. In the police report, it says she left home around seven-thirty to drop something off. Do you know what it was?"

She shrugged. "I'd imagine it was some paperwork for one of the financial planners. She was always crunching numbers for them, so it must have been something they needed for a client. At least that's all I can think of." She was thinking that the only financial planner Darcy could have been helping was Kent, and he'd been devastated when he found out she'd disappeared, so she never thought anything of it. But what if...no, she refused to think he had anything to do with it. He was kind of a jerk though.

"Is Kent here today?" I asked.

"Y...es," she stammered, thinking that was weird, she'd never mentioned his name. "He's in his office."

"Great. Do you think he'd mind if I asked him a couple of questions?"

"I'm sure he'd help if he's not with a client," she said. But she was thinking he wouldn't like it at all, and worried she'd get in trouble if I barged in on him. Getting yelled at by Kent was never a fun experience. One she tried to avoid at all costs. On second thought, maybe she'd better tell me to make an appointment.

"It's okay," I said. "I'll talk to your boss first. He's the one I'm here to see. I'll have him show me where Kent's office is when we're done."

"That would actually be really great. I'll let Todd know you're here."

"Thanks," I answered. She picked up the phone and soon ushered me toward the big boss' door. The first thing I noticed when I walked in was the view. His desk was nicely situated on the left side of the room instead of centered in the middle. From here he could look out the big windows and see the lush, green golf course and the park with a playground on the other side of the buildings.

He stood to greet me as I came in. "Hi Mr. Baxter, I'm Shelby Nichols. Thanks for seeing me on such short notice."

"That's quite all right," he said. He was thinking it was kind of strange that the police were looking into Darcy's disappearance after all these years, but maybe they had a lead. He sure hoped so. "What would you like to know?"

I had a sinking feeling that this was a dead-end. "I'd like to know why Darcy was coming back to the office that night. What was so important that it couldn't wait until the next day?"

"That's a good question. As I recall, I think she had a report for someone in the office."

"Was it Kent?" I asked.

His brows raised in surprise. "Yes that's right, it was for him. I can't remember what she was working on, but you're welcome to ask him yourself. He still works here."

"That would be great," I said. "Do you think her disappearance had anything to do with her job?"

"Absolutely not," he said. "I asked myself that question several times back then, but I never could come up with any reason for it. You always wonder if she ran off with someone...but if she did, it wasn't anyone from this office."

"Then what do you think happened?"

He shrugged. "I honestly don't know. It could have been anything. All I know is that when she didn't come home after an hour or so, her husband came to the office looking for her. He found her car in the parking structure with the keys and all her personal stuff in it, and hurried inside to our offices. The building was still open because Kent was here, but Kent hadn't seen her, so they called the police, and then they called me." He swallowed, remembering that night and how bizarre it was that she'd just disappeared like that. He'd never forget the way Scott fell apart, little by little as the night wore on, and how he stayed there all night waiting for her to show up.

They'd scoured the grounds and even brought in a dog to pick up her scent, but it lead nowhere. It still creeped him out just a little to walk into that parking structure late at night, knowing that was the last place she'd been seen alive.

"Is there anything else you need?" he asked.

"Um...so you think she's dead?"

He glanced at me quickly before looking away. "I think if she were alive, she would have come back. She had a great family, two kids, a good husband. From what I knew of her, she wouldn't have left them willingly. So...yes, I think she's dead."

I nodded, grateful for his honesty. "Thanks, that's all I have for now...could you introduce me to Kent?"

"Sure," he nodded. "But why are the police looking into this? Do you have a new lead?" His hope that I did took some of the heaviness of her disappearance away.

I hated to disappoint him, especially when he felt so bad. "We might have something, but it's a long shot, so please don't say anything. I'm not sure it will pan out, but I've decided to look into it anyway."

"Oh...that's good. Will you let me know if you find anything? I'd sure like to know what happened to her." That night had haunted him for a long time. Even talking about it now unsettled him.

"You bet...I'd be happy to."

He smiled with relief and stood. "Kent's office is this way."

I followed him out the door and down the hall. Luckily, Kent's door was open, so we just walked in. He glanced up with surprise to see me with Todd, and hoped I was a new client with lots of money to invest. However, as Todd explained my reason for being there, his lips thinned with distaste. He wasn't happy that I wanted to question him about that night, mostly because it was something he'd worked hard to forget.

"Thanks for talking with me," I said with a gracious smile. "I promise I'll only take a minute of your time." I knew it didn't matter how long I actually took, but telling people it would only take a minute made them a lot more likely to cooperate.

"Sure. Have a seat." He gestured to the chair in front of his desk and sat down. "It's been a long time since Darcy disappeared. Have you found something new?"

"Yes," I lied, but only because he had surprised me with his directness. "But it's not a lot to go on, so I need you to tell me what you remember from that night. Darcy was supposed to meet with you, right?"

"Um...no. That's the weird thing. Everyone thinks that because I was working late that night. They think it was me she was coming to see. But I never told her she had to bring me anything. I know she'd been working on a report for me, but unless she took it home by accident, there was no rush to get it to me that night."

"Hmm...that is strange," I agreed, noting that he was certainly doing a lot of explaining for someone who wasn't involved.

"Yeah. I never understood what she was doing here at all." He was thinking he knew exactly what she was doing here and it was most likely his fault. The familiar pang of guilt flooded him with anger. He never should have given her that ultimatum about needing that report on his desk first thing in the morning, but it still didn't make him responsible for her disappearance. It wasn't his fault.

"Okay...let's assume for a minute that she was bringing that report for you. Can you think of anyone else in the office who would know she was coming back that night? Was there someone she may have told, or who may have overheard you telling her you needed that report on your desk by morning?"

His breath caught and his gaze snapped to mine. How did I know that? The flash of anger in his eyes changed to disbelief, before he dismissed it as a fluke. "I suppose she could have confided in someone who worked here, but I don't know who."

"Whatever happened to that report? Did you ever find it?"

"No. It never showed up here, so if she had it, she must have taken it with her or something, because it wasn't in the car either."

"Wow, that's nuts," I said. "What was in the report? Was it something worth kidnapping her for?"

He shook his head. "No. It wasn't that important. It was just a calculation of projected taxes based on growth for a portfolio I was working on for a client."

"Did your client ever get the report?"

"Sure. I re-worked it for him myself."

"Okay," I nodded. "So she wasn't taken because of your report."

"No," he said firmly. He was starting to lose his patience with me, so I knew I'd better hurry before he shut up entirely.

"Your company takes up the entire fourth floor, is that right?" At his nod, I continued. "From your experience, do any other tenants in the building work late, or are they pretty much out of here by five o'clock?"

"I think most of them are gone by six, but sometimes people stay late."

"Do you remember if her car was the only one in the parking structure that night?"

He heaved a sigh. "That was a long time ago, but I'm pretty sure there were a few other cars there, probably between four to eight. I think the police questioned everyone who was still here in the building, just to see if anyone had seen her. They didn't find anything. Now...if you're done, I have work to do." He was thinking for a police detective, I hadn't done my homework or I'd know the answers to all these stupid questions, and wouldn't be wasting his time.

Wow, the secretary was right, he was a jerk. "Well, thanks for your time." He grunted, and I quickly walked out the door. As I left, the secretary made me promise to let her know if I found anything new. After confirming that I would, I took the elevator to the first floor. With time before my next appointment, I stopped to scan the register on the wall near the elevators to see who the other tenants were.

The realization that her abductor could have been anyone in this building hit me hard, and I knew Kent was right that I should have talked to the detective before I came here. If he or the private investigator Scott hired had done their work right, it made sense that they would have checked out the people in the rest of the building. If there was a connection, they would have found it.

At this hour it was quiet in the corridor with most everyone hard at work in their offices. I read the names of the tenants out loud, noting there were five altogether. I got to the last one and a sudden chill swept over me, making my arms break out in goose bumps. My breath hitched, and I rubbed my arms, while turning in a slow circle. The outside doors were closed with no one else in sight. On a whim, I read the last name aloud once more, and again felt a cold touch like a soft breath against my cheek, only this time it carried the smell of gardenias.

Chapter 4

I gasped and, with a surge of adrenaline, raced out the door and into the fresh air. After a few deep breaths, my heart slowed, but my legs still shook. What was going on? Had I really smelled gardenias again? Needing to put some distance between me and that building, I headed toward the courtyard that was at the middle of the building complex.

The center of the courtyard held a large fountain surrounded with trees, shrubbery and flowers. Hearing the pleasant gurgle of water soothed me, and I questioned my sanity. Was my mind playing tricks on me? I sat on a bench to collect myself and tried to reason it through. There had to be a logical explanation for all of it.

Feeling the chill in the air and smelling those flowers was all in my head. For some reason, I'd personalized Darcy's death, probably because we had so much in common. So it was only natural that I'd feel a connection to her and my imagination was just overdoing it.

That's all...no way was she haunting me. Only...now I had a clue I couldn't ignore. I definitely needed to check out tenant number five in that building, Marketing Solutions,

LLC. But how could I go back there? Just thinking about it brought goose bumps to my arms again.

I glanced at the other office buildings in the plaza and turned toward building three. Darcy's husband, Scott, worked in number three so I headed in that direction. Hesitating in front of the doors, I took a deep breath and hurried into the lobby.

After punching the sixth floor, I kept my gaze away from the listing of tenants. Whatever was going on, I wasn't quite ready for another freaky incident. I got on the elevator and tried to relax. When the elevator doors opened on the sixth floor, my composure had returned, and I found Scott's architecture firm located in the suite to the right. A friendly receptionist led me to the office where Scott sat at his desk with a large computer monitor. It was in the center of a spacious room with lots of light and large windows.

He quickly stood to greet me, and I entered with my mind wide open so I'd know what I was up against. In his mind, he was prepared to treat me with polite indifference, but that changed when he saw me. For a split second, he thought I was Darcy, but the similarities ended after a second look. Still, the fact that I looked like her surprised him. Some of his outward distrust disappeared, but he still kept his guard up. He wouldn't be completely sold on my merits until we had a nice little chat.

He was thinking that after looking at my website and reading about me in the newspaper, he felt better about his daughter hiring me. He'd found out I occasionally worked for the police, and that went a long way to dispel his distrust, especially with the rumors that I had 'premonitions.'

At first he'd been concerned that I was out to take advantage of his daughter, but now it looked like I was legitimate, and that made him more open to my investigation. Even if he didn't want to admit it, a small part of him hoped that maybe I could succeed where the others had failed.

That didn't sound like a man who had murdered his wife.

We exchanged greetings, and Scott pointed to a medium-sized box on the side of his desk. "I put the documents from the private investigator in this box for you. Everything he found out is in there. You're welcome to keep it for as long as you like." He was thinking it wouldn't matter if I give it back. He'd kept it too long as it was.

"Thank you, I really appreciate it."

"I hope it helps." He caught my gaze, wanting to emphasize his point. "I didn't realize Tiffany was going to hire someone or I would have shared this with her a long time ago."

I smiled and nodded. "I understand, but just so you know, she told me this was something she needed to do. I think she needs some kind of closure so she can move on with her life."

"And you think you can give it to her?" He'd heard of psychics feeding on the vulnerabilities of others with false promises, and wasn't about to let me try anything like that on his daughter.

"I don't know, but I'd like to try."

He liked that I hadn't agreed to something I couldn't know, and his mouth creased into a curt smile.

"Can we get started?" I asked. "I'd like to hear in your own words what happened that night."

"Sure," he agreed, and we both sat down. I sensed immediately how emotionally draining this was for him to relive the worst day of his life. His story matched up with everything I already knew. He told the events clearly and concisely, only leaving out the pain and fear he'd felt, and I knew it was the truth.

"How long did you wait after the police investigation to hire the P.I.?" I asked.

"About two weeks," he said. "At first, I knew they were taking it seriously and doing everything they could. There were even some leads they followed up on, but nothing came of them. That's when I got frustrated with the way they handled it. It was like they kept putting me off, but now I know it was because they had nothing to tell me. That's when I hired the P.I."

"Did you ever receive any strange phone calls?"

"No. I kept waiting for something. Hoping actually, but there was never anything like that. I've never told anyone this, but somewhere along the way it just hit me that she was gone." He couldn't say dead even now. "It was the weirdest thing, but as I stepped back from the situation, I realized the feeling had been there for a while, and I just knew it here." He placed his hand over his heart.

I nodded and sent a sympathetic smile his way. "One more thing. Do you know anyone who works for Marketing Solutions on the first floor of her building?"

"No, I don't."

"Do you think Darcy might have had contact with anyone who worked there?"

"No," he said, his brows drawn together. "Why?"

I shrugged. "Let's just say I have a feeling that someone in the company is connected to her in some way. I don't know how, or why, but I'd like to find out."

He raised his brows. To his knowledge, no one had done more than the cursory Q and A with the tenants in Darcy's building. If I had a 'feeling' about it, he was more than interested in what I could find out. "You can check the files from the police and my P.I. to see if they interviewed anyone from there. But I never heard of a connection."

"All right, I will. Hey...did Darcy like gardenias?" I asked on a whim.

His face paled. "Yes. She did. In fact, she loved the way they smelled. How did you know?"

I didn't know quite what to say, so I went with the truth. "As I've worked on this case, I've smelled them a few times...weird huh?"

"Yeah," he agreed, thinking it would probably freak him out if he were in my place. But hearing that also had a soothing effect on him. He hoped I'd finally find out what had happened to her. He hated to think that she had died painfully, but it was worse thinking her killer was still out there. It also made him a believer that I really was psychic. How else could I have known that?

"Well...thanks for your time, and for this." I picked up the box. "I'd better get going."

"Wait," he said. "How much is Tiffany paying you?"

"Um...one-fifty an hour, but she gave me five hundred and I'm going to see how far I can stretch it."

His smile widened. "That's nice of you, but how about I give you another five hundred to stay in the loop. That way I don't have to go through my daughter to find out what you know." He pulled out his wallet and took out five hundred dollars along with his business card.

I shrugged. "Sure, but wouldn't talking about my investigation give you an excuse to talk to her more often, especially with the wedding coming up?"

"You don't know how much I would like that, but she doesn't always tell me things. I have to admit, I wasn't real happy that she hired you, so I doubt she'll want to tell me much about your investigation. Paying you will guarantee that I'll know what she knows. Oh...and Tiffany doesn't need to know about this. Okay? We'll keep it our secret."

"Fine," I agreed, taking the money. He made a good argument, and if I were in his place, I'd probably do the same.

He showed me out and even offered to carry the box for me, but it wasn't heavy, so I declined and got on the elevator with a promise to keep in touch. It wasn't long before I was back in the parking structure and unlocking my car. I slid into the front seat and maneuvered the box onto the passenger seat. In the process, my bag fell off my shoulder spilling the contents of the police file onto the floor.

After getting settled, I picked up the papers and noticed several photos of her car. They showed the car door open with the keys in the ignition and her purse on the passenger seat. I studied them for a moment and glanced up, realizing why it looked so familiar. I was in the same parking structure. This was where she'd been abducted. For some reason, I hadn't put it together.

I glanced back at the photos and noticed the number four on the wall above her car. The hairs on the back of my neck stood on end. I glanced up and right in front of me was the number four. My heart started to race and my mouth went dry. What were the chances of that happening? Of course, the space was empty or I wouldn't have parked here. Still, it seemed like more than a coincidence, and a jolt of panic spiked through me.

Hardly daring to breathe, I grabbed the keys from my purse and, with shaking hands, got the car started. I backed out a little too fast, but managed not to hit anything, and got the hell out of there. This case was freaking me out. What had happened in the dead file room I could almost believe was a figment of my imagination. It was creepy down there anyway. But that didn't explain what had happened in the lobby today, or the few times I'd smelled gardenias. The fact that I'd parked in the exact same spot where they'd found her car nearly put me over the edge.

I turned on the radio to get my mind off the creep factor and concentrated on driving responsibly. A gas station on my right caught my attention and I pulled into a parking place. Inside, I filled the largest cup I could find with Diet Coke and added both vanilla and cherry flavorings. It was good, but didn't quite do the trick, so I found my favorite candy bar and got that too.

Back in my car, I took a big bite of chocolate paired with caramel and nuts. I didn't know what was going on, but chocolate always made it better. I enjoyed each bite and sighed when it was gone, but at least now I felt fortified and ready to get back to work.

Meeting with the retired detective was next on my list, but since I was meeting at his house, I figured I didn't have to worry about anything weird happening there. On a whim, I rolled down my windows to enjoy the breeze and sang along with the radio. By the time I arrived at Geoff Parkers' house, I was pretty much back to normal.

The man who answered the door had a gruff look about him. He was medium height and barrel-chested with a square jaw and unshaven face. His thick gray hair stuck up in a few places, and splotches of red stained his worn flannel shirt. He noticed my gaze on his shirt, and a smile broke over his face, making him seem less formidable. "You must be Shelby." He opened the screen door. "Come on in. The wife and I are putting up tomatoes, but we just finished a batch so this is perfect timing."

That explained the red stains. "Thanks so much for meeting with me."

"No problem. Let's go into my workshop. That's where I keep everything."

I followed him into a room where clocks of all kinds hung from the walls. A work bench with desk lamps and magnifying glasses took up most of the space, and tools I'd never seen before rested in a meticulously organized chest. "Wow. Do you work on these?"

"Yeah, it's a hobby of mine. Only now, instead of clocks, I've switched to watches. Take a look at this beauty."

He turned on the desk lamp and held a watch under a magnifying glass. He gently popped open the back, showing me the intricate gears inside his newest creation.

"So...you made that?" I asked.

"Yeah. I like putting all the pieces together...kind of like a puzzle." He was thinking it was also like doing detective work, but without all the blood and death. He liked this better. "Anyway, have a seat. Can I get you anything? Coffee? Soda?"

"Oh no, I'm good thanks." I sat down on a chair beside his work bench, and he pulled a box from a corner.

"This is everything I kept, so let's get down to business." He was thinking that after all these years, he could finally pass on what he'd found and be done with it. "After you called yesterday, it reminded me of all the extra research I'd done and kept these last few years. That case was one of the hardest I'd ever come across, and I always felt bad that it went unsolved.

"You have to remember, when the leads dry up, and more homicides are committed every day, it's easy for unsolved cases to get pushed to the side. Right before I retired last spring, I went back over the unsolved cases and picked that one to look at one more time. I hoped with fresh eyes maybe I'd see something that I'd missed before.

"That case was hard on me, and I felt like I hadn't done my job right, or maybe I would have found something.

Anyway...I took another look, but nothing had changed, so I changed my perspective. That's when I found something."

He took out four folders and laid them side by side on the table. "These are copies. The originals with all the rest of the information are still in the dead file room." He opened the first file, showing the photocopy of Darcy's picture. "This is your case, but these..." he gestured to the others and opened them one by one, "are three other missing person reports. They all occurred after Darcy's disappearance."

I glanced at the pictures, noting they were all pretty women in their late twenties to mid-thirties. I shuffled through the pages and found they had all disappeared under suspicious circumstances. One was out jogging, another had gone to the grocery store and never come back, and the third never showed up at work. The cars in which the two women had disappeared were not left behind with keys like Darcy's. They had been abandoned, leading the investigators to believe the women may have run off. One of them was going through a divorce, and the other wasn't married. The jogger had a husband and three kids, and they hadn't found a trace of her anywhere.

"I know they don't look related," Geoff said. "But just take a look at the dates."

As I scanned each date, my pulse quickened. "They all disappeared in October."

"Now check the years."

I glanced at each year and could hardly believe what I was seeing. "If you start with Darcy's file there's a two year gap, but since then, these have happened every year, ending with last year at this time." I didn't state the obvious, but a chill ran up my spine.

"If this is a pattern, it might happen again...this month," Geoff said. "But what do I know? I turned this over to one of the detectives before I left, but I don't know if he followed through on it or not."

"Who was the detective?"

"Wilkinson. Do you know him?"

"No. I don't think he's still there, but I can ask Dimples...a...Detective Harris. He's the one I work with." I glanced at Geoff and his eyes crinkled in the corners.

"Dimples?" he snickered. "Yeah I know who Dimples is." He wasn't going to let me live it down. He laughed again. "You don't call him that to his face, do you?"

"Oh...no...of course not," I sputtered.

He chuckled even more. "You're a terrible liar." He was thinking Harris probably hated it. But if he let me call him that, then he was either crazy, or he had a big crush on me. After looking me over, he'd bet on the crush.

"He has a girlfriend," I said.

Geoff's eyes narrowed and his brows drew together. That was weird. "Is that so?" he asked. Then it clicked. "Wait a minute...are you the lady with the premonitions?"

"Oh...so, you've heard about me?"

He chuckled. "Yeah...there aren't too many people like you who do consulting work for the department, so yeah, I've heard plenty."

"Was it good?" I had to ask.

He smiled. "What do you think?"

Since he wasn't thinking anything one way or the other, I went with my gut. "Probably good, with a little weird thrown in?"

"You got that right. Not everyone in the department thinks you're for real, but I figure what does it matter?" He shrugged. "You get the bad guys, everyone's happy." His thoughts shifted to what he remembered hearing about me getting arrested for murder, and his smile drooped a little.

"Well...just so you know, I'm back on the payroll. I've got my badge back and everything."

"Badge? What badge?" He didn't think that made any sense. Most consultants didn't have badges.

"Yeah, my honorary badge. Here, I'll show you." I pulled my ID card out of my purse and showed it to him.

He glanced at it and tried not to smile. This was not a badge, it was an ID card. "That's not a bad picture. You look pretty good." He kept his mirth under control, thinking he didn't want to hurt my feelings by pointing out my mistake.

"Um...thanks." I quickly put it away, knowing a red flush of embarrassment stained my cheeks. "Is there anything you can tell me about Darcy's case that's not in the file? Did you interview anyone that seemed suspicious but you couldn't pursue because you didn't have enough to go on?

He thought for a minute before replying. "No. At first, everyone looked suspicious, but then after a week went by with nothing, it was like all the leads dried up. They went nowhere, and our investigation came to a stop. I think the husband may have hired a P.I. You should talk to him."

"Yeah, I talked to the husband before I came here, and he gave me everything the P.I. had on the case."

"Oh, that's good," he said.

"What about the other tenants in the office building. Did you interview any of the employees that may have seen something that night?"

"Well...let's see. I'm pretty sure we canvassed the area for witnesses, but with the car in the parking structure, it's not visible from any of the buildings, so that really cut out any eyewitness reports. As far as the other tenants in the building...I don't remember any that stood out."

"How about the Marketing Solutions Company on the first floor?"

He rubbed his head and frowned. "To be honest, that doesn't ring a bell. You might have better luck reading the file. We were pretty meticulous about our findings."

I nodded. "Okay. I'll get right on it. Do you mind if I take these other files? I'm interested to know if any of them got solved."

"Yeah, that's fine. In fact, I'd be glad to see someone working on them. Who knows? If one of them has been solved since I left, that might mean that Darcy's killer is in jail already, and all you need to do is link them together." He seriously doubted that, since they weren't solved when he left last spring, but he didn't want to discourage me. He also didn't want to scare me off. This was October...the same month and time-span between killings. It meant the killer could strike any day now. Since all the victims had light-colored hair and blue eyes...just like me...it could get a little creepy.

Why did he have to think that? I was already creeped out enough as it was. He also thought they were dead...murdered. It took all my will power to suppress my shudder and put the folders in my bag. "If you remember anything else, please don't hesitate to call me." I handed him my business card.

"Sure," he said. "And feel free to call me if you need anything." He was thinking he'd come out of retirement to help me if he thought it would do any good. Still, he was glad I was on the case, and he hoped I could find out what had happened to those poor women. "One more thing...if you do figure it out, will you let me buy you a drink?"

He was sincere about that, and it hinted of a respect between colleagues which brought a lift to my spirits. "It would be my pleasure," I agreed. We shook hands and I hurried out to my car, ready to get started on the files.

On the drive home, I couldn't help thinking that instead of one missing-person case, I now had four. But I decided my first priority was to my client, Tiffany Shaw. If I found something that connected the disappearances to each other, I wouldn't hesitate to look into it, but I wasn't going to waste my time. For now, I would concentrate on Darcy. After all, wasn't it her energy I kept feeling? At least I had one good clue, even if it did come from a dead person.

Once I got inside Marketing Solutions, I could use my mind-reading skills to find the person linked to Darcy Shaw. It might even be the killer. Wouldn't that be great? But even finding the killer wouldn't do me much good unless I had solid evidence linking him to Darcy's death, and the thing I needed most to prove that, was her body. So, not only did I need to catch the killer, I needed to know what he'd done with her. This could get dicey. I mean...what if he'd chopped her up into tiny little pieces? Eww...that would be awful.

I pulled into my driveway and dragged my heavy bag inside, then went back out to get both boxes and carried them into Chris' office. Before taking a second look at the files, I woke up my computer and googled the marketing company. After it came up, I eagerly clicked on the website.

The company looked like a computer software business that used their software to design websites, send out email campaigns, and research strategies to promote small businesses. It was a small company with only thirteen employees besides the president and vice-president who turned out to be brothers. Wow, this was perfect. I could use my consulting agency as the reason to set up an appointment. Once inside, I could meet the staff and hopefully get an idea of who might be connected to Darcy.

With a burst of excitement, I called and made an appointment for the next afternoon. That settled, I took out the folders and looked through them, comparing everything I could to determine if anything else besides the dates was related.

An hour later, and no further in my search, I decided to put in a quick call to Dimples. He picked up and I told him about my meeting with Detective Parker. "He said he gave all four files to Detective Wilkinson. Do you know what he did with them or where he is? I know he's not there now, but if you could tell me where he went, I could talk to him about this. Maybe he found something new."

"Um...I'm afraid he moved to Arizona," Dimples said. "But I might be able to find a phone number."

"Oh...all right. That should work. Was he a good cop?"

"Yeah, he was good. He just got tired of living in the city, and with his wife's health problems, it made it easy to move to a drier climate. Okay...here it is." He rattled off a number. "I don't know if that one will still work, but you can give it a try."

"Sure, thanks," I said.

"Um...I don't know what happened to his case files, but I imagine they're still here. Since you found the first file in the dead files room, that's probably where the others are too. You might want to come back and take a look...unless you're too scared to go back down there."

I could hear the teasing smile in his voice. "Ha! Not me, I can go down there just fine."

"Good," he said. "When do you want to come in?"

"Well, let's see...it's about one...I could...oh damn! I forgot about lunch!"

With my heart racing, I disconnected and sprinted to the bathroom. Thank goodness I'd put on my make-up and a cute outfit this morning. In seconds I'd fluffed up my hair and applied a thin coat of lipstick before grabbing my purse and running to the car.

If I hurried, I'd only be a few minutes late. It usually took time to get seated, so that would work in my favor as well. I just hoped Kate wouldn't be mad. It would be just like her to dock my fee of five hundred dollars for being late. I sped down the freeway and got off the ramp downtown in record time, grateful not to get caught for speeding.

I pulled up in front of the valet parking and jumped out, barely waiting for my claim ticket. Inside, it was packed with people waiting for tables, and I scanned the area for any sight of Kate. Not finding her, I hurried to the hostess desk and gave her my name. "Oh, I just seated your party a few minutes ago, they're this way."

Whew! That was close. I'd made it and was only sweating a little. Hopefully it wouldn't show too much, and all that rushing around would give my complexion a healthy glow instead of a wilted one. Guilt that I'd hung up on Dimples swept over me, but if he knew I was meeting Kate, he'd understand.

I followed the hostess to the table and spotted Kate looking perfect and elegant seated beside a man whose back was to me. She caught sight of me coming to the table and smiled, telling her companion I had arrived. The man beside her turned in his chair and politely stood. Shock slowed my progress. He was the spitting image of Jon Passini.

"Sorry I'm late," I said breathlessly, and quickly moved into the empty chair.

"That's all right," Kate answered. "I've just been telling Alec all about you. Shelby, this is my associate, Alec Passini."

He smiled and gave my hand a quick squeeze. "So nice to meet you."

"Nice to meet you too," I said. Now that I was closer, I could see the differences. Alec was younger with a leaner build and narrower face. He had the same dark eyes, but instead of anger and resentment, his held warmth and kindness. What was going on here?

"Kate told me you knew each other in college," Alec said.

"Yes...that's where we got to be such good friends." Keeping a smile on my face while I said that proved difficult. Kate was thinking that my smile looked more like a grimace and she was glad Alec wasn't watching me too closely.

"It was my first year in college," Kate began. "And Shelby's last. Then she got married and left for law school."

Alec turned to me, his brows raised in interest. "So you're a lawyer too?"

"Uh...no. It was my husband that went to law school."

"Oh, I see...so what did you graduate in?"

"I didn't graduate because we got married and I had to work while my husband went to law school." I glanced at Kate to find a smug smile on her face, and knew she was enjoying this way too much. I was going to kill her for this.

"How is Chris anyway?" she purred.

"Good," I said.

She glanced at Alec. "Chris and I worked at the same law firm, so it was fun to renew my friendship with Shelby. I think we were both surprised to see each other again after so long. But anyway, Shelby's got her own business now," Kate explained, noticing the anger in my eyes. "She's quite successful. What do you call it again?"

"I'm a paid consultant, but what I do is more like a private investigator. It's called Shelby Nichols Consulting Agency."

"How interesting," Alec said. "What kinds of things have you done?"

"Oh...mostly snooping into other people's business...that sort of thing." I caught the look of surprise on his face and smiled. "Just kidding. What I do isn't all that interesting. Just lots of sitting around in a car for hours and spying on people. But that's enough about me, tell me about you two. What brings you here from Seattle? Kate said you're working on something together?"

"Yes," Alec answered. "We're looking at a way to merge our companies and came here for some legal documents."

Kate jumped in like I didn't know what was going on, and explained how they were trying to reach an agreement between their shipping companies. "We're hoping a merger will be beneficial to both of us."

"Nice," I said. "Well, I hope it works out then."

We chatted throughout our lunch, and at one-fifty, Alec excused himself for a meeting he had to attend. After he left, Kate dropped all pretense of being my best friend. "So what did you pick up?" she asked.

It was tempting not to tell her everything, but since she was paying me the big bucks, I had to give it to her straight. I wasn't sure what to say about Alec's brother, Jon, and his visit to Uncle Joey. I had a feeling it was all tied together somehow. Maybe I'd better leave Uncle Joey out of it until I knew what was going on.

"Well, for starters, I picked up that you two have been sleeping together." She hadn't been expecting me to say that, and her neck and face turned red and splotchy. "But I won't tell Uncle Joey that part if you don't want me to, although it might explain a few things."

"Things? What things?" she asked.

"Well...I don't think he planned on having feelings for you, so it's kind of put him in a bind."

Kate's eyes widened with hope. "So all of this isn't just a show? He really does care about me?"

"Yes. In fact...he thinks he's in love with you. His job...from what I could pick up...is to make sure you go through with this merger. Once that's accomplished, the plan is to take control of your share so his company can take over, or something like that. It's a little complicated, and I'm not sure I've got all of it right. All I know is that he doesn't want to go through with it now, but if he doesn't, he's afraid he might die. He's also afraid that if he tells you that he was going to double-cross you, even though he had a change of heart, you'd probably want him dead too. So, I guess he's in a tight spot."

I didn't tell her that his boss was his older brother, and he really wasn't afraid Jon would kill him, although I did pick up some definite fear there. Because of that, I had to believe that blood might be thicker than water, since I wasn't sure his love for Kate would be enough for him to stand against his brother's plan when it came right down to it. "I guess you'll have to decide if you want to be with him, and what you're willing to give up for him. Otherwise, I'd just tell you to stop the merger...which might be a good thing anyway."

Kate was thinking what a mess this was, but now that she knew what was going on, she could figure out what to do. She could make sure she didn't lose her company. Deciding what to do about Alec might be a little harder, but she was sure she could think of something.

She opened her purse and pulled out five one-hundred dollar bills. "Here's your fee." She handed it to me and added, "I'll give you five hundred more not to tell Uncle Joey."

"What? You can't be serious. You know how Uncle Joey feels about double-crossers."

She pursed her lips. "Yeah, but this isn't double-crossing, this is personal. Now that I know what's going on, I can take care of it myself. I don't need him involved." I didn't agree right away so she continued. "If you must tell him something, at least tell him a shortened version and leave out the part about Alec being in love with me."

I shook my head. "You know, I truly believe that being in love makes people stupid, so I'll try and forget you tried to bribe me."

She gasped and her mouth dropped open. Shock that I had the audacity to call her stupid sent her pulse racing. Who did I think I was anyway? She made a move to snatch the cash back out of my fingers, but I knew it was coming and quickly stuffed it in my purse.

"Geez Kate, calm down," I said. "All I meant was that sometimes people do crazy things when they're in love. You don't want to get on Uncle Joey's bad side now do you? Besides, you should be happy to know Alec's really in love with you. That's positive, right?"

Her mouth moved like a fish out of water, but no sound came out. That was a good thing since what she was thinking wasn't very nice. I took that as my cue to leave. "Well, thanks for lunch. If you need anything else, let me know." I probably shouldn't have said that last part, but I couldn't resist.

Turning my back on her wasn't the best idea, but since we were in a crowded restaurant, I figured I'd be safe. Although it didn't stop my ears from burning with her insults, so I put up my shields. I didn't have to listen to that crap, and she probably had no idea I could do that. It made me feel powerful and in control. Outside the restaurant, I had to wait for the valet to bring my car and I tensed up, worried that Kate would come out before I left. That would be awkward. Thankfully, he brought my car around pretty quick, and I jumped in.

I drove away, making a quick decision to stop by Uncle Joey's office while I was downtown, and then maybe stop by the precinct after that and apologize to Dimples. Uncle Joey needed to know what Kate had gotten herself into, and how it was probably related to his situation. I'd also have better luck finding out the parts he didn't want me to know if I talked to him in person.

At Thrasher Development, I exited the elevator and breezed inside, but Jackie wasn't sitting at her desk. Without her there to announce my arrival to Uncle Joey, I rounded the corner behind Jackie's desk to call his extension. After several rings, it went to voice mail, so I hung up without leaving a message.

Where was everybody? The 'ding' of the elevator sounded out in the hall and I heard some people exit the elevator and come toward the office. Not wanting to get caught behind Jackie's desk, I took a couple of steps, but didn't make it around the chair before they entered the office.

A commanding woman with thick, dark hair and artfully applied makeup entered with a younger man at her side. "Hello, you must be Jackie," she said. "We've spoken a few times over the phone. I'm Julia Passini and this is my accountant, Howard Anderson."

Yikes! Another Passini? She barely looked old enough to be Jon and Alec's mother, but with the same dark eyes, it had to be true. I smiled pleasantly. "Hello. Actually, I'm Shelby Nichols, but it's nice to meet you. Um...do you have an appointment with Uncle...uh...Mr. Manetto?"

Her eyes narrowed. She'd caught my slip and her smile faltered. "Where is Jackie?" She was thinking I looked guilty about something and trying to cover it up. From her experience, relatives were always trying to get something for nothing, and I had called him "uncle," so I was probably up to no good.

"I don't know," I quickly explained. "I just got here myself and thought I'd leave a note. That's why I was standing here behind her desk, looking for a notepad and pen? But I'm sure she's around here somewhere. Would you like to wait in the conference room while I check? I'll be happy to look for her while you wait." I knew I was talking too much, but her obvious disapproval put me on the defense.

Before she could answer, footsteps sounded in the hall and Jackie came around the corner. She stopped in surprise to find us all standing there.

"Jackie!" I said, relieved. "There you are. This is Julia Passini and her accountant Howard. They just got here."

Jackie raised a brow at me, but politely greeted them, asking that they follow her to Uncle Joey's office for their scheduled appointment. They disappeared down the hallway and I let out my breath. From Jackie's mind, I realized that they were early and Uncle Joey wasn't even there yet. I also picked up from Julia Passini that she had come early on purpose in order to snoop around in Uncle Joey's office if she got the chance.

If Jackie left her there alone, that's just what she'd do, so I hurried down the hall. Sure enough, Jackie came out and pulled the door closed behind her. "You can't leave them in there alone," I whispered. "They'll look through Uncle Joey's things."

Jackie studied me for a moment and without a word, pushed the door back open. Sure enough they were standing beside Uncle Joey's desk, with Julia reaching for the top drawer. Her eyes widened slightly, but other than that, there was no outward indication that she'd been caught snooping. Instead, she picked up a photo of Miguel, like that was what she'd been reaching for. "Who is this handsome young man?" she asked.

I didn't think Jackie should tell her the truth, but before I could open my mouth Jackie answered. "He's my son, and since Joe and I are together, Joe's grown quite fond of him."

"Ah...I see. How very nice for you." Julia didn't miss the mama-bear-menace in Jackie's tone, nor did she miss the implication that Uncle Joey belonged to Jackie. "I'm sure Joseph is very lucky to have you and your son in his life."

Howard took a seat in a wingback chair, hoping we hadn't noticed how close to the desk he'd been standing. He was thinking Julia had a lot of guts to come into Manetto's territory, but with her husband's death, it was time to settle the overdue accounts. He just hoped Jon hadn't screwed it up for her. She needed to get on Manetto's good side or she was toast.

"Shelby?" Jackie said.

"Huh?" Oops. She had asked me something, and I'd missed it.

"I just asked if you'd mind getting some bottled water from the break room for our guests."

"Oh, of course. I'll be right back." I hurried out, relieved Jackie was staying to keep an eye on them. She had lots more authority than I did, so I didn't think Julia would try anything with her there. I also picked up that Uncle Joey was supposed to get back in five to ten minutes, so it wouldn't be long now.

Wanting to warn Uncle Joey, I took my time getting the water and was rewarded when he came in a few minutes later with Ramos. "Shelby. What are you doing here?"

"I just stopped by to tell you about my lunch with Kate, and it's a good thing too, because when I got here Julia Passini and her accountant, Howard, showed up. They got here early to snoop around, so Jackie's been entertaining them in your office. I came out to get water for them, and decided to wait so I could warn you."

His eyes narrowed. "Did you pick up anything?"

"Yes."

"Come in here." He ushered me into the conference room for more privacy. "What did you get?"

"What I picked up mostly came from the accountant. He was thinking that with Julia's husband dead, it was time to get on your good side and not let Jon screw things up."

Uncle Joey pursed his lips. He was wondering how many Passinis he would have to deal with before this was over.

"Actually there is one more," I said. "The man Kate's been dealing with is the other son, Alec."

"Oh...I see," Uncle Joey said. "Now it's all starting to make sense." He glanced at me thinking it was a good thing I was there and that maybe he was being foolish for leaving me out of it. "I'd better get in there and rescue Jackie. I'll call you when I'm done, and you can tell me all about your lunch with Kate."

"Okay...but just so you know...she's in love with Alec."

"She loves him?" he asked. "This just gets worse and worse. Do you know what he wants from her?"

"Yeah...well...I think so."

Uncle Joey let out his breath. "Fine. I want a full report later, but right now I need to go. I'll call you." He was thinking this was worse than he thought, and nobody challenged him and got away with it.

He left the room and turned down the hall, buttoning his jacket and managing to grow taller and more confident with each step. Just as he opened the door, I realized I still held the water bottles in my hands. I took a step forward, but Ramos stopped me.

"Wait," he said. "I'll take them in."

I hesitated, glancing up at him. "All right. Thanks." He came to my side and took the bottles, his gaze never leaving mine.

"Just a word of advice," he said in a low voice, leaning in close. "I think you'd better stay away for a bit. For your own sake." He was thinking that there were some secrets Manetto kept that even Ramos didn't know. It would be bad for me if I found out what they were, and with my luck, that's just what would happen. Some things were meant to stay buried.

"You mean like the past, or what's happening now?"

"Is there a difference?" he asked, a sardonic smile on his face. "Maybe I'm just being overprotective. After you got shot...let's just say I wouldn't want to see it happen again."

"Yeah...me either. But if you need my help, you'd let me know, right?"

"Shelby," he growled, shaking his head. "Leave it alone. I don't want you to get hurt, and this is dangerous. We'll be fine."

I gave in, not pointing out that Uncle Joey might not agree with him, but my heart warmed to know Ramos cared about me. "All right. But be careful."

"Always," he said.

We were standing close enough that it was easy to take a deep breath and inhale the scent of his musky aftershave. His head bent slightly toward mine and his gaze went to my lips. I froze and let out a small gasp. With him this close, my heart rate doubled and I couldn't seem to think straight, let alone breathe.

The sound of a door closing brought me back to reality and I flinched away. My face flamed with guilt and my heart raced even faster. I glanced up to find Jackie coming down the hall with narrowed eyes and pursed lips. She was wondering what the hell was going on. I was a married woman! What was I thinking? She stood there glowering at us for a good five seconds before she grabbed the bottles from Ramos, shook her head, and then turned around to head back to the office.

I swallowed and glanced at Ramos. "Uh...see ya." I started toward the door.

"Shelby, wait," Ramos said. "I'm sorry...it...it won't happen again." He was thinking he'd been blind-sided by the smell of my hair, but he'd try and be good, even if it wasn't how he normally behaved. He just hoped that someday he got to kiss me at least once before he died. It could happen at any moment with the way things were going, but...

"What? Are you kidding me?" I caught his smile and smacked him in the arm. "You're terrible."

"What? What did I say?"

"Nothing."

He was thinking, *that's right*, and I could only shake my head. With a groan, I told him goodbye and hurried out the door to the elevators, his chuckle trailing after me. Once the doors swooshed closed, I leaned against the wall and shook my head some more. That was close. Too close. What was I thinking? Where was my brain? The fact that he wanted to kiss me certainly gave me a rush, and I tried not to let it go to my head. Still, I couldn't help the goofy smile that spread over my face.

Chapter 5

The smile was still there as I entered the police station. I hurried to Dimples' desk, but he was gone, and a small worry that I'd have to deal with Bates crept over me. I glanced in that direction, but his desk was empty too, so maybe it wasn't so bad. I found one of the other detectives and told him I needed to check the dead files. He shrugged and told me to go ahead before returning to his paperwork, but I caught that he was glad it was me going down there and not him. That room gave him the creeps.

Dang! Why did he have to think that? I was feeling all brave and courageous up to that point, but now dread clenched my stomach into a tight ball. Would something weird happen to me again? I wasn't sure I could take another one of *those* kinds of incidents without falling apart and screaming my head off. I sighed and pulled out the paper from my pocket with the missing women's names, then started down the stairs to the basement.

Gingerly, I opened the door to find the light still on. Had it had been on all this time? I shrugged, not feeling bad about leaving the light on...not after what had happened.

Since I had to go inside again, I decided to do it fast. Just go in, grab the folders, and get out of there. No lingering to look at the files for me.

As I entered, the musty smell hit me first, bringing with it the remembered panic. Hesitating, I focused on my task. With a deep breath, I hurried to the cabinets, half expecting to feel a chill in the air and maybe even smell some flowers, but when nothing happened, my breath wheezed out and the tension drained from my shoulders. Moving methodically from cabinet to cabinet, I soon had all three folders in my nervous hands.

The only thing that dampened my success came from realizing that with the files here, it meant they were unsolved. Still, I hoped that somewhere inside was a clue that would link them together and point to the killer. Besides the company in Darcy's building, it was the only other lead I had. I rushed to the door with only a slight twinge of nervousness and pulled it open. Relief flooded over me when I stepped into the hall. This time, I reached back in to turn off the light and hoped I'd never have reason to go back inside that room again.

I made it back to Dimples' desk in one piece and sat in his chair. Taking a moment to glance around, I decided that no one cared what I was doing there, so I quickly found a piece of paper and wrote Dimples a note to let him know I'd taken the files. With that out of the way, I gladly left the building.

It was great to get home after such a hectic day, and sudden weariness washed over me. After what I'd been through today, I had no desire to do much of anything, so I stacked the files in the den and changed into a comfy pair of jeans and a tee-shirt.

My appointment with the Marketing Solutions Company wasn't until tomorrow afternoon, so I had plenty of time before that to go over the files. Right now, I just didn't want to think about it. My cell phone rang and I contemplated not answering, but seeing that it was from Thrasher Development, I quickly picked it up.

"Hello Shelby," Uncle Joey said. "Do you have a minute to talk?"

"Yes."

"Good. So...what does Alec want from Kate." I told him the gist of it and heard him sigh. "Did you tell Kate?"

"Yes. She even offered me money not to tell you." I had no loyalty to Kate and it felt good to tell him the truth. "She wants to handle it her own way, but I don't think she knows about Jon and Julia coming to see you, right? So it's probably not a good idea to let her take care of it. Besides, I'm not sure Alec would hold up under the pressure from his family, no matter how much he loves Kate."

"Hmm..." Uncle Joey said. "Julia came to do damage control after my little meeting with Jon, so I don't think they're on the same page, and I don't think either of them knows that Alec has feelings for Kate. There might be a chance to use this to my advantage."

"How?" I asked.

"I have a plan, but it looks like I might need your help after all."

"Really?" Sudden unease washed over me. Now that he was asking, I wasn't so sure I wanted to help. Especially since Ramos had wanted me to stay out of it. But how could I turn him down? "Uh...sure. What do you need?"

He noticed my hesitation and huffed out a breath. "Don't worry, Shelby. What I have planned won't be dangerous, and you could bring your husband. In fact, now that he's my lawyer, it makes perfect sense for him to come."

"Chris? Wait. I know about your agreement, but if you're asking me to help you, Chris might not think that's part of what he agreed to." There was silence on the other end of the line, and nervous tension clenched my stomach. Oops.

"It doesn't matter what he thinks," Uncle Joey growled. "He's coming as my lawyer. The fact that you're coming with him is part of his job."

I sighed. Now Uncle Joey had us both over a barrel. He was like the king of conniving dudes. "So what is it you want us to come to?"

"I'm holding a small dinner party for the Passinis tomorrow night where we'll be celebrating our up-coming merger. It's at my house with all of my friends, so there's nothing for you to worry about. You'll be perfectly safe and hear everything I need to know."

"So you're going through with the merger? You know they'll try to take over Kate's side of the business, right?"

"Yes. But that's not going to happen. I have it all figured out."

"Okay," I agreed, knowing that if anyone could get the better of a situation, it was Uncle Joey. "So the party's at your house? That should be nice. What time?" The only time I'd been to his house, I thought I was going to die, but I still remembered how amazing it was. It would definitely be nice to see it again under different circumstances.

"Seven."

"Okay. I'll tell Chris." I wasn't sure how happy Chris would be about it, but since we were going together, he couldn't be too upset. Plus there was food involved. "What's for dinner?"

Uncle Joey snorted. "I'm not sure...but something Italian."

"Oh good, I love Italian food." I realized I was excited and it kind of shocked me. "Is it formal, as in suit and tie?"

"Yes."

"Great. That will work, we'll be there."

"Good," he said. "And just so you know, besides the Passinis, Kate will be there along with a few of my other associates."

"Oh yeah...right," Damn! Kate with my husband in her sights curbed my excitement.

"Don't worry, Shelby," Uncle Joey said. "I'll make sure Chris doesn't sit next to her. Besides, if she's in love with Alec, it won't matter."

"That's true. But you're forgetting that I have to listen to her all night long. We didn't exactly part this afternoon on the best of terms you know."

"But she knows you can hear her, so maybe it won't be so bad."

"That's true," I agreed, but I didn't believe it for one minute. Now that she knew I could hear her, it was like a secret weapon. She could think whatever she wanted and have the pleasure of insulting me without anyone else knowing. I'd just have to tune her out if I could.

"Good. I look forward to seeing you tomorrow night." He disconnected and I sighed. Dinner didn't sound too bad, even if Kate would be there. So that left telling Chris. I had a feeling that was going to be the hard part.

The rest of the day went normally enough. I got a phone call from Billie asking me if I could meet her at the Attorney General's office for an interview she had with him the next day. Since it was an hour after my appointment with Marketing Solutions, I told her I could, and we disconnected.

I had dinner all ready, but as usual, Chris was late getting home from work. Since Josh and Savannah had other things going on, we couldn't wait, so we ate without him. By the time Chris got home, they had both left, so while he changed his clothes, I microwaved a plate of food for him to eat.

While he ate, I told him about my day, starting with my visit to Darcy's employer, followed with my visit to her husband, and finally, what I'd learned from Detective Parker. By the time I got done, he'd finished his food.

"Wow. So you think it might be a serial killer?" Chris wasn't too happy about that. If I figured out who it was, it could be dangerous.

"I don't know. I guess it's a possibility. I've got an appointment with Marketing Solutions tomorrow, so I'll see if anything stands out."

"You've had a busy day. Weren't you supposed to go to lunch with Kate too?"

"Yes." I nodded and proceeded to tell him all about it. I started with getting there late, and ended with her wanting to bribe me with another five hundred dollars not to tell Uncle Joey. "I told her I'd ignore that since being in love made some people stupid. She didn't like that much, so I don't think we left on the best of terms, and now that we've been invited to dinner at Uncle Joey's house, I'm not so sure it was very smart of me."

"Huh? What are you talking about?"

Poor Chris. His life would be so much easier if he wasn't married to me. "Oh...well...I went to Uncle Joey's office after lunch to tell him about Kate and ran into Julia Passini. She's Jon and Alec's mom?" Chris got that glazed look in his eyes that spelled trouble, and I hurried to explain what I'd overheard her thinking, and how the Passinis were planning a merger with Uncle Joey's shipping company which Kate ran, and how because of that, Uncle Joey planned to invite us to dinner. "He wants both of us to come. That's good, right?"

"Um..." Chris narrowed his eyes. "Wait a minute. Our agreement is that if I help him with his cases, he leaves you out of it. It seems to me that asking you to eavesdrop on the Passinis isn't part of that agreement."

"Well...he's kind of gotten around that part. See, it's actually that I'm coming with you since you're his lawyer, not the other way around. And since I'm going to be there, Uncle Joey just needs me to listen to the Passinis so he can make plans that don't include him getting killed. He promised it wouldn't be dangerous."

Chris was thinking that Manetto getting killed wasn't so bad and maybe we shouldn't go.

"Chris...that's not helping."

"All right, all right. But it really bugs me that he's got both of us in his clutches, and I feel like a chump that I fell for it, and worse, that he pulled one over on me. How did this happen?"

"Kind of puts a new light on what I've been going through these last few months, huh?"

He twisted his lips. "Yeah, I guess. So what time is this big dinner?"

I told him the time and place, adding that dinner was going to taste great to help him feel better.

"Hmm..." He glanced at me with narrowed eyes. "So...you know what's for dinner?"

"Yes...something Italian."

He chuckled. "Of course! I should have known."

"Oh...I didn't think of it that way." I laughed, then shook my head to think I'd told Uncle Joey how much I loved Italian food. I mentioned this to Chris and he could hardly believe it.

"I'll bet he loved that."

"Maybe," I said, shrugging. "We were talking on the phone, so I don't know for sure."

Chris snorted. "I didn't mean that literally."

"Ha, ha. I knew that. I'm just messing around with you." I playfully hit him in the arm so he'd believe me.

"Uh-huh. So...is there anything else besides food that I'll get for going? You know...for compensation?"

"Sure," I said, playing his game. "You get to come with me. That's a plus, right?"

He smiled. "Yeah. You're right. So maybe it's not so bad that I'm Manetto's lawyer. At least in this situation." He was thinking how good it would feel to be there where he could keep an eye on me, and not have to hear how it went from me later. Yes, this was good. I wouldn't be able to leave anything out, or lie to him, because he'd be there.

"I don't lie to you," I said, although I couldn't say the same about leaving stuff out. "And mostly what I leave out isn't important."

"Right," he said. "Thank goodness for that."

I didn't like the direction this was going, so I changed the subject. "So," I said, kissing his cheek. "You want to get started on that compensation now or later?"

"Depends," he answered. "How long will the kids be gone?"

The sun rose the next morning with the promise of another beautiful autumn day. After getting the kids off to school and a quick shower, I settled in to look over all the files, hoping to find a bigger connection than the one I had.

A couple of hours' work later left me empty-handed and frustrated. Maybe they weren't connected at all, and the fact that they each disappeared in October a year apart was just a coincidence. I sure couldn't find anything that stood out. At least I had that appointment with Marketing Solutions, or I'd feel like a complete failure.

I drove to The Corporate Office Plaza and pulled into the parking structure, this time making sure I wasn't parked anywhere near number four. It meant I had to walk further, but that didn't bother me. Stepping inside the lobby, I glanced at the directory and followed the signs to Marketing Solutions, LLC.

A wide double-door with the name in bold letters above stood before me, and I couldn't help the shiver of dread that ran down my spine. Darcy's killer could be inside. I might come face to face with him. How was I going to handle that without giving myself away? On the other hand, maybe I was just being optimistic and this lead wasn't going anywhere. Thinking of it that way settled my nerves, and I knew that no matter what, I wanted to find Darcy's killer. That mattered more than any unpleasantness I might face.

I stepped inside and smiled with confidence, giving the receptionist my name and appointment time. She ushered me into the company president's office where he shook my hand and offered me a plush leather chair in which to sit.

"Hi Ms. Nichols, I'm Craig Hanley." He was thinking I looked like someone he could work with and hoped he could make the sale. His perfectly white teeth could have glowed in the dark when compared to his handsome tanned face. He gave me his spiel about what his company could do for me and how his program could easily double my revenue. "How many people do you employ in your consulting business?" he asked.

"Um...just me," I replied, knowing that wasn't what he wanted to hear. "But I can always hire more once my business takes off. I could probably use a new website too."

"Great. You're just the kind of person I think we can help." He explained his marketing process and, I had to admit, I was seeing all kinds of dollar signs behind my name...I mean...*brand*. It was amazing how quickly my business could grow in just a few months. I was ready to sign up right then, until he named his starting price. At least I kept my jaw from dropping to the floor. Still, he must have caught something from me because he got quiet and pursed his lips. He was thinking he hoped he hadn't just wasted his time. What did I expect? His rates were reasonable, even if they seemed high, and you got what you paid for.

"That sounds good," I said, surprising him. "But before I commit to anything, can I meet your staff and the marketing manager who'd be helping me?"

"Of course," he replied.

He led me to a small space of cubicles where several people were busy at their computers. Besides the receptionist and the woman who was head of sales, the rest of the employees were men. He took me around to each desk and explained who everyone was in relation to the accounts they managed. "We work as a team, and a lot of times we help each other with our accounts, so at this point, I can't tell you who would be handling your account specifically.

I managed to meet every person there, but didn't get a read on anything that would lead me to a serial killer. None of these people seemed inclined to do anything like that. So what was the connection? Why had Darcy wanted me to come here? It didn't make any sense unless there was something I needed to pick up, but what?

My time came to a close and I had to tell the president that I wasn't ready to sign up yet. Maybe I shouldn't have come under the pretense of wanting to hire his company since I couldn't ask any questions about Darcy and her disappearance. Now I couldn't do that without giving my real motive away.

As a last-ditch effort I asked, "Is this everyone in your company?"

Craig thought that was a weird question, but maybe I was one of those people who liked to be thorough. He might as well tell me the truth. "Actually...no, my brother Sean isn't here, and we have people who work remotely as well. But let me assure you, we have clients not only in the United States, but all over the world."

"What does your brother do?"

"He's involved with developing and upgrading our platform and the systems we use."

"Oh, so...he's your computer guy?"

"Yeah, mostly." Craig was thinking his brother was a royal pain in the butt, mostly because he was too smart for his own good. But it was Sean's program they used, so Craig had to pay him the big bucks and pretty much let him do his own thing, which irritated the hell out of him.

"I'd like to meet Sean before I make my decision. Is that possible? Does he come in to the office?"

Craig couldn't understand why meeting Sean was important, but if it got my business he was willing to see what he could do. "Yes, he comes in at least twice a week, sometimes more." He was lying about that. Unless there was a problem, they were lucky to see him once a week. "Let me have our receptionist set up the appointment for you."

"Great." I followed him back to the receptionist's desk and waited while she got Sean on the phone. He answered, and from what I could hear from her thoughts, Sean was not happy to come into the office to meet a potential client. Wasn't that what his brother was supposed to take care of? He finally gave in, but said it had to be Monday because he was going to be unavailable for the next two weeks.

"Would Monday work for you?" she asked. "I'm afraid that's the only free day he's got until November."

"Uh...sure...what time?"

She put the phone back to her ear and told me ten a.m. At my nod, she told Sean I had agreed and quickly disconnected. "Here's a card with the appointment time on the back in case you need it."

"Thanks." I turned to Craig who'd been waiting politely during the exchange. "I guess I'll see you Monday then."

"Good." He smiled and nodded, thinking he'd better make sure Sean's office was dusted and tidy. He couldn't remember the last time Sean had been there. Maybe he could get the receptionist to do it this afternoon.

I walked back to my car, hoping that meeting with Sean wasn't going to be a waste of time. But he sounded like a smart recluse with lots of money. That could mean something. Plus, he'd said he was unavailable for the next two weeks. Did that mean he was busy planning an abduction and murder?

A chill went down my spine. Maybe by Monday, I'd know what had happened to Darcy. But then what would I do? Without evidence I couldn't do much. I'd probably have to spend time watching and following him. If I could find the bodies that would do the trick, but just thinking about how I'd do that gave me the creeps.

I checked the time, realizing I only had fifteen minutes to get downtown to the Attorney General's office. I hoped Billie wouldn't be too mad if I was a little late. I had to circle the block twice before I found a parking space, and I ran a half-block to the building, out of breath and a little sweaty. I spotted Billie, relieved to find she was still seated in the waiting area.

"Hi, sorry I'm late," I said.

"It's okay. It might be a few more minutes before we get in." She was thinking that her ploy hadn't worked, and she felt a little guilty for asking me to come when she didn't exactly have an appointment.

I stared at her, more than a little put-out. "You don't have an appointment do you?"

Her head snapped toward me, a guilty flush creeping up her neck. "Uh...well...not with Grayson Sharp...but I thought maybe we could talk to someone in his office."

"Like who?"

She shrugged. "I don't know...probably his secretary...I mean...his executive assistant. I figured with you here, it didn't matter because you'd pick up on something."

I took a deep breath and let it out, trying not to get too upset with her. A woman came down the hallway and glanced our way. Billie jumped up and smiled. "Hi Addie, I'm Billie Jo Payne. Thank you so much for seeing me. I know how busy you are, but I only have a few questions."

Addie just stared at her before answering. "I have five minutes to answer your questions. That's the best I can do. Next time, you have to go through our public relations department."

"I will, I promise. Thanks for your time," Billie said. She glanced around the room. "Can we come to your office where it's private?"

Addie pursed her lips, but gave in and motioned us to follow her down the same hall from which she'd come. At the end, she opened an office door with "Office of the Attorney General, Grayson Sharp" emblazoned on it and ushered us inside.

She took her place behind the desk, and we sat opposite her on a couch clearly meant for those with appointments to see the attorney general. She gestured toward his door. "He's out for the rest of the day, and your five minutes are almost up. What can I do for you?"

Billie stood and began to pace the room. "There have been allegations against Grayson Sharp, including unauthorized use of campaign funds, to tampering with evidence, and bribery, mostly from large business owners for what could be called illegal activity. Can you confirm or deny these allegations?"

"Yes," she answered. "There's nothing to it. These allegations are nothing but smoke." She knew it wasn't true, but now was not the time or place to voice her real opinion. "If you want to talk to Grayson, you'll have to come back another time when you have an appointment."

"I tried to make an appointment weeks ago. He won't see me."

"Maybe not personally, but he is holding a press conference tomorrow morning specifically about these allegations. If you want answers, come back then. That's the best I can do." She was worried that this was getting out of hand. She'd overheard a few of his phone calls, and Grayson seemed to be hiding something. She'd also caught him at her computer a couple of times, but he'd always said he was just checking a few files she'd sent for him. Did that mean something?

"Thanks," I said, joining Billie. "We'll do that." I leaned toward Addie and whispered, "Just remember, people with power sometimes think they are above the law. If you see or hear anything that seems suspicious, like phone calls or him using your computer for something, let us know."

Her eyes widened and she glanced at me with apprehension, wondering who the hell I was, and how had I known she was worried about that.

"I'm a special consultant," I said. I took out one of my business cards and handed it to her. "Don't hesitate to give me a call. I'm sure I can help you out. Plus...I'm really good at keeping things confidential." I glanced at Billie and nodded toward her. "So is Billie. With both of us on your side, we can help if you get in a bind."

Billie didn't have a clue what was going on, but she nodded her agreement anyway. I stood and quickly exited, Billie on my heels. Soon, we were outside and walking down the street toward my car.

"Okay," Billie began, stopping me. "What just happened in there?"

"I know...crazy huh?" I smiled and raised my brows.

Billie shook her head and twisted her lips with impatience.

"Okay, okay," I began. "I got a feeling that Addie had knowledge of some information that might implicate the attorney general, so I went with it. I have no idea what it is, but being the attorney general's secretary, I'm sure she's privy to all sorts of things. Just think! She could be your mole...your deep throat! This could be the scoop of the year."

"So you think she'll call because she knows more than she's saying?"

"Yeah."

She huffed out a breath, not real happy with me. This was her story, and it felt like I'd scooped it from her, maybe because I'd given Addie my card and hadn't told her to call Billie. That meant Addie would call me first and that was just not cool. Oops.

"You gave her your card too, right? So she can call either one of us."

"No. I never gave her my card."

"But she knows who you are," I said. "I'm sure she'll call you if she can't get a hold of me. So it's all good. Plus, she'll see you at the press conference tomorrow. You can give her your card then. That will help her make up her mind about what to do, and then she'll probably call you. Besides, it doesn't matter who she calls, I'm not going to meet her without you anyway."

"Are you sure?" she asked.

"Of course," I agreed. "This is your story and I don't want to take it from you...even though you did ask for my help...don't forget that part."

"Oh...yeah," she said, instantly contrite. "I am glad for your help. If she decides to call, this could be the break I need to get the scoop on this story." She glanced back at the office. "You know...you're right...this is kind of exciting. It's like I have my very own informant...that is so cool."

I smiled, relieved that she wasn't upset with me anymore. "Girl...you are moving up in the world." We shared a laugh, then parted ways with a promise to call with any news. I drove away happy to know I'd helped Billie, and confident that whatever happened next, we could work through it together.

I got home in plenty of time to fix something for the kids to eat and get ready for the big dinner at Uncle Joey's. Right before I got in the shower, I gave Chris a call to make sure he was remembering and wouldn't be late. He assured me he could hardly forget, and said he'd be home soon.

While fixing my hair and makeup, I had to decide which dress to wear. Since I only had three that would work, it wasn't too hard to figure out. I pulled the blue dress from my trip to Orlando out of the closet and put it on. I looked fantastic in it and, because I knew Kate would be there, I wanted to look my best.

I hadn't worn it since the poker game with Carson where I'd won a cool million dollars. I looked it over carefully, grateful that it didn't show any signs of blood from the shootout. That brought back the image of Carson lying dead with a bullet between his eyes. My stomach clenched and my knees went a little weak. Did I really want to wear the dress that reminded me of that? On the other hand, it also reminded me of Ramos, and how he'd saved my life. Maybe if I concentrated on that part it wouldn't be so bad.

"Wow," Chris said. "You look great. When did you get that dress? I don't think I've ever seen it before."

"Oh...thanks," I said. He didn't know that Ramos had bought it for me in Orlando. Feeling slightly guilty about that, I'd hid it in the back of the closet along with the shoes. Now I had to lie. "I found it a while ago on sale. I was saving it for a special occasion and I figured, why not wear it now, you know? Do you think it will work?"

"It depends," he answered. "On who you're trying to impress." He was thinking it was because Kate would be there.

"Huh...you got me. But it's not just Kate...I like to look good."

He chuckled. "Well...I don't mind as long as it doesn't cost me an arm and a leg. But to be honest, I think you look good in anything." His voice softened and he added, "And nothing."

My heart melted. He was so good to me, and most of the time, I probably didn't deserve it. I put my arms around him and held him tight, then pulled away to brush his lips with a soft kiss. "Thanks honey. I sure do love you."

"I love you too. Don't forget that if Kate does something to make you mad, okay?"

I sighed. "Don't worry. I'll be good, even if she is thinking something that will make me want to hit her."

"She wouldn't do that...I mean...she knows you'll hear her. I'm sure you'll be fine."

I didn't want to point out that he was giving her way too much credit...just like Uncle Joey, so I let it go. Still, it made me even more determined to prove myself the better woman.

We took my car, since it was nicer, and hopped on the freeway. I had the address in hand since the only time I'd been there was kind of a blur. I'd been scared to death that time, so it was comforting to go back with Chris by my side.

As we neared the big house, excitement overcame my anxiety. This was nothing like the last time, and if I'd known then that I'd be coming back like this now, I wouldn't have believed it. "Wow, this is kind of crazy, isn't it?" At Chris' furrowed brows, I explained. "That I'm coming back, and it's so different than the last time."

Chris twisted his lips into a frown. "Yeah. I get that. It still feels a little wrong to be here though. Kind of like taking the first step into the dark side."

I chuckled. "I know what you mean. Are you nervous?" I asked.

"I'd be lying if I said I wasn't. But I'm also...intrigued."

"That's exactly how I feel." I reached over and squeezed his hand. "Here's the turn."

Chris pulled into the long driveway and followed it to the circular drive in front of a huge house. A young man waited, ready to open our doors and park the car. He helped me out and Chris soon joined me. I took his arm and we followed the walk and up two steps to the spacious entrance.

Ramos stood in front of the door, and I was sure he had more than one weapon hidden under his jacket. His cool nod and hard eyes made him seem more dangerous than ever, but I still caught a quick thrill of pleasure that I'd worn the blue dress he'd bought me before he shuttered his thoughts.

"Shelby...Chris," he said. "Follow me. Mr. Manetto's waiting for you."

We passed through the hallway and it was just as I remembered from before. Beautiful hard-wood floors with

Persian rugs and antique furniture. High ceilings with hanging light fixtures set off the dark-wood wainscoting that framed the ceiling and floors. Ramos led us past the door to Uncle Joey's office and ushered us into a beautifully furnished dining room.

The lavish table was set with china and fresh flower arrangements. Contemporary artwork hung from the walls, and a large picture window overlooked the beautifully manicured yard. The Passinis, David Berardini and his wife, and a few others were already there. Jackie noticed our arrival and hurried over to greet us.

She offered us champagne and took us to the Passinis for introductions. Kate stood beside Alec and, with her red hair falling in soft curls around her shoulders, along with a sea-foam green and copper dress, she easily stood out. She caught sight of us and turned her gaze to Chris with a sexy smile. She kept her gaze on him, practically oozing with an undercurrent of physical attraction, and giving him a look of undisguised admiration. It set me off. She wasn't supposed to look at my husband that way.

"Julia," Jackie began. "I believe you met Shelby Nichols at the office yesterday."

"Yes," Julia responded. "So nice to see you again."

"You too," I said, pulling my attention away from Kate and her traitorous thoughts. "Allow me to introduce my husband, Chris." Julia tilted her head in a polite nod. "Chris, this is Julia and her sons Alec and Jon Panini."

"Passini," Alec and Jon both said at the same time.

"Oh! Yes...of course," I said. "I'm so sorry. I guess I just got...well...they are quite similar and...anyway..."

Kate snorted and her lips twisted into a sardonic smile. She found my discomfort highly amusing. How could I make such a terrible blunder? She wasn't going to let me forget that one anytime soon.

"Nice to meet all of you," Chris said, stepping in to rescue me. He took Julia's hand in his and said warmly, "I'm Mr. Manetto's lawyer, but don't let that put you off." His rakish smile caught her off guard and she responded with a flirtatious smile of her own.

"I'll try not to hold it against you," she said. But she was thinking how handsome he was, and how nice it would be to hold herself against him. Shocked, I slammed my shields down. What the freak?? Wasn't she old enough to be his mother? Good grief! If I had to hear one more sex-laden thought about my husband, I might just turn around and walk out of there...dragging him with me of course.

Kate caught the murderous glint in my eyes and snorted again. I let down my shields enough to hear her thinking she was surprised at how easily I let other people upset me, especially considering that the evening had barely begun. Couldn't I control myself better than that?

I gritted my teeth and clenched my fists, managing to hold back my anger. Her gaze caught mine, and she waited for me to explode, or mess up again, but I wasn't going to give her the satisfaction. "Nice to see you again, Kate," I lied. "How are you?"

"Good," she said. Her gaze settled on Chris and she smiled sweetly. "Chris, I didn't know you were Uncle Joey's lawyer."

"Yes," Chris answered. "A lot of things have changed since you left. How are you enjoying Seattle?"

"Things are going great. I run a shipping company there and I'm finally getting the hang of it."

"Wow," Chris said. "That's a big change from filing court petitions and representing clients. How did that happen?"

"Well, let's just say Eddie Sullivan was in no position to run it, so I took over. To be honest, I couldn't have done it without the help of my manager, Zack Riordan. He's been amazingly helpful and an indispensable asset to the company."

She glanced at Alec and smiled. "In fact, we're doing so well it looks like we'll be merging our company with Alec's. It will bring us twice the profits with less cost. We won't be bidding against each other for the same contracts either. It's perfect." Kate was thinking Uncle Joey held all the cards on this deal, so they had effectively cut off any pretense Jon might have had of taking over her part of the company. He just didn't realize it yet.

Alec was thinking how hard it was to be caught in the middle of his family and the woman he loved. He was resigned to his fate, but if there was a way he could get out of looking like he'd set Kate up, he'd take it in a heartbeat.

I promptly zoomed in on Julia's thoughts. Relief came through that this was all going so well. It was the only way she could see her way clear of the mounting debts her husband had left her. Hot anger shot through her. Why did he have to die and leave her with this mess? Stupid man! He was supposed to take care of her. Now look at what she had to do.

The wave of anger toward her husband caught me off-guard. Wow, she was really upset. I tuned into Jon's thoughts to see if he felt the same way. While he was grateful Uncle Joey had gone along with the merger, he was thinking he'd have to be careful that Alec did his part with Kate so they could off-set the terms of the agreement with a few stipulations of their own. Hmm...this was getting complicated.

Uncle Joey joined our little group, and I felt Chris tense up beside me. While his features stayed relaxed and personable, his animosity toward Uncle Joey came through loud and clear. Luckily, Uncle Joey didn't speak directly to Chris, and we were soon taking our seats at the table.

As I glanced around the table, I took note of all the people there and realized Ramos was missing. Where was he? I got a little angry that he wasn't included, but then realized that, as Uncle Joey's bodyguard and hit-man, he didn't exactly fit with this group and probably wouldn't have liked it anyway. Still, as his right-hand man, it seemed like he should have been there.

I was strategically seated next to Jon and Julia, which gave me the opportunity to pick up their thoughts more readily. I did my best to get them talking, but I could only do so much. At least now I knew they were having money problems. Kate and Alec were sitting together with Alec clearly showing his interest in Kate. There was one time that Jon studied Alec with narrowed eyes and wondered if there was more to his act. Alec caught his glance and gave him a slight nod, which seemed to appease Jon's worries.

But it wasn't just an act, and Alec was growing tired of the whole thing. He didn't need his father's business to succeed. He could make plenty of money on his own, and this charade was wearing him down. As soon as the papers were signed, he planned to get out of the family business and strike out on his own. If his brother managed to take the business out from under Kate, he wouldn't be around for it. Then maybe he could convince Kate the merger had nothing to do with the reason he'd fallen in love with her.

As dessert arrived, Uncle Joey stood to offer a toast. "First of all, I'd like to thank the Passinis and the rest of you for coming to my home, and joining me to celebrate the merger between our two companies. May this merger between the Passinis and the Manettos be a blessing to both our families."

Everyone raised their glasses, and I caught Julia's relief that Manetto had made it official. She'd thought he would, but until he had said those words, she hadn't been sure.

Now all she needed was his signature on the paperwork. But it looked like it was going to happen as they'd planned, and she allowed a small sense of satisfaction to brighten her smile.

Julia stood and raised her glass. "To Joseph Manetto. He was a good friend of my late husband, Bernard Passini, and I know this merger would have made my husband proud."

As we raised our glasses again, a loud curse startled me and I jerked in surprise, making champagne slosh over the edge. No one else reacted, so I knew it was only in someone's mind. I covered my slip-up by smiling and heard it again. This time I knew it came from Jon. I shot a quick glance at him, catching the murderous set of his jaw and pursed lips before he caught me staring.

The transformation of his handsome face into a pleasant smile would have made me doubt what I'd seen was true. But lucky for me, I knew it was all a show and that he was furious. How could his mother betray his father like that? His father hated Manetto. If he knew what she'd done, he'd be rolling over in his grave. With him gone, they shouldn't have to keep paying Manetto. Jon shouldn't have let her talk him into this. But it was too late now. He'd have to do damage control and figure out a way to take Manetto out of the equation.

Whoa! Someone wasn't happy. Did that mean he was going to kill Uncle Joey? When he thought about taking him out, it didn't seem like he meant death. But what else was there?

With dinner over, a few people began to leave. Chris glanced at me and raised his brows thinking *can we go now?* I smiled and nodded my agreement, glad to know he was just as anxious to leave as I was.

As we stood, Uncle Joey caught my gaze and motioned us over to his group. I didn't really want to join them since he was talking to the Passinis and Kate. But I just smiled and nodded, then glanced at Chris. "We've been summoned."

"Figures," he said. "Let's make it quick and get out of here."

"I couldn't agree more."

Uncle Joey made room for us beside him and, rather than looking at me, he focused his attention on Chris. "We're just talking about the merger. I'm flying to Seattle on Monday to sign the paperwork and wondered if you could join me."

My breath caught. He couldn't make Chris do that! It was dangerous. "No," I blurted. "He can't go."

Everyone stared at me in surprise, even Chris. "Umm...sweetheart," he said, glaring at me before turning his gaze to Uncle Joey. "Let me check my schedule and see what I can do." He was thinking that I should keep my mouth shut and let him handle this.

"I'd appreciate it," Uncle Joey said. He leveled me with a cold stare. "I just need my lawyer to make sure the papers are in order before I sign them."

"Uncle Joey, you don't need Chris for that," Kate chimed in, a little offended. "I'm a lawyer too. I've been working on the paperwork with Alec's lawyers. I'll make sure everything is done right, and you can read over every little detail with me before you sign."

Uncle Joey studied Kate before he nodded his agreement. "Hmm...you're right. That should work." He put his hand on Chris' shoulder and pursed his lips into a wry smile. "I guess you're off the hook. That should make Shelby happy."

I felt the blood rush to my face, but decided to make light of it. "Uncle Joey, you are such a tease."

No one moved a muscle. How could I say that to a mob boss and live? Even Chris was waiting for Uncle Joey's reaction. To my great relief, Uncle Joey laughed. "Shelby...you are a treasure. And I mean that in the best way." He took my arm. "I hope you had a wonderful time tonight. Thank you for coming. Let me see you both out." I caught a stray thought from Julia that if I wasn't related, I'd probably be going to my execution...in fact, I still might.

Uncle Joey ushered me and Chris out of the room and down the hall. Dropping his voice, he said, "I take it you heard something that's made you nervous."

"Yes...I did," I said, grateful he wasn't as bad as everyone thought. "I'm not sure you should go through with this merger. Jon isn't real happy with his mother. He doesn't think his father would approve. In fact, he thought his dad hated you. He's going through with the merger, but he's hoping to figure out a way to take you out of the equation. I don't know if that means he's planning to kill you to do it, or what. That part wasn't real clear."

Uncle Joey let out a breath. "All right. Thank you Shelby."

"What are you going to do?"

"Make plans of my own."

"Do you need me to come?" I asked, feeling Chris stiffen beside me.

"No," he answered. "That won't be necessary. I'll have Ramos with me, and if what you say is true about Alec being in love with Kate, I'm sure we can use that to our advantage."

"It's true. He does love her."

"Good. Then we should be fine."

"All right," I said. "But don't trust anyone... and watch your back."

"I will," he answered.

Chapter 6

We drove home in silence. Since Kate had gotten Chris off the hook, did that mean I owed her one? Ugh, I hated being in her debt.

Chris was another story. He was miffed that I'd offered to go with Manetto, especially after the way I'd blurted that he couldn't go. That was embarrassing. At least Manetto took it all in stride. But that was pretty stupid of me. Even he was nervous about how Manetto would handle my comment about the teasing part. It made him sweat just to think about it. Sometimes I was just so clueless...

He glanced at me and noticed my wide-eyed stare. "Oh shit! Uh...sorry. I didn't mean...well, I guess since I'm thinking all those things I meant them, but I would never say you were stupid. I mean...I don't think you're stupid...not at all. It's just that...you know...that was a little tense back there."

"Yeah...I know. I get it." I knew I shouldn't feel bad, but that didn't make his thoughts any less hurtful. I should have put up my shields once he got started, but I already knew without hearing his thoughts that he wasn't happy with me...just not the stupid and clueless part. I guess I did say stuff I shouldn't. "Stupid, clueless, and naïve...I guess that's me in a nutshell."

"Shelby...you know I didn't mean it."

"Yeah...I know. It's my fault that I heard, so just forget about it. Okay?"

Chris sighed deeply. He knew from my tone of voice that he'd hurt my feelings. He also knew apologizing wasn't going to help. I put my shields up after that, like I should have earlier. Was I a glutton for punishment, or what? It must be the stupid part of me. I closed my eyes and sighed. Now I was feeling sorry for myself.

Chris reached over, took my hand, and rubbed his thumb across my knuckles. "I remember the first time I saw you at that frat party. You took my breath away. I couldn't take my eyes off of you. I even forgot I was there with another girl. Remember how long we just sat there and talked about everything? From then on I couldn't stop thinking about you." He pulled my hand to his lips and kissed it.

"What?" I asked, shocked. "I thought talking to you for so long was my idea. You really felt that way?"

He smiled and shook his head. "Shelby, you have no idea. I tried to seem like I was all macho and everything, but you really had me tied in knots. Now, times like tonight and seeing you in that gorgeous dress...well...you still make my heart race. The luckiest day of my life was meeting you at that party. I just...I want you to know that I'm sorry I made you feel bad. You're an amazing woman...you're not perfect...thank God...because neither am I, but you're perfect for me, and that's all I need."

We pulled into the garage and Chris cut the engine. He glanced at me and noticed that my eyes had filled with tears. Even though they were the good kind, Chris groaned and quickly got out to open my door. He pulled me out of the car and held me close. With his strong arms around me, my distress was forgotten, and I sank into his arms in complete surrender.

"Thanks honey," I said, pulling back just enough to look into his warm brown eyes. "I love you so much." Our lips met in a crushing kiss that turned my insides to mush and curled my toes. Needing to breathe, we finally pulled apart.

"Let's go inside," Chris said.

"Oh baby, oh baby," I giggled.

When I woke the next morning, Chris was already up and cooking breakfast. It was Saturday, and the smell of bacon hit me like an elixir, dragging me to the kitchen. Savannah and Josh were already up, and the table was set. I gasped in surprise. This was a minor miracle in my house, and I couldn't help clapping my hands with joy.

The rest of the weekend went by in a blur, and it wasn't until Monday that I got back to my case. I hadn't heard anything from Uncle Joey, so I figured no news was good news. Today was my appointment with Sean Hanley, and I quickly got ready to meet him. I hoped he was the one so I could close the case, but on the other hand, meeting with a serial killer kind of freaked me out...if that's what he was. At least we were meeting at the office, so I didn't need to be afraid anything bad would happen, right?

As I slipped on my shoes, my cell phone rang. The caller ID said it was Billie, and I quickly answered. "Hi Billie. What's up?"

"You'll never believe this, but Addie, the Attorney General's secretary, just called me. Did you watch the interview Saturday at the A.G.'s office?"

"Uh...no."

"You didn't? I thought for sure you'd watch it."

I grimaced from her disappointed tone, hoping I wasn't in too much trouble. "Sorry, but I had a lot going on over the weekend." I didn't dare tell her I'd forgotten all about it.

"Oh...well, I got in a couple of good questions, and I really think I've got him scrambling. Addie seemed quite upset about the whole thing, and she called me late last night to set up a clandestine meeting. She wanted to make sure no one saw her, so we decided to meet at Gracie's Tavern around nine-thirty tonight. It's kind of out of the way, so that seemed like a good place to meet. She wanted you to come too. Can you make it?"

"Sure," I agreed. "I'll be there."

"Good." She gave me directions and we disconnected.

I let out a sigh and rushed to finish getting ready. At least Addie had called Billie first, so that was a plus. I also hoped she actually had something concrete to go on so I didn't have to push her into a corner by reading her mind. That would make Billie happier about the whole thing, and I wouldn't have to lie about my facts.

As I contemplated my next move with Sean, I realized that if I felt like I was in too deep, maybe I could ask Billie to help me. I'd helped her, so turn-a-bout was fair play, right?

Once again, I pulled into the parking structure where Darcy had been taken. Too bad I wasn't really a psychic, then maybe I could pick up some kind of latent energy and figure out what had happened. Oh well...I didn't really believe in that stuff. Of course, what was so different about it than reading minds?

Did that mean that since I could read minds, a whole bunch of other stuff was possible too? I'd never thought of it that way, and it kind of made me sick to my stomach. Could it be true? What if people really did have premonitions, or were psychics, or ghost whisperers. In fact, just the other day in the Reader's Digest, I'd read about people who'd suffered brain injuries. One woke up speaking with an accent; another saw mathematical patterns, and one more played the piano for hours with no musical training. I was probably like them, although I'd never heard of anyone reading minds. Of course, if they knew what was good for them, they'd keep it to themselves.

I entered the lobby and made my way to Marketing Solutions. I walked in and the secretary smiled, thinking that Sean hadn't made it in yet and wasn't I early? I checked my watch. It was nine fifty-nine. What was early about that? In fact, for once, I wasn't late. "Hi," I greeted her. "Shelby Nichols...here to see Sean."

"Yes. Hi Shelby. He's not here yet, but he should be walking in any moment now. Would you like to take a seat until he gets here?"

"Sure." I sat down where she could see me waiting and glanced around the room. I hated waiting, but tried to get my thoughts in order for the upcoming interview. I had to admit that my palms were a little sweaty just thinking about how this meeting might go. What if Sean was the killer? I'd have to be careful that I didn't give anything away since I certainly didn't want him stalking me next.

The door flew open, and a man in jeans and a graphic tee shirt strode in. His hair was cut short, and he was clean-shaven and wearing wire-rimmed glasses. He was fairly good-looking in a boyish sort of way and, with sneakers, looked like he belonged in a band or something.

Relief poured from the secretary, so I knew this was Sean. He blinked a few times, like he wasn't sure where he was, then glanced at me and smiled, surprised. "Uh...hi...you must be Shelby Nichols. I'm Sean." He extended his hand.

"Yes. Nice to meet you." I shook his hand, surprised to find such a firm grip.

"So...um...you wanted to talk to me?" he asked. At my nod, he continued, "Let's go into my office then." I followed him into a spacious office with windows overlooking the golf course. The room was bare of any personal items like photos or knick-knacks, and the desk didn't even have a computer on it. The secretary must have cleaned it though, because there wasn't a speck of dust anywhere, and I could still smell the scent of lemon furniture polish.

Sean hastily sat behind his desk and motioned for me to take the seat facing him. He studied me with shrewd eyes, thinking I was the first customer who'd ever wanted to meet him, and wondered if there was another motive besides the obvious one.

"I don't get into the office much," he began. "I work at home, mostly. So, what can I do for you?"

"I appreciate you taking the time to meet with me. I hope it didn't interfere with your busy schedule too much."

"No...it's okay," he said. Something about me set off his internal alarms. What did I really want from him?

Damn. This wasn't going very well. "I don't know if you know about my business, but I have a consulting agency and I'm considering hiring your company. I always make it a practice to meet everyone I plan to work with, just to see if it's a good fit for me. I met everyone in your company, but when I found out you were the brains behind the system, I wanted to meet you too. Does that make sense?"

"Oh...sure." He thought it made a lot of sense, and he was flattered that I appreciated his contribution. He'd better do what he could to sell me on it. "The system we use is top-notch, and I make sure everything's up to date." He hadn't done an update for a while, but unless Craig found a problem, he probably wouldn't. As long as the program got the job done and made him lots of money, he was more than happy to leave it alone.

"Great," I said. "So, you actually wrote the code for this system? You must know a lot about computers."

"Yeah, I graduated in computer science." He was thinking he was mostly self-taught because he was so smart, and hadn't actually graduated, but I didn't need to know that.

"So...are you working on any new programs?"

My question caught him by surprise and he glanced at me sharply. "Maybe. Why?"

I shrugged. "I don't know. It just seems that since you don't come here very often, you must have something else you're working on."

"Like what?" His heart rate jumped. Did I know something? How? He was a genius, no one knew about that part of his life. It was the reason he never got caught.

"Oh...you know...in case I wanted to invest? Like...get in on the ground floor of a future computer program and make lots of money?"

"Oh...I get it. Sorry...I can't talk about that." Relieved, he settled back in his seat. "Intellectual property contracts and all that, so it looks like you're out of luck." Now that he knew that's why I was interested in him, he could relax his guard a little and study me. He liked what he saw. "So what's your company called?"

"Uh...Shelby Nichols Consulting Agency," I answered, suddenly nervous.

"And what do you do?"

"Lots of things," I shrugged. "Most of my jobs are helping people find things out. Lately, I had a mom call to find out what her daughter did after school while she was at work. Stuff like that."

His eyes narrowed. "Like a private eye?"

"Not exactly." I knew admitting that would be a mistake. "I'm more like a consultant. But I could move into that if I had some help. First I need to get my name out there, then

I could hire people to work for me and do that kind of stuff too. That's why I was thinking about hiring your company."

"Right," he said. "Well...if that's what you want to do, then you really should hire us."

"Yeah...it's looking more and more like that's the way to go."

He smiled, pleased with himself. "Good. Well if that's all, I need to get going."

"Thanks for meeting with me."

"No problem. Glad I could help." He stood and once again shook my hand. "I hope this turns into a lucrative relationship for both of us."

"Yes...well...I'll let you know," I said. As I walked to the door, I picked up a sense of satisfaction from him that grew into a feeling of euphoria. He was scrambling since his latest target had moved and blown everything he'd worked for all to hell, but with my blond hair and blue eyes, I was the perfect replacement.

I left his office door open and caught that he was going to check out my address and phone number to begin the stalking process. This was perfect timing since his last candidate had moved away right from under his nose a few days ago. He guessed he'd overplayed his hand and scared her too much. But with me it would be different. Since he didn't have a lot of time left, he couldn't employ his full arsenal before the deadline, which was probably for the best and could possibly heighten the challenge. He was even thinking, *let the games begin*, and mentally rubbing his hands together.

Oh hell! I was his next target? Damn! It was him! I faltered just a bit but managed to walk out of there without fainting or anything. The outer door shut behind me, and I leaned against the wall to support my shaking legs. This guy needed to be stopped. Right now. If I followed my instincts, I'd march right back in there and punch him in the stomach and then kick him in the balls. Once he was lying on the floor, I'd kick him a few more times and then stun him with my stun flashlight. He'd be sorry he ever thought about hurting me.

That mental image helped get me out of the building and into my car without once checking to see if he followed me. Let him come. He'd picked the wrong girl to mess with this time. He thought he was so smart, hah! He wouldn't know what hit him.

I drove home with a new purpose, knowing that whatever he planned to throw at me, I'd have to have a counter-plan. Or I could just ask to meet with him again, tie him up real tight, and ask him questions about where the other women were buried. Even if he didn't answer, I'd know.

I still might want to torture him a bit anyway, or at the very least, stun him a couple of times. But I could do that. I'd just have to pick the right time and place. Maybe I could even use the basement room in the same building as Thrasher Development. I'd spent some time tied up down there and knew firsthand what a perfect spot it was.

I'd probably need some help. I wasn't sure Chris would agree to do what I wanted, but he might if he knew I was the next target, although he didn't have much experience with kidnapping and torture. Dimples was out of the question, but what about Ramos? He had all the necessary skills and lack of conscience that would make him the perfect partner. The only problem with that was not telling Chris anything about it. Could I do that? I wasn't sure. I only knew that I wasn't going to be anyone's victim, and I wasn't going to end up dead. So that meant being proactive.

Of course, once I knew what Sean had done with the bodies, how was I supposed to get him arrested and help the police build a case against him unless he came after me first? Since I didn't want that to happen, it left the door open for him to bring charges against me. I could hardly leave him alive if that were the case, but I couldn't really kill him, no matter how much I might want to. Hmm...I might just need Chris for this after all. He'd know how to build a case without getting me in trouble. But how could I torture him then? Damn! I'd probably have to leave the torturing part out.

There had to be another way to get the results I wanted, but right now, I wasn't thinking rationally, mostly because deep down, I was scared to death. It creeped me out to think I was his next target, especially when I could imagine all sorts of horrible things he may have done to the other women.

I got home and went directly to the den where I kept the files of all the missing women and opened them up. I had a small whiteboard and taped each picture to the top and wrote their names in dry-erase marker beneath. Then I wrote "Sean Hanley" below that and circled it. Next, I drew lines between each woman's picture to Sean's name with the date of disappearance on the line.

I propped the whiteboard on the desk against the wall and studied it, feeling a sense of control wash over me. This was my storyboard, just like the one Kate Beckett used on my favorite TV show, Castle. She always figured it out, and I could too. Too bad I didn't have Richard Castle standing beside me right now, telling me how to catch him. I needed to lay a trap, but the only thing that really made sense was using myself as bait. I didn't really want to do that much, but with Ramos as back-up it could work.

I spent the afternoon thinking up different scenarios to catch Sean that didn't involve letting him get me first. In all of them there was just too much that could go wrong, and it didn't leave me with many options besides just grabbing him like I first wanted to.

I looked up Sean's address and phone number to add to the storyboard, and found it on google maps so I'd know exactly where he lived. Maybe I could drive by on my way home from my meeting with Addie and Billie later tonight and check it out. If he had a big yard, maybe the victims were all buried there. Or maybe I could sneak in while he was gone and take a look around. Thoughts of doing that kind of made me sick, but if I got Ramos to help me, it could work.

My kids got home from school, so I took the storyboard off the desk and turned it around against the wall by the side of the desk where no one would see it and left the room. I was ready for a break, and talking to my kids and getting dinner ready would help ground me. I hurried into the kitchen where Josh was guzzling milk straight from the jug. It was almost empty, so I only shook my head and let it go.

"You know...you could have some cookies with that," I said.

He shrugged and kept guzzling. Savannah rushed past me, heading up to her room where she could cry in peace. Whoa. What was going on with her? I followed her to the bottom of the stairs.

"How was school?" The words popped out of my mouth before I could call them back. I inwardly cursed, knowing it was about the worst thing a parent could ask their child if they wanted to know the truth.

"Fine," Savannah said, but inwardly she was thinking it was crappy and about the worst day she'd ever had in her life, and life sucked, and all she wanted to do was listen to her music and cry and never go back to school again.

"What happened?" I asked, hoping she'd open up.

"Nothing! I said it was fine." She continued up the stairs to her room, and I had no alternative but to follow her if I wanted to get her to talk to me.

"Yeah...well, if the way you're snapping at me is any indication, then fine isn't quite the right word to describe it. How about crappy? Does that work better? What was so crappy about it?"

"Mom..." she whined, turning back before she entered her room. "Are you doing that premonition thing on me again? I don't like you doing that. It's like...invasion of privacy."

"No honey, not at all. I'm just concerned because you seem a little upset and I'd like to talk about it...if it would help." Since I didn't really have premonitions, saying that wasn't lying.

"You wouldn't understand," she said, thinking no one my age could ever remember what seventh grade was like, especially since cell phones and the Internet weren't even invented back then.

I almost blurted that she was wrong and it wasn't that long ago, but let it go. "I remember seventh grade very well," I said. "It was one of the worst years of my life. I was always getting picked on by the older kids and sometimes the boys were really mean. Other times, the girls were even worse, especially my friends. I hated that."

"You hated seventh grade?" she asked. "Then why did you tell me it was going to be fun?"

"Because I hoped it would be fun, and I didn't want to discourage you before you even got started." The glare in her eyes softened, so I took that as a good sign and continued, "So just tell me one thing that made today so bad."

She let out a sigh and heaved her backpack onto the floor, leaving the door open for me to follow, then threw herself onto the bed and stared up at the ceiling. Grateful, I sat on the edge of the bed and listened as she began to talk. As all her frustrations spilled out, I got her to move over so I could lie down beside her.

An hour later, she was feeling good enough to help me fix dinner. As we got started, I picked up from Josh that he was relieved to see us out of her room. He was starving and had debated about asking what was for dinner earlier, but he didn't want to interrupt our 'girl' talk. What was it with girls anyway? They were always so hard to understand. One minute they were nice and happy, and the next they were screaming and crying. He didn't get it. Now it looked like Savannah was turning into one of them. That was tough, and he thanked his lucky stars he wasn't a girl.

That thought coaxed a laugh out of me, and I glanced at him with a knowing smile.

"What?" he asked. "What'd I do?"

"Nothing," I answered. "I can just tell that you're hungry, that's all."

He shook his head, thinking he'd never understand women. "I'm going to go shoot some hoops," he said. I nodded and he left to go outside where we had a basketball hoop set up against the garage.

Chris pulled up a few minutes later, shocking me that he was home early. He quickly changed and joined Josh in the driveway while Savannah and I finished dinner. As we sat around the table for dinner that night, I sighed with gratitude for my family. We had our challenges, but having them in my life was worth everything.

Around nine o'clock, I got a text from Billie reminding me about our meeting with Addie. I'd totally forgotten and had to rush to get ready. Chris wasn't happy I was leaving, but since it didn't have anything to do with Uncle Joey, he couldn't complain too much.

"Just call me if you're going to be later than eleven," he said.

"Oh, I'm sure it won't be that late."

"Good. How's the investigation going anyway? Was today your appointment with that guy from the Marketing Company?"

"Yes. It went well, and I found out some stuff, but I don't have time to tell you about it now." I'd put off telling Chris about that meeting because I hadn't decided exactly what to tell him. Now that would have to wait until I got back. "I'll fill you in later."

I rushed to make it to Gracie's Tavern by nine-thirty and pulled into the parking lot only a few minutes late. For a Monday night, the place seemed a lot more crowded than it should have been. Thankfully, Billie spotted me and waved me over to her table. I slid into a chair and smiled at Addie whose pale face and haunted eyes underscored the quick smile she gave me. I picked up on her anxiety and the subsequent stomachache she suffered. She was thinking that if we ever let anyone know she was the source of this leak in the Attorney General's office, her career would be over. She still wasn't sure she could go through with it.

Billie was ready to get down to business and get this done, totally missing Addie's reluctance. As she opened her mouth to ask Addie what information she had, I spoke up. "You can trust us, Addie. Neither of us will ever tell anyone where we got this information. That's a promise."

I glanced at Billie with raised brows and she quickly responded. "That's right. As a journalist I don't have to reveal my sources, as long as the information is accurate. So your secrets are safe with me."

Addie licked her lips. "How will you put it in the paper then?"

"Oh we always say it's from an anonymous source." She didn't add *'close to the attorney general'* like she was thinking. "No one will know who gave it to us, so you'll be fine."

Addie glanced between the two of us, then sighed and leaned forward. "Okay. Here's what I've got. First of all, I overheard Grayson talking to one of the businessmen who contributed quite a bit to his campaign about getting the charges dropped against him. I don't know exactly what that means, but you can guess. After you left last Friday I got suspicious about something.

"A while back, I caught Grayson at my computer a couple of times. He brushed it off, but on Friday, I decided to check all my files. I found one I didn't know about and opened it up. It showed two men's names that I recognized as campaign contributors along with files showing inquiries into their businesses. The inquiries all came in at different times, in various stages of investigation, and were based on things like tax evasion, retaliating against witnesses, and obstructing justice. They're all felonies. When I checked the public records to see what became of the charges, I found out our office had never filed them. It looks like they were given to Grayson, and he put them on my computer."

She licked her lips nervously. "From how big the files were, I don't think Grayson could have put them there from just the few times I caught him, unless he somehow found out my password. But I change it every month and these files spanned about six months' time. So I don't know how he did it."

"Hmm," Billie said. "Unless he got your IT guy to give him your passwords. Then all he'd have to do is stay late or come in on a weekend and use your computer."

"So do you think the reason he put everything on my computer was so it would look like he never got them and it was my fault?" Addie asked.

"Could be," Billie said. "So what did you do with the files?"

"I copied them onto a thumb-drive," Addie answered. "And it's a good thing I did too, because this morning when I checked my computer, they were gone. He must have come in over the weekend and deleted them."

"Wow," Billie said. "That was close."

"Tell me about it." Addie sighed and opened her purse. She took out the thumb-drive and handed it to Billie. "It's all there. After everything I've done for that man, he pays me back like this? It's unbelievable. I guess you never really know someone as well as you think. I believed in him. I thought he was a good man." She was thinking how stupid she was to turn a blind eye to his above-the-law attitude. She could see it now, but she'd mistakenly let the power go to her head as well. Now look where it had gotten her.

"Thanks," Billie said. "You won't regret this."

"Just keep my name out of it." With a nod from Billie, Addie stood and quickly left the tavern.

Billie glanced at me. "What a story. This is great." Before I could respond, her phone rang. "Um...it's my boss. I've got to answer it."

I nodded and gathered my things to leave. Billie's hand on my arm drew my attention back to her, and I found her eyes round with surprise and shock. I hadn't been listening to her conversation, but from her expression, I knew something big had gone down.

"What is it?" I asked, my stomach clenching with dread.

She put her phone away and pursed her lips. "There's been an explosion...in Seattle. A yacht owned by the Passini Shipping Company blew up about an hour ago. They're saying Joe Manetto was onboard."

Chapter 7

"What?" I felt the blood drain from my head. "What do you mean? He was on a yacht? What happened?"

She shook her head. "The only thing my boss knows at this point is there was some kind of a party on the yacht...and it went down from an explosion. Apparently several people made it off, but others are missing. I guess the rescue operation is still underway so it's too early to have a list of names."

I took a deep breath. "Okay." This was awful, but I had to believe that Uncle Joey and Ramos had survived. They were smarter than to let themselves get blown up, right? They'd survived worse things, hadn't they? Just then my phone rang, and my heart skipped a beat. Maybe it was him or Ramos telling me they were okay.

"Hello?"

"Shelby! It's Jackie. Something terrible has happened," she sobbed. "Kate called. There was an explosion on the boat. She doesn't know where Joe is. I need to know...Joe told me about you...that you have premonitions. I need to know if he's okay. Can you come to the house?"

"Yes. Yes, of course. I'll be right there." My throat closed into a tight lump. Hearing Jackie's frantic voice made it all real. If Kate had called and didn't know where Uncle Joey was, did that mean he was really dead?

I glanced at Billie. Her brows were drawn together in concern and she was thinking I seemed almost a little too upset if Manetto didn't mean anything to me. Who had just called me? Where was I going? I cleared my throat and swallowed. "I've got to go."

"Who was that?" she asked.

"I'll... tell you later," I answered, knowing she would never let it go unless I gave her a promise of some kind, even if it was a promise I didn't intend to keep. Without waiting for a response, I hurried out of the tavern and jumped into my car.

I drove to Uncle Joey's place in a daze, still not believing it had happened. If it had...and they were dead...tears gathered in my eyes, but I blinked them away. I wasn't ready to believe Uncle Joey or Ramos was dead. Not yet. The Passinis had planned this. Their plan all along must have been to get Uncle Joey to sign the merger and then kill him. I didn't think for one minute the explosion could have been an accident, but if Kate was still alive, did that mean she was on their side? It wouldn't be the first time she had double-crossed Uncle Joey.

I turned into the driveway and my stomach clenched. What was I going to tell Jackie? She thought I had premonitions, so I had to tell her something. Even if it wasn't the truth, I knew I had to tell her Uncle Joey was still alive. No way could I tell her he was dead. He couldn't be dead.

The walk to the front door seemed to take forever, but was also too short once I got there. Before I could ring the bell, the door flew open and Jackie grabbed me. She held onto me like I was a life boat and she was a sinking ship.

"It'll be okay," I murmured, patting her on the back, and my eyes filling with tears. "It's okay," I said over and over. "I'm sure he's fine."

Her breath caught and she stepped back. "You are? You're sure he's fine?" Hope brightened her tear-filled eyes.

I nodded and smiled, wiping away my own tears. "Yes...pretty sure. Let's go inside."

She swallowed and stepped aside as I walked past, closing the door behind me. I followed her down the hall and into a comfortable sitting room. "Thank you so much for coming," she began. "I was going crazy here by myself."

"When did you find out?"

"Kate called to tell me, just before I called you. She said she'd call me back as soon as she knew more, but she hasn't called yet."

"Did Kate say what happened?" I asked.

"She sounded out of breath, and she was shivering, like she'd just been pulled out of the water. She said the yacht was anchored near the docks, not too far from shore. Then there was a big explosion, and the boat started to sink. Alec helped her get into a lifeboat, but she couldn't find Joe and Ramos in the confusion."

"Did she see them after the explosion?"

"I don't know. She wasn't making a lot of sense."

"She was probably in shock," I said, knowing firsthand how that felt. "But if she saw Uncle Joey and Ramos after the explosion, that means there's a good chance they got off the yacht before it sank, especially if they could swim to shore. They might be on the beach somewhere."

"Is that what your premonitions are telling you?" Jackie asked, sounding desperate.

"Yes." I nodded. "Either that, or someone else helped them off." Of course, I had no idea, but it could be true. "Let's see if we can get through to Kate again. Do you have her number?"

"Um...it's on my phone." Jackie picked up her cell, but her fingers were shaking and she couldn't get the numbers right.

"Can I try?" I asked. With a grateful sigh she handed the phone to me and I quickly brought up Kate's cell number and pushed call. It rang several times before it went to voice mail. I left a message that I was with Jackie and to call us back right away.

After I disconnected, Jackie reached for the phone. "I haven't tried Joe's cell phone yet. Maybe I should do that."

"Oh...yes, that's a good idea." I handed it over and watched as she pushed in his number. She held it to her ear, and we both listened with baited breath, hoping he would answer. It went to voice-mail and Jackie's face crumpled, but she left a tender message for him to call her, telling him how much she loved him and he'd better not be dead. She disconnected, then pushed in another number. From her thoughts, I knew it was Ramos' cell.

The same process repeated without him picking up, and she left another message, only this time it wasn't so sweet. "Damn it Ramos!! You or Joe better call me or you're in deep shit!" She clicked the phone off and sent it spinning across the coffee table, then glanced at me. "That felt good."

"I'm sure it did." I smiled, wishing I could yell at them too. "How could they let this happen?"

"I know!" Jackie agreed. "This is horrible. How could they do this to me? If you weren't here, I don't know what I'd do. I'd probably go crazy. I hate this. I hate waiting around for the phone to ring."

She took a deep breath and began pacing back and forth across the floor like a caged animal. "Joe did tell me something before he left. He said if I heard any bad news not to worry, he had plans in place that should keep him safe. But then he ruined it by telling me that if anything did happen to him, he made sure in his will that I'd be well provided for. Damn that man! What am I supposed to think?"

I was saved from answering by the phone ringing. Jackie dove for it and I held my breath as she answered. I knew from her thoughts that it wasn't Uncle Joey or Ramos, and my shoulders sagged. She hung up and explained it was Ricky. Then the phone began to ring again. This time it was David Berardini saying that he and his wife were coming right over.

Jackie sighed and flopped onto the couch, drained and exhausted. "I guess the news is out. Everyone's coming over to wait for word."

"Yeah? That's good. It means you won't be alone." At her stricken expression, I quickly continued. "While you wait for Uncle Joey to call. Which I'm sure he'll be doing any time now." Jackie stared at me with disbelief in her eyes. She wondered if I was the real deal or not? Just then it sure didn't sound like it.

"Can I get you anything?" I asked. "Like a drink or something to eat?"

"Yes," she said, nodding absently. "I think some wine would be good. It's in the kitchen."

"Great. I'll be right back." I hurried out, glad for something useful to do that would hopefully take her mind off me. I found the kitchen without too much trouble, and after checking the cupboards, found a bottle of Cabernet and poured a generous amount into a glass. By the time I returned, David, his wife, their son Nick, and Ricky had all arrived.

Jackie gratefully took the wine and almost drained the glass. She was thinking she could have used something stronger, but needed to keep her wits about her when Joe called. I perked up to hear that. At least she was being positive.

"You all need to know," Jackie announced. "That Shelby said Joe was going to be fine." She glanced at me and smiled. "So even though things look bad, there's nothing to worry about. You all know how much Joe trusts Shelby."

They all turned their gazes to me. Everyone but David's wife comprehended that Jackie was talking about my premonitions, and their relief hit me like a tidal wave. I managed a weak smile and a nod, but they still waited for me to say something.

I swallowed, hoping I could phrase my response so that it didn't sound like I was lying through my teeth. "That's right, and you know Uncle Joey. He's been in lots worse situations before and he always manages to come out of them just fine. This is no different. In fact, he knew the Passinis were planning something, so I'm sure he was ready for it."

"Shelby's right," Ricky added. "We have to believe in the boss."

That seemed to break the tension and everyone began asking questions at once. Nick came to my side, his brows drawn low and his gaze hard. We'd spent some time together in Orlando, and he'd seen me win a poker match with my premonitions. Still, he was a little skeptical. "So...is this another one of your premonitions? Or are you just saying this to help Jackie." He'd seen my hesitation and shifty eyes. That meant I was probably lying.

"Listen Nick," I whispered. "I'm doing my best here. I'm just as shook up as the rest of you. All I know is I have a feeling it will be all right, and I'm going with it. If I'm wrong, we'll know soon enough, but I sure hope not."

His lips twisted, but he accepted my explanation with a short nod. "Good to know."

The shrill tone of the phone ringing froze everyone in their places. With all eyes focused on Jackie, she quickly answered, then held out her arm toward David, who reached out to steady her.

"Are you sure?" she asked. There was a long pause before she spoke, but from her thoughts, I knew it was Kate and the news wasn't good. "Yes. I think that's a good idea. Shelby? Well, she's here..." Jackie glanced at me while she continued to listen. "Okay, I'll do it. I'll call you when I have the information."

She lowered the phone and leaned against David, who helped her to a chair. After sitting, she took deep breaths to compose herself, then closing her eyes, she began. "That was Kate. They're still searching the area, and they've rescued a few people, but right now Joe and Ramos are officially missing." She glanced at me, struggling to hold back the tears that filled her eyes. "She wants me to get on the next flight out, and she wants Shelby to come with me."

Now everyone turned their gazes to me. "Uh...me? Are you sure?"

"Yes. I don't know why, but she said it was important that you be there. Will you come?"

I nodded. "Um...sure. Of course."

Jackie closed her eyes and sighed. "Good. Thank you Shelby."

"I'll check the flights and book them," David offered, taking out his phone.

"Thanks." Jackie wiped the tears from her cheeks. "While you do that, I need to call Miguel. He needs to know what's happening, and I don't want him to hear this from anyone else."

She went into Uncle Joey's office for privacy and I sat down on the couch. I knew Kate wanted me there because I could figure out what had happened by listening to Julia or Jon. I wasn't sure how that was supposed to help, since we already figured that they'd planned the whole thing. Still, it would be nice to know what was going on. I still couldn't believe that Uncle Joey and Ramos were dead...I just couldn't, but if I found out the Passinis had done something to make sure Uncle Joey and Ramos didn't survive, I might want to shoot them myself.

"Okay...you're all booked," David said. "I've got you on the eight-twenty flight to Seattle. Ricky will pick you up at six-thirty."

"Okay. I'd better go home and get packed. Tell Jackie I'll see her in the morning."

It was nearly midnight when I pulled the car into the garage, and I hoped Chris wasn't too upset with me that I hadn't called. Then I realized that if he'd gone with Uncle Joey, he could be dead or missing too. I found him sound asleep in bed. The bedside lamp was on and his hair was tousled with his face half turned into the pillow. He must have sensed me watching because he stirred, moving his arm and flopping to his back. His eyes fluttered open and he glanced at me in confusion.

"What time is it?" he asked.

I threw myself into his arms. "Oh Chris! You'll never believe what's happened."

The breath whooshed out of him and he made a strangled sound. "You're...cho..king...me."

I loosened my arms and rolled off his stomach onto my side of the bed. He grunted, and with blinking eyes, pushed himself into a sitting position. As soon as he was settled, I flung my arms around his waist and laid my head against the crook of his neck.

"What's going on?" he asked, pulling me tight.

"Uncle Joey and Ramos are missing....and they might be dead." As I told him how I'd found out from Billie that the yacht they were on had blown up, and how Jackie had called minutes later to ask me to come over, tears filled my eyes, and my voice shook. I blinked them away, hoping Chris wouldn't notice how upset I was. "I think the Passinis must have planned the whole thing."

"But what did Jackie want?" Chris asked.

"I guess Uncle Joey told her I had premonitions, so she wanted to know if he was still alive."

"Damn...so what did you tell her?"

"I basically told her they were both alive." I sniffed and wiped my nose with a tissue.

Chris frowned and twisted his lips, thinking that was a dumb thing to do.

"I know, but you would have done the same thing, so don't judge me too harshly."

"I didn't..." He sighed, knowing he couldn't lie to me. He also knew that now wasn't the time to get upset with me for listening to his thoughts. "Okay...maybe you're right." He brushed my forehead with a kiss. "But this whole thing...it's crazy. I wonder what really happened."

"Yeah. It was kind of a shock. It also made me realize you could have been there. You could have gotten blown up!" I hugged him tighter. He winced, and I immediately loosened my hold.

"I didn't though..." he said. "I'm fine." He was thinking I could have been there just as easily...I could have been the one getting blown up.

"But that's the thing," I said. "Maybe if I'd been there I could have saved them. I would have known what the plan was and stopped all those people from getting killed." Hot remorse washed over me. I should have gone with Uncle Joey.

"No, don't think like that," Chris said. "If the Passinis planned to blow up the boat, you couldn't have stopped them. And don't think for one minute you're responsible for anyone's death. It had nothing to do with you. Nothing at all."

"Maybe," I said, not convinced. "Do you think they're really dead?"

"I don't know," he answered, careful to keep his thoughts neutral...even if this was good news. "I'm confused. You said Kate called first. What happened to her? Wasn't she on the boat too?"

He'd been thinking it was good news for us if Uncle Joey was dead, and it kind of made me feel bad. "I don't know...I think so."

"Since Kate got off, do you think she was in on it?" he asked.

"Not really, but I have no idea. Who knows what Kate is capable of? But don't forget that Alec Passini is in love with her. If he was in on the plans, he probably made sure she got off okay. I don't think Alec would have left her to die, no matter how much his mom and brother might have wanted it."

"Then maybe the explosion really was an accident."

"Maybe...but I doubt it. Jon Passini hated Uncle Joey and planned to take him out. I just didn't know how he was going to do it. Uncle Joey must have signed the merger and that was all they needed to kill him off."

"Are you sure the Passinis got out alive? That would tell you whether it was an accident or not."

"Hmm...I think Kate would have said, but I don't know for sure. I guess I'll find out tomorrow."

"Yeah. It should be on the news in the morning."

"Well...actually..." I hesitated, hoping Chris would understand, but not holding my breath. "Jackie asked me to fly to Seattle with her in the morning and I said yes." He stilled, a little shocked, and opened his mouth to object. I cut him off. "I have to go. I told her I would, and I'm already booked on the eight-twenty flight with her."

"Why did you do that? Especially since Manetto didn't want you to go in the first place."

"Jackie needs me...and Kate asked if I'd come."

Chris let out a deep sigh. "So you're going to get involved in this mess? What if it puts you in danger? Have you considered that?"

"Yes, but I don't think it will be dangerous, and I want to help if I can. I want to know what happened, and I want to know if they're really dead. Because some part of me would feel really bad...and I know you think it's great...but I don't, and this is...this is really hard for me." The tears I'd been holding back ran down my cheeks. "Please try and understand." I sniffed, and Chris reached for a fresh tissue.

"Here." He handed it to me and closed his eyes in resignation. "When will you be back?"

"I don't know. But I'm sure it won't be long."

He was thinking that I'd said the same thing when I'd stayed in Orlando, and that little escapade had ended up lasting more than a week, never mind that I'd nearly died. Now I was doing it again. How was he supposed to feel good about that?

"I'm sorry, honey, but it's something I have to do. Don't worry. This is different. I'm sure I'll be fine."

"You say that now," he answered. "But the truth is...you don't know. You don't know what Kate has planned. You don't know if the Passinis are done with their schemes, and you don't know what's happened to Manetto and Ramos. There are too many things that could go wrong, and it drives me nuts with worry."

"Well...if it makes you feel better, I think I'll be safer there than here." Looking at it that way, now was probably the best time to tell him about my visit to Marketing Solutions.

Now Chris was really confused. "Huh?"

"Remember my appointment with Sean Hanley at Marketing Solutions this morning?" He nodded, so I continued. "Well, after talking with him I found out that he's the guy. I think he killed Darcy Shaw and a few other women as well."

"What? That's huge. It means you've solved the case. I guess the hard thing will be proving it."

"Yeah. But that's not the worst part..." I fidgeted with the blanket, not wanting to look Chris in the eyes. He picked up on my reticence and was wondering what I had done this time.

"It wasn't my fault," I began. "But since I fit the bill and his other target moved, well...he's probably coming after me now."

"What the hell!" Chris said, jerking upright and turning to catch my gaze. "You're his next victim?"

"Looks that way. It kind of freaked me out to be honest, but at least by going to Seattle for a few days, I won't have to worry about him killing me, right?"

Chris couldn't speak. Besides a few swear words, all kinds of thoughts were going through his head, mostly about how I couldn't even stay out of trouble when Manetto wasn't involved. How in the world did I do it, and how was I going to get out of it this time, and what the hell!

"Chris! That's not helping."

His shoulders sagged and he sighed. "Oh Shelby...what am I going to do with you?"

I woke at five-thirty the next morning and could hardly open my eyes. After grabbing a quick shower and pulling on my clothes, I packed my carry-on case with everything I thought I might need for a couple of days. By six-twenty, I was ready to go, but I couldn't leave without telling Savannah and Josh goodbye. They weren't happy when I woke them up, but let it go when they found out I was leaving for Seattle. I told them it was sudden, but I hoped to be back sometime in the next few days.

I gave Chris a long kiss. "I'll call when I get there. And thanks again for checking out Sean Hanley while I'm gone."

"Sure. As long as you call Harris as soon as you get back and let him know."

"I will."

After another kiss, I headed out to the waiting limo. Ricky drove, and Jackie sat in the back. The other passenger surprised me. "Nick? What are you doing here?"

"My father didn't want you two going alone, so I'm your back-up."

"Oh." For some reason, that helped relieve some of the nervous tension in my stomach. "Good. I'm glad you're coming."

"I agree," Jackie said. She didn't look like she'd slept at all, but there was deep anger lodged inside her heart that seemed to sustain her. She was determined to get to the bottom of this and take care of it just like her Joe would, and if the Passinis thought they could get away with murder, they were in for a rude awakening.

"Did you hear anything more?" I asked.

"No," she answered. It was sounding more and more like Joe was gone, but until she had proof, she wouldn't stop searching. Besides, if Joe thought it would be in his best interests to disappear for a while, he would. In the meantime, she wasn't going to let the Passinis get away with it.

I didn't know exactly how she was going to do that, but I was grateful she wasn't despondent or crying. She had a backbone of steel, and wasn't afraid to fight for what she wanted. She'd even hired a hit-man to threaten me once, and stood up to Uncle Joey to boot. I almost looked forward to seeing her take the Passinis down.

The plane landed in Seattle to overcast skies and a big chance of rain, totally fitting my somber mood. We took a taxi to the hotel where Uncle Joey and Ramos had been staying, and a small hope that they were hiding out in their rooms gave me hope. Jackie marched up to the clerk and told her she was Mrs. Joe Manetto and wanted the key to her husband's room. The clerk stammered that she'd need to see some ID first, and Jackie pulled out her driver's license and a credit card.

As the clerk examined them, I glanced at Nick, my brows raised in surprise. They were married and I didn't know? When did that happen? Nick shrugged, but his eyes were wide with surprise. This was news to him. Maybe Uncle Joey and Jackie had kept it under wraps to protect her. Whatever the reason, it put a new spin on their relationship, but also made it uncomfortable to be there. I mean, how could I tell her congratulations, or I'm so happy for you, if he was gone.

Once the clerk gave Jackie her key, she waited while Nick and I got checked in as well. Our rooms were on the same floor and across the hall from hers. We took our key cards and hurried to the elevator. On the way over, I caught a glimpse of the back of an older man with silver hair and my heart raced. Was that Uncle Joey? He turned his head and my elation fell. Nope. Not him.

Jackie and Nick waited in the elevator for me, so I hurried to catch up. The doors opened on the fourth floor, and we eagerly stepped out, following Jackie to Uncle Joey's room. I picked up that she was secretly hoping he would be there too, and this was all a ruse to trick the Passinis.

With shaking fingers, she slid the card into the lock and pushed the door open.

"Wait," Nick said. He slipped into the room like a bodyguard checking for bombs. Not about to wait, Jackie breezed in right after him. She couldn't let another minute to go by without knowing if Uncle Joey was there. I followed behind, hoping she was right, and noticed the room was neat and tidy.

Nick came back from checking the bathroom, and Jackie opened the closet to find Uncle Joey's suitcase and a few shirts hanging up. She opened the dresser drawers and found more articles of clothing, then slipped into the bathroom where his toothbrush and shaving supplies sat on the counter. With each discovery her mouth tightened and tears threatened to fall.

"I'm going to put my things away in my room," I said. "But I'll be back in a minute."

Jackie nodded, grateful to have some time alone, and Nick and I left. My room was directly across the hall, with Nick's next door. "Which room is Ramos'? I asked him.

"That one next to Manetto's."

"Too bad we can't get in there, but I guess it wouldn't be any different from Uncle Joey's room."

"Probably not," Nick agreed.

I slipped my key card into the slot and opened the door. To my surprise Nick followed me inside. "I've been thinking about a plan," he said. "I want to go to the dock and see how the investigation's going. Maybe you'll get some kind of premonition while we're there that will help us know where they are."

"Uh...maybe," I said.

Nick shook his head. "I just can't believe that Manetto and Ramos were taken by surprise. Unless they were locked up in a room or something, I think they would have gotten out." He still couldn't believe they were dead, but it was looking more and more like that was what had happened.

"What about Kate? Are we meeting up with her?"

"Yes. Jackie's supposed to call her when we get to the dock. In fact, she might already be there."

"We should get going then," I said.

"Okay. I'll meet you in the hall outside Jackie's door."

He left, and I sat heavily on the bed, tired from not sleeping much and full of anxiety about what we were going to find. I slipped my phone out of my pocket and quickly called Chris to let him know I had arrived safely. He was especially happy to hear that Nick had come with us as a bodyguard of sorts. I told him I'd call him later tonight and disconnected. I quickly unpacked and, after using the bathroom, opened the door to find Jackie and Nick already waiting in the hallway for me.

We took a taxi straight to the dock where the rescue operation was still in progress. As we exited the taxi, the wind picked up, sending bursts of cold right through my clothes. I pulled the hood of my jacket up over my head and shivered as drops of water pelted into me with the breeze.

Were Uncle Joey and Ramos out there somewhere submerged in a watery grave?

Two search and rescue boats circled a bigger boat in the distance. I scanned the dock and spotted Kate at the end of the pier. She stood beside a man who held a radio and looked like he was in charge. She was talking to him animatedly, and from her thoughts, I knew she wasn't happy with the way he was handling things.

As we walked toward her, she caught sight of us and immediately ran over. Embracing Jackie, she broke down in tears. She was thinking it looked like both Ramos and Uncle Joey had died in the explosion. Facing this alone was too much, and having us there unleashed the torrent of tears she'd been holding back.

"I'm so glad you're here," she said, pulling away, and wiping her eyes. Including all three of us, she continued, "They searched the bay for survivors all night and sent them back out at first light this morning, but no one's turned up yet. I don't know what to do."

"How far out was the yacht?" Nick asked.

"See that big boat?" She pointed toward the water. "That's where they say the yacht went down."

From here, it didn't look so far away that a person couldn't swim to shore, and my hopes surged. "Has anyone else turned up since it happened?"

"Yes. A couple of people, but that was early this morning. They're saying that they haven't spotted anyone alive since then, so there couldn't be any survivors left. The next step is to send divers down to the wreckage." Thank goodness Kate didn't add *to look for bodies*, like she was thinking.

Jackie stood motionless under her umbrella, gazing out over the water. Her thoughts swirled from despair that they were dead, to hope that maybe they had gotten away. She swallowed and turned to Kate, resolved to get to the bottom of it. If they really hadn't made it out, she needed to find who was responsible and make them pay. "I want to know exactly what happened last night."

"Okay," Kate said. "There's a coffee shop down that way. We could get out of this rain and talk there."

Jackie nodded solemnly, and all of us followed Kate back toward the parking lot. A sidewalk ran around the lot, and we trailed it to the street, where it emerged near a small, weathered coffee and sandwich shop.

The inside surprised me with a wall of windows fronting the bay, offering an amazing view. We found a table and sat, all of our gazes drawn to the boat anchored near the spot of the sunken yacht. A waitress arrived to take our orders and, as soon as she left, Kate began to talk.

"It was a beautiful day yesterday, with the sun out and no wind at all, perfect for a party out on the yacht. The party was to celebrate the merger, which Uncle Joey signed on Saturday. I think the Passinis invited everyone they knew to come, which seemed kind of crazy to me, but the yacht was huge. It had three decks, and before we left the dock, it was crowded with people wandering all over the place.

"I spent most of the evening with Alec, but I saw Uncle Joey and Ramos many times. Looking back, it seems like either Julia or Jon was with them the entire time, but I can't be certain. Anyway, just before midnight, we heard an explosion, only it was kind of weird and muffled. But it rocked the boat and it started to list sideways. Soon, everyone was screaming, and the captain yelled over the speakers that the yacht was taking on water and telling everyone to head for the life rafts.

"That's when I realized I'd lost track of Uncle Joey. It seems like I'd just barely seen him, but when I tried to find him again, I couldn't see him anywhere. I was on the middle deck, so I yelled his name over and over while I rushed to the lower decks. As the water rose, Alec pulled me toward the life rafts, but I refused to leave without finding Uncle Joey first. That's when Alec realized he couldn't see Julia or Jon anywhere either.

"At that point, Alec pulled me toward the last remaining raft. He threw a life jacket over my head and literally dragged me across the boat. The captain had already boarded and was waiting till the very last second for any stragglers. We barely managed to push away before the yacht tilted into the air and sank."

Kate's eyes held that faraway haunted look as she remembered the events of last night. I'd never seen her so pale, with big dark circles under her eyes. As I studied her, I realized she seemed ready to collapse. She kept blaming herself over and over for this catastrophe, thinking she never should have pushed for the merger.

"So when did you find the Passinis?" I asked.

"Oh...when we finally got to shore, we found Julia with some of the other survivors who had left before us. I searched the crowd for Uncle Joey and Ramos, but when I couldn't find them, I called you." Her remorseful gaze met Jackie's. "I didn't know what else to do."

"Did they pull many survivors out of the water?" Nick asked.

"Yes," Kate said. "Apparently, there were several who jumped off the yacht and started to swim for shore. Jon Passini was one of them. I still can't believe how fast it went down after the explosion. It seemed like only a few minutes passed... and there was nothing I could do. I felt so helpless." She had given up, and thought since they hadn't turned up yet they were both dead.

Jackie's sharp, indrawn breath and tear-filled eyes caught at my heart. She'd seen the same thing in Kate's expression, and grief threatened to overwhelm her. "If they killed my husband..."

"You can't give up yet," I said. "We still need to talk to the Passinis." I caught Kate's gaze. "We need to question them...in person. If they were involved...I'll know."

That seemed to jolt Kate out of the shock Jackie's revelation had caused. "That's right. I think they're all at the yard office trying to straighten things out. They should still be there. We can take my car." She was thinking that with my mind-reading skills, we'd know if the Passinis had made this happen. If this was their fault, she'd show them they couldn't double-cross her and get away with it. She hoped in her heart that Alec wasn't involved, but she had no doubts about Jon, and she couldn't wait to confront him and maybe pump a bullet or two into him.

Jackie was thinking the same thing about shooting Julia, the only difference being she didn't have a loaded gun in her purse like Kate, who seemed more than ready to use it. Nick was a little more level-headed, thinking he knew ways to make people disappear, and he hoped Kate and Jackie wouldn't lose their composure and start a fight, but he'd be ready just in case. He'd covered up things before...he could do it again.

Yikes! This could get dicey. I'd have to make sure I didn't blurt out anything that could escalate this meeting into a gun battle.

The Passini Shipping Company yard offices weren't far and, with Kate driving like a maniac, we arrived in minutes. She was already suffering from post-traumatic stress disorder, and thoughts of the Passinis killing Uncle Joey were sending her over the edge.

Relieved to arrive in one piece, I hopped out of the car and took deep breaths through my mouth to calm my racing heart. It was difficult considering I was surrounded by people whose thoughts centered on hacking off a few fingers or arms, followed by breaking a few ribs and noses, then finishing up with shooting a few bullets right between their eyes.

Most of these violent thoughts were focused toward Jon, although Jackie included Julia in the shooting-between-the-eyes part since she didn't like her much. I tried to remember that when most people were upset, they thought worse things than they would ever do, but with these strong murderous thoughts coming from both Kate and Jackie, I wasn't so sure I could count on that.

Chapter 8

With my stomach in knots, I dutifully followed behind Kate and the others into the building. Kate rushed past the secretary who stuttered a greeting and wisely got out of her way. At the end of the hall, Kate threw open the door and barged inside the office, startling everyone there.

A man explaining some paperwork at the large desk stopped mid-sentence, and Julia straightened from her position of studying it. Both Jon and Alec jumped up from their chairs beside the desk. Alec's eyes held true concern for us, while Jon's narrowed in open contempt, and Julia's widened in surprise.

"We need to talk," Kate blurted. "Did any of you have anything to do with the explosion? Did you orchestrate the whole thing? Did you want Uncle Joey to die?"

"Kate," Alec said, taking hold of her arms. "What's going on? Why are you all here? Did you find his body?"

"No," she said. "But it doesn't look good."

"I want to know what happened last night." Jackie stepped in front of us, her tone hard and cold. "Every single detail. I'll know if you don't tell me the truth, and you'll be sorry you ever crossed a Manetto."

Julia's face turned pale, but she pursed her lips before glancing at the man seated behind the desk. "Please leave us." Sensing a dangerous current in the room, and eager to escape whatever the hell was going on, he fled out the door, shutting it behind him with a bang.

Julia turned to face us, her back ramrod straight. "Of course," she said. She was thinking this looked bad, but she had nothing to do with it. "Jon, Alec, please find chairs for our guests. We have much to discuss, and I for one am too tired to do this standing." With her guard relaxed, I noticed that exhaustion made the wrinkles stand out around her mouth and eyes. She took the seat behind the desk vacated by the man who'd left and waited for all of us to sit before she began.

"First, let me assure you I had nothing to do with the explosion. Besides the loss of life and injuries, that yacht was worth millions. Do you think I would be stupid enough to blow it up? I had just successfully signed a merger that would breathe new life into our struggling company. Why would I ever do anything to jeopardize that? We had far more to lose than we ever had to gain if we intended to kill Joseph. This is a horrible tragedy, and I intend to get to the bottom of it. From what I have been able to find out, it looks like it was nothing more than a terrible accident. But believe me, if it wasn't, I will find out what really happened. I'll make it a personal vendetta to find those responsible and make them pay."

Julia was telling the truth. She believed it had to be an accident.

"I've never been more scared in my life," she continued. "It was worse, knowing that if anyone got hurt, it was my fault. I tried to wait until everyone was off the yacht before I left, but with it sinking, and people screaming, I didn't know what to do." Julia's eyes filled with tears as she recounted the traumatic experience.

Now that I knew Julia wasn't to blame, I turned my focus to Jon, but found his thoughts closed behind a cloud of confusion. If he orchestrated the whole thing, it was likely that he hadn't told his mother any of the details, and I knew he was hiding something.

"Jon...where were you when the explosion happened?" I asked.

He glanced at me, sensing a threat in my tone. Why was I there with Kate and Jackie anyway? He hadn't given my presence much thought, but now he grew suspicious. "With a few of my friends on the upper deck. We were playing pool. The explosion rocked the boat, and everyone scrambled down the stairs to see what was going on. I found the captain, and together we sounded the alarm to evacuate. While he radioed for help, I got the lifeboats released and people loaded inside. In no time at all, the boat was sinking. I did what I could to get people off, but it sank so fast there were some who had to jump overboard. I was one of them."

He was telling the truth, but there had to be more to it. I just needed to get more specific with my questions. "What do you think caused the explosion?"

He shrugged. "I have no idea. One of the engines must have caught fire or something."

"But if you were anchored on the bay, the engines wouldn't have been running would they?"

"Oh...I guess not, but I don't know. Seriously, I have no idea how it happened." He started to sweat as the realization hit him that he looked guilty as hell.

"Did you see Uncle Joey and Ramos after the explosion?"

He thought back, but came up blank. "No, I didn't. The last time I saw them, they were talking to someone I didn't know, probably one of Kate's friends. I might have seen them after the explosion, but honestly, everything happened so fast it's hard to remember. It's all a blur."

"Did you cause the explosion to kill them?" I asked.

"No! I swear it wasn't me. It must have been an accident." He was thinking he may have wanted Manetto dead, but not like this. He was smarter than that. Manetto's people would have killed him...and they still might...given as how it looked like he'd set the whole thing up.

Julia came to the same conclusion and stepped in front of Jon. "We had nothing to do with this. If someone planted a bomb, then we were set up. That is the only explanation."

She and Jon were both telling the truth, and I could hardly believe it. "But who would do that, and more important, why?"

"What are you saying?" Kate grabbed my arm and jerked me toward her. "Don't tell me you believe them. They set this up. It's the only thing that makes sense."

I locked my gaze with Kate's. "I know that, but they didn't do it Kate. They're telling the truth. It was either an accident, or someone else caused it. But it wasn't them."

Her brows drew together and she stared at me with incredulity. How could I be right? Everything pointed to them. They had motive and means. If I wasn't there to read their minds, she'd be convinced they were guilty no matter what they said. But now...wait...was I in on it? Was that...

"No!" I interrupted. "Don't even go there."

She flinched and dropped her gaze, then shook her head. "This is...sorry. I just...I'm so confused. I don't know what to think."

Jackie stepped to my side. "So they didn't do this?"

I glanced at Jon and Julia, who were looking at me like I was an alien or something. They were grateful I was taking their side, but it spooked them since they had to agree they looked guilty. Alec had a hard time believing Jon hadn't done it either, but all he wanted to do was hold Kate in his arms and comfort her.

"I know it looks like they did it," I began. "But someone set them up. Now it's up to us to figure out who that is."

Jackie sighed with defeat and glanced between me and the Passinis. She was thinking that if Joe hadn't trusted me so much, she wouldn't believe a word I said, no matter how convincing I made it sound.

"All right. I'll take your word on it, but just in case..." Jackie turned to Julia and Jon. "I want you to know that anything Joe signed is still legally binding. Only now instead of him, you will answer to me. Just so we're perfectly clear on this...if he is dead, I am his successor. Now I suggest you help us figure out who did this before I decide to end your sorry lives for killing my husband. I'll be in touch."

We left the building and I knew both Jackie and Nick were having a hard time believing the Passinis were innocent. Jackie wanted to kill them anyway, but she could wait for the right opportunity. Kate trailed along behind, and I picked up that part of her wanted to stay so she could be with Alec, and the other part was in shock that Jackie was Uncle Joey's wife and successor. How could Uncle Joey marry Jackie and put her in charge? For some reason, Kate had always hoped that when the time came, he would still pick her.

We got in Kate's car and she pulled out of the parking lot. "Do you want to go back to the hotel?"

"No," Jackie answered. "Let's go back to the marina. I want to know if they've found anything new since we left."

Kate nodded, and a few minutes later we were back at the docks.

By now, the rain had stopped and the wind had died down. As we stood on the dock, the dark clouds parted and a few rays of sunshine hit the water out in the bay, giving the water a golden hue. The man Kate had been talking to earlier noticed us and made his way over. He was thinking that he hated being the bearer of bad news, but it was part of the job.

Kate introduced us and he nodded before speaking. "I have some new information. Our divers reached the lower levels of the yacht and found a couple of bodies. We're in the process of bringing them up. It will take the rest of the day to retrieve them, but if they have any identification on them, we can let you know. I just need the names of your missing relatives and a phone number where you can be reached."

Jackie seemed to shrink a little and Nick quickly put his arm around her. Kate told him Uncle Joey's name, but the only name for Ramos she knew was...well...Ramos.

"His name is...Alejandro Ramos," I said, my heart breaking. Telling the detective Ramos' name was like confirming that he was really dead.

The detective glanced at me and nodded. "Thanks. You might as well go home. There's nothing you can do here. We'll call you with any information we have once we bring up the bodies." He was thinking that these were the only bodies left since all but a few people on the list had been accounted for, and from the looks of the remains, they'd been involved in the explosion.

I gasped and my hand came to my mouth. I couldn't seem to catch my breath, and a small sound of distress escaped my lips. They really were dead. Jackie thought I must have had a premonition about Joe, and fear tightened her throat, but she swallowed past it and nodded at the detective.

No one spoke as Kate drove us back to the hotel. Kate knew I'd picked up on something, but wasn't ready to know what it was. Jackie and Nick figured the same thing, but wanted to wait until we were back in the hotel to hear it. I didn't want to tell them what the detective had thought, so I tried to compose myself and act normal. I didn't know if I should tell them. Just because the detective thought everyone but those in the boat had been accounted for didn't make it true. I should probably just keep it to myself.

Kate pulled into the parking structure beneath the hotel and turned off the engine. "What should we do now?" she asked.

"I think we should try and figure out who planted the explosives," I said. "Maybe we could get a list of guests from the Passinis. Kate, did you invite people too? Jon made it sound like you had some friends there."

"Yes. I invited most of the office workers from our shipping company. Uncle Joey thought that would be a good gesture."

"Did they all make it out?" I asked.

"Yes, I'm pretty sure they did, but I can call Zack and find out. He's my manager I told you about. I'm sure he'll know."

"Let's go to my room to talk this through," Jackie said.

"Sure," I said.

Nick glanced at Jackie, taking in her drawn, tired face, and hurried around to her door, opening it to help her out. She gratefully took his hand and let him lead her to the elevators. He was thinking that if Manetto really was gone, this was the least he could do for his wife.

Tears flooded my eyes, and I blinked rapidly to keep them back. I couldn't cry now. There would be plenty of time for that later. Now I needed to be strong.

"What happened?" Kate asked under her breath. She'd seen my reaction and knew how hard I was struggling.

"Nothing...I'm just afraid they're really dead."

Kate thought I was probably hiding something I'd heard. "Do Nick and Jackie know you can read minds?"

"No," I answered sharply. "They think I have premonitions, and I want it to stay that way."

Nick held the elevator door for us, noticing our angry expressions. Something was up with Kate and me, but he held his silence, determined to ask me about it later. If Manetto really was gone though, he was relieved Jackie was taking over and not Kate. He couldn't work with Kate, and he didn't think anyone else would want to either.

Hearing that sent a sharp sting of sadness over me, made worse when I caught Jackie's continual thoughts of *don't let him be dead, don't let him be dead,* running over and over in her mind. It was enough to make my stomach churn until I was ready to throw up.

Nick took the key card from Jackie and opened her door. I followed behind with reluctance and moved to sit on the small couch near a square wooden table and chairs. Nick opened the small fridge and got out a couple of mini bottles, offering them to us. Jackie gratefully took hers, thinking if this was as bad as it looked, alcohol might help deaden the pain. Kate took one as well, but I declined.

"Did you get a premonition Shelby?" Jackie asked. "Do you think they're dead?"

My gaze locked with hers, and sadness nearly overwhelmed me. With a rush of anger, I pushed it away and tried to think positively. "There's still a small chance they got out. So until their bodies are recovered, we still have reason to hope, right?" I glanced at Jackie. Tears streaked down her cheeks, but her clear gaze settled on mine like a lifeline. "Didn't he tell you that if it sounded bad, not to believe it?"

"Yes." She nodded. "He did tell me that, but..."

"Then that's what we're going to do," I said. "Until we hear from the police, we shouldn't give up hope."

"All right," Jackie said, composing herself. She glanced at Nick. "Why don't you talk to Julia or Jon and get a list of their guests?"

"I'll take care of it," Kate said. "And I'll get a list of the guests from our company as well." She glanced at Jackie and her composure faltered. "Jackie I swear I'll find out who did this and make them pay. I promise."

Jackie nodded, but her face crumpled and she began to cry. At that, Kate burst into tears. "This is all my fault! I'm so sorry Jackie!" Kate threw her arms around Jackie and sobbed. Jackie patted her on the back and they both cried together. Feeling their grief and hearing their sad thoughts opened a hole in my heart, and tears streamed down my face too.

Watching us, Nick's eyes filled with tears. Mortified, he stood and hurried toward the door. "I need to make some phone calls. I'll be back." He quickly exited the room, thinking about calling to update his dad, and grateful to get away from our tears.

Jackie pulled away from Kate and grabbed some tissues off the night stand. After blowing her nose and wiping her eyes, she turned toward us. "We need to stop this. I can't believe my Joe is dead. He wouldn't have let this happen, and neither would Ramos. Until we find their bodies, I refuse to grieve. Now...let's get to work. Besides the Passinis, who the hell would dare kill my husband?"

Her outburst put a stop to my tears, and Kate and I both grabbed a few tissues. Jackie picked up her mini-bottle and took a big swallow

Kate had already finished hers, and rummaged in the fridge for another, but decided against it since she had work to do. I glanced inside the fridge and found a Diet Coke. Yes! I promptly grabbed it and popped it open.

After finishing off her bottle in one long guzzle, Jackie sat down in the armchair and let her head fall back. Her initial enthusiasm had dried up, and she couldn't stop the tears from leaking out of her eyes. Seeing this, Kate pursed her lips and moved to the door.

"I'm going to get those lists together," Kate said. "I'll call and we can meet up later."

"Good idea," Jackie answered. "If you don't mind," she said. "I'd like to be alone for a while."

"Sure," I agreed. "I need to call home anyway."

I followed Kate out of Jackie's room and shut the door. In the hallway, she paused, her lips turned down in a frown. "Tell me the truth. Did you hear the detective think they were dead?"

"He thought so...but only because most everyone had been accounted for."

She nodded and turned to leave. Before she got to the elevator, she stopped and glanced over her shoulder. "You'll let me know if they find anything, okay?"

"Sure," I agreed and watched her get on the elevator. With a huge sigh of my own I opened my door and hurried inside. I kicked off my shoes and headed straight to the bedroom where I flopped down on the bed. The emotional turmoil I'd gone through left me exhausted. I debated about calling Chris and filling him in, but I just wasn't ready to do that. Saying they were probably dead out loud made it too real, and I just didn't want to face it. Instead, I snuggled up with my pillows and fell asleep.

Loud knocking on my door woke me. I checked the time, realizing I'd been asleep for two hours. I hurried to the door and cracked it open. Nick stood on the other side, so I pulled it open and let him in. "Did you find out anything?" I asked.

"Not yet. Do you want to get something to eat?" he asked.

Since it was nearly four in the afternoon, and I'd been up since five-thirty that morning with nothing to eat all day, I realized I was starving. "Sure. Let me get my purse."

As we stepped out into the hall I hesitated. "What about Jackie?"

Nick shook his head. "I already talked with her. She'll have something brought up if she gets hungry, but right now, she just wants to rest."

I could hardly blame her for that. We took the elevator to the lobby and ended up in the hotel dining room for dinner. I got a burger and fries, but after the first few bites, I couldn't eat anymore. With Uncle Joey and Ramos' deaths looming over me, I just didn't have an appetite. When Nick's plate was empty, I met his gaze. "After all this, do you still think they might have made it out?"

Nick narrowed his eyes, worried that I might start crying again if he told me the truth. "Yeah, sure," he lied. "Ramos is a very resourceful person. If anyone could make it out, it's him."

I liked what he said, but knew he didn't believe it. Tired of the whole thing, I suddenly wanted to find out what had happened, good or bad. "Maybe we should go back to the docks and see if they've made any progress."

"All right," Nick said. "The police and divers should still be there. What about Kate? Where did she run off to?"

"To get the guest lists. She was supposed to call, but to be honest, I think she wanted some alone time with Alec."

Nick considered it. "Lucky for her he wasn't involved, but I'm not so sure I trust that the Passinis didn't have something to do with it. How good are your premonitions anyway?"

"Real good," I said. "I wish it was them; it would make this whole thing easier."

"That's for sure. I called my dad and asked him if he knew of anyone who'd want Manetto dead. He said there were lots of people, but that didn't mean they'd actually kill him. Not when it meant certain death since we'd end up killing them." He snorted. "You know something funny? He didn't know Manetto and Jackie were married."

"Really?"

"Nope. But my mom did. She even knew Jackie was next in line to run the business. How do you like that? She didn't even say anything."

I smiled. "Good for her. Was your dad disappointed it wasn't him?"

"No, especially since my mom was so happy about it."

"Makes sense to me," I said.

"You ready?" he asked.

"Yeah...let's go."

It had started to rain again, and the dreary afternoon held little warmth. I shivered as we pulled into the parking lot and found only one police car left. The detective from earlier was sitting inside and motioned us over to get in out of the rain. Nick slid into the front seat, and I sat in the back.

"Good timing," the detective said. "I was just leaving."

"Did they recover the bodies?" Nick asked.

"Yes. There were two. At the moment, they're still out on the search boat, but they'll be taking them to the morgue.

They didn't tell me if they found any IDs on the bodies, and from what I understood, they might have been close to the explosion." He was thinking that for one body, there wasn't a lot left to ID.

"Crap," I said, feeling the blood drain from my head.

"Are you all right, Miss?" he asked, concern tightening the crinkles around his eyes.

I swallowed and laid my head back against the seat. "Yes. Please continue."

"With the explosion so close to the rooms, it looks like they were unable to get out before the boat sank. We'll probably need your help to identify them, but the bodies won't be ready for you to see until morning. I have to advise you that they will be difficult to identify. That long in the water makes bodies decompose pretty fast. We'd have to rely on a tattoo or a chipped tooth or some other identifiable mark. Barring that, we can always get dental records, but remember...that takes time."

"We'll come in the morning," Nick said.

My thoughts immediately went to the bullet wound Ramos had taken while we were in Orlando. I knew exactly where that was, but looking at his decomposing dead body was something I didn't want to do. Not now, not ever. I closed my eyes and swallowed. Was he really dead? How could this happen? I thought for sure they'd made it out.

Nick noticed my distress and thanked the detective. He got out of the car and helped me out. Keeping a hold on my arm, he led me back to the car and I slumped into the seat, light-headed and a little nauseated. We drove back to the hotel in silence. At my door, Nick hesitated. "Will you be all right?" he asked.

"Yes. Thanks. I'll see you tomorrow."

He nodded and I hurried inside, not wanting him to see my tears. I thought of the last time I'd seen Ramos at the office and how he'd tried to kiss me. I'd pulled away, and he'd joked about wanting to do that before he died, and now it would never happen. Memories flooded over me. I remembered the thrill of riding behind him on his motorcycle. His smile as he ate fish tacos like they were going out of style and the look on his face when he saw his brother for the first time in fifteen years.

Sobs escaped my lips, and I no longer tried to hold them back. He was gone, and I'd never see him again. And Uncle Joey? He was gone too. After all this time of trying to get out from under him, now...it was over. They were dead.

Taking a deep breath to get under control, I knew it was time for a hot bath. I filled up the tub, and scooped the bath salts out of my luggage, grateful I'd had the foresight to pack them. Soothing eucalyptus and uplifting spearmint flooded my senses, and soon I was lying in the comfort of soft, hot water. At least now the tears had a place to run.

I didn't get out until I had refilled the tub with hot water a few times. Now my fingers and toes were shriveled like prunes, but at least my tears had dried. After drying off, I pulled on my pajamas and snuggled in bed with my phone, finally ready to call Chris without blubbering like an idiot. I was sad and needed to hear his comforting voice.

"Hey Shelby," he answered. "How are things going? Did they show up?"

"Oh Chris," I said, tears immediately running from my eyes. "It looks like they're really dead. The detective said the divers found a couple of bodies in the lower rooms near the explosion. With everyone else accounted for, they think it must be Uncle Joey and Ramos. They've taken them to the morgue and Nick and I are supposed to identify what's left of them in the morning."

"Wow. I can't believe it."

"I know. It looks like it's really them." I sniffed, then grabbed a tissue and wiped my nose. "I feel so bad. And guess what? Uncle Joey and Jackie were married...she told them at the front desk that she was his wife and I never knew. Now he's dead, and she's all alone." I couldn't stop the tears from falling, but at least I wasn't sobbing anymore.

"Oh, honey...I'm really sorry to hear that." Chris took a deep breath. "I never thought he'd really be dead. Are you sure it's them?"

"Well...actually...no. They didn't say there was any identification on the bodies, that's why they want us to come to the morgue in the morning...but I'm not sure I can do that. The detective said that after being in the water so long, they probably wouldn't look very good, and just thinking about looking at them like that is giving me a stomachache."

"Then don't go. I'm sure Nick and Jackie can handle it. Anyway, you're not part of the family. It shouldn't be you that has to identify them."

"I know," I said. Was that an accusation?

"So...do you know what happened? Did the Passinis do it?"

"That's the strange part. It's not them. We confronted them, and I know they didn't do it. They're just as confused as we are."

"What?" he asked. "That doesn't make sense. Who else had the motive and means to carry it out?"

"Exactly," I agreed. "This is a nightmare. Not only are they gone, but we have no idea who killed them and why."

"Maybe it's time for you to come home."

"But...I need to find out who did this."

Chris sighed. "I know...but Shelby...listen to me, this could get dangerous. What if you figure it out and that person decides to kill you. There's so much that could go wrong, and...I don't want you to get caught in the middle of something you can't get out of. Right now you can leave. With Manetto gone, there's nothing holding you there."

"But there is," I said. "I can't walk out on Jackie. I have to see it through. At the very least, I have to know if they're really dead." Now it was my turn to sigh. In my mind I knew what he said made sense, but my heart was still breaking to think they were dead, and I knew he'd never understand that. "So, I'll see how it goes tomorrow. I'm going to try and get some sleep now. I'm exhausted."

"That's a good idea, and...Shelby...I'm sorry you're so sad. Let me know what happens tomorrow, okay?"

"Yeah. I'll call you." I said it without much warmth. He wanted me to leave, but I wanted to stay, and the comfort I'd called him for wasn't there, leaving me empty and disappointed.

"Hey," he said. "I love you. I wish I was there to hold you tonight. This is a shock. I'm sure you never expected this to happen. If you need to stay a little longer we'll figure it out, okay? I'm sorry if I said the wrong thing, but you know how I felt about Manetto, right? Anyway, I'm still sorry you're hurting."

"Thanks Chris. This is just...hard, and I feel really bad."

"I know...and it's okay that you feel bad."

The tightness in my chest loosened and I was able to breathe freely again. I asked him how things were going at home with the kids and, for a moment, forgot all about Uncle Joey and Ramos.

"I found Sean Hanley's address," Chris said. "And I checked his records, but besides a couple of speeding tickets, he's clean."

"That's interesting. Thanks for doing that. When I get back we'll have to figure out what to do and go from there."

"No honey...the first thing you're going to do is tell Harris...then we'll go from there. Okay?"

"Sure," I agreed. Thinking about taking on a serial killer without knowing Ramos had my back kind of freaked me out, and I was ready to turn the whole thing over to Dimples.

We talked for a few more minutes, then said goodbye and I finished getting ready for bed.

Snuggling under the covers, I turned out the lights and closed my eyes, but sleep eluded me. I kept seeing images of Ramos and Uncle Joey. It was like they were haunting me. Then I'd see images of Sean Hanley coming after me with a knife and a crazy gleam in his eyes, ready to cut my heart out.

Finally, I turned on the television to take my mind off my troubles and watched a nature show, glad to find one without lions or wolves sneaking up on little lost sheep. Hours later, my eyelids got heavy and I turned it off, at last ready to stop thinking and fall asleep.

Chapter 9

My eyes fluttered open the next morning, and all at once, the reality that Ramos and Uncle Joey were dead crashed over me. I sniffed and rubbed my chest over my aching heart. Part of me believed they were dead, and the other part wondered when I had given up. I was usually a pretty optimistic person, so why had I quit believing they'd made it out? I mean...those bodies might not be theirs. They could belong to someone else, right?

I sighed, knowing the odds of that were pretty slim. As strong and capable as Uncle Joey and Ramos were, they were still human, and the business they were in certainly didn't help. I had to face it. Maybe this time their luck had run out, and they really were gone.

Nick sent me a text saying he'd be leaving for the morgue soon, and he asked if I wanted to go. I told him not really, but asked him to knock on his way out just in case I'd changed my mind. When the knock came, I was dressed and ready to go, but after opening the door, I couldn't quite make myself step out into the hallway.

"You ready?" he asked.

I sighed. From his thoughts, I knew he didn't really want to face this by himself, but he also didn't want a blubbering woman with him either. "You know...I don't really want to go. What about Jackie? Did you talk to her?"

He glanced at the door across the hall. "She didn't answer my phone call, but..."

"Oh no...do you think she's all right?" He pursed his lips, hating that I interrupted him. Why did women always do that? I snapped my mouth shut and waited for him to continue.

"She answered my text, telling us to go on ahead. I think under the circumstances she's doing fine, but going to the morgue is definitely not a good idea."

"Yeah...I agree. In fact, I don't think it's a good idea for me either. Maybe I'll wait with Jackie and see if there's anything she needs while you're gone."

"All right," he agreed. "I shouldn't be long."

After he got on the elevator, I took a deep breath and walked over to Jackie's door. I worried about her being alone for so long and wanted to see if she'd let me in. I raised my hand to knock, but heard a low voice and froze. Was that a man's voice? I listened carefully for a full minute, but when I heard nothing more, decided it was probably just the TV.

Maybe I should give her a little more time. I went back to my room and got out my ice container. I needed a soda something fierce. With money and my keycard in my pocket, I followed the signs to the ice machine, loaded my ice container, and bought a diet soda. The machine next to it had chips and candy bars, so I bought a salted nut roll and some chips for later. Nuts weren't as bad as chocolate, so I didn't feel too guilty about eating that for breakfast.

Juggling my ice and treats, I rounded the corner back to the hallway where my room was located. Glancing up, I caught sight of someone entering the room across the hall from mine. Was that Ramos' room? It had to be pretty close, but from here, I couldn't tell. It could just as easily be the one next to it. Just in case, I hurried down the hall and listened at his door, but even holding my breath, I couldn't hear anything.

I sighed. It must have been a different room and I was just imagining things. The same as how I thought I'd seen Uncle Joey when we checked in yesterday. It was probably just wishful thinking. Stepping across the hall to my room, I rearranged my purchases and ice so I could get the keycard out of my pocket. Just as I pulled the card out, the soda slipped out from under my arm. As I jerked to catch it, the ice container tipped, spilling ice all over the floor. In my effort to stop the ice from falling, the whole container slipped from my hands, scattering ice and my candy bar halfway down the hall.

"Well damn!" I cursed. With a low growl, I picked up the container and started shoveling ice inside. Then got down on my hands and knees to hurry things along and hoped no one came out of their room right then to see me like this. Nearly done, I noticed my bottle of soda had rolled into Nick's doorway and crawled over to retrieve it. I froze to hear the sound of a door opening and inwardly cringed. Great! I'd just been caught crawling on the floor with my butt in the air by a stranger. How embarrassing.

"Babe."

I screamed and jumped at the same time, twisting around with my heart hammering and my breath catching. "Ra...Ramos?" I couldn't seem to breathe right, and tears gathered in my eyes.

He stepped toward me, warmth flooding his dark brown eyes and his mouth turned up in a sexy smile. My heart nearly gave out. He reached for me, gripping my arms and helping me to my feet. My legs were shaking so bad I could hardly stand on my own. Still, I threw my arms around him and held on for dear life. With his grip solid and strong around me, I dared to believe he was real. After a moment his arms relaxed and, breathing in his scent, I finally loosened my death grip.

"You're not dead," I mumbled, blinking back tears. I pulled back just enough to glance at his face and notice the small cut and bruises along his jawline.

"Nope." His lips twisted into a half smile. "But I'm sorry you thought I was." He was sorry, but at the same time, he was thinking how great it felt that I cared enough to cry over him. And here I was, wrapped in his arms and holding him close. It was enough to make him think he could probably kiss me and get away with it.

"Don't even think about it," I gasped, and tried to pull out of his arms.

He chuckled, but didn't let me go. "So...do you want me to help you clean this up, or what?"

I glanced at the floor, then back at him. "The ice?"

He nodded, raising one eyebrow and thinking that maybe something was wrong with me. I didn't seem to be handling this too well.

"Ramos!" I pulled away and smacked his arm. "I thought you were dead! Where the hell have you been?"

"Let's go in Manetto's room. I'll explain everything."

"So he's alive too?"

"Yeah, he's in there. We've mostly been staying in my room this whole time."

"Why did you hide from me...from all of us?" I asked, my eyes filling with tears.

He glanced up and down the hall, not wanting anyone to see him. "I'll explain inside." He picked up my soda, chips, and candy bar, then motioned me toward Manetto's room.

"Fine," I said. "Just give me a minute." Before he could say another word, I grabbed my keycard out of my pocket and slipped inside my room. I leaned against the door and sighed, feeling the tears run down my cheeks.

I hurried into the bathroom to splash cold water on my face and get under control. Even though this was a good kind of shock, I still needed some time to calm down, especially since I didn't want Ramos to see me crying like this.

What I needed was my Diet Coke. I drank a glass of water instead, and felt better. After washing my face with a cool washcloth, I freshened up my makeup and added a touch of lip gloss.

Feeling more in control, I opened my door and crossed the hall to Jackie's room, noting that the ice and container were gone. After a quick knock, Jackie opened the door, her thousand-watt smile nearly blinding me.

"I'm so glad you know," she said, opening the door wide and ushering me in. "After you all left yesterday, Joe came in. He'd never planned on letting me believe he was dead, not for one minute, but he had to wait until all of you were gone to tell me."

"Shelby," Uncle Joey said, greeting me with a quick hug. "Come on in. Have a seat, and we'll explain what's going on."

For some reason, tears prickled at the backs of my eyes, but I held them away, and smiled instead. It came as a shock to find him looking so good. Where were the cuts and bruises on his face from being in an explosion and barely escaping with his life? What in the world was going on? Did they know who planted the explosives?

Ramos gestured toward the small couch. I sat down, and he sat beside me. His warm presence helped settle me down. Still, a million questions ran through my mind, and even though I was a little shell-shocked, anger started to climb into my heart. If Jackie had found out yesterday, why did it take so long for them to tell me? Last night would have been good. I'd cried buckets of tears and told Chris they were dead.

"Why did you keep this from me for so long?" I blurted. "Do you realize how bad I've felt thinking you were both dead?" My voice had gone up, and unwanted tears filled my eyes. Embarrassed, I tried to blink them away before anyone noticed.

"Shelby," Uncle Joey soothed. "I'm so sorry. I didn't mean to distress you. I would have told you sooner if I'd had a chance, but I didn't want you to give it away to the Passinis or the police that we were still alive. Once Jackie told us you didn't think the Passinis were involved, I didn't want it to get out until I had a plan."

After a short silence, I let out my breath and my shoulders relaxed. "Okay, I get it. Just tell me what happened. How did you escape alive?" I flopped back against the cushions like I didn't care. Uncle Joey was thinking how gratifying it was to know that I did care. Guess I hadn't fooled him, and I felt kind of bad that I wasn't showing how happy and relieved I was that he and Ramos were alive, but there was a matter of pride and hurt feelings involved here, and it was going to take me a minute to get over it...although sitting next to Ramos and his solid warmth helped.

"To begin with, being on a boat left me feeling vulnerable, so I didn't like that. I always say no matter where you are it's nice to have an exit strategy." He nodded toward Ramos. "So I had Ramos hire a speedboat for the night and set up a signal for the driver in case we wanted to leave early."

"Wow...that was lucky."

He snorted, thinking it wasn't luck, just good planning. But there was a drawback to the whole incident. "It might not have mattered if we hadn't gotten out of that room," he added.

"You got locked in a room?" That surprised me.

"Yes. Looking back, it was pretty stupid of us, but it all worked out in the end. Anyway, we got a note from Julia asking us to meet her in one of the rooms on the lower deck. She claimed to have proof that her husband was murdered and wanted our help.

"Naturally, we decided to check it out. We both had our guns, so we thought we'd be okay. We entered the room and found one of the Passini security guards down, and another slumped over a desk beside a briefcase of some kind. While we were checking on them, the door clicked shut and we couldn't get it to open.

"That's when we discovered that the briefcase was full of explosives, and there was about a minute left on the clock."

I inhaled sharply. "How did you get out?"

Uncle Joey nodded at Ramos to finish the story. "I don't know anything about disarming a bomb, so I tried breaking down the door. It wouldn't budge, so we shot holes in the door to weaken it, and kicked it out. We barely made it out into the hall and a few steps toward the stairs when the bomb went off. It knocked us off our feet and sent debris flying everywhere. Then the yacht lurched as water began pouring in.

"Within seconds water was spraying over us. We got to our feet and struggled toward the stairs. With the way the boat had tilted, I wasn't sure we were going to make it out alive. By the time we climbed up the stairs to the upper deck, the yacht was going down fast. We didn't see anyone else on board, so we jumped into the water and started swimming. I flashed my light to signal the boat we'd hired and he came and got us."

"Wow, that's incredible. Where did you go?" I asked.

Uncle Joey picked up the narrative. "Since I didn't want anyone to know we'd survived, I had him let us off at another dock and we stayed in a cheap motel for the night. We came back here the next day... yesterday, and saw all of you get in a taxi. Jackie said you went to the pier and then to the Passini shipping office."

"And she told you I found out it wasn't them," I said.

"Yes," Uncle Joey said. "But I have no idea who else it could be. I guess that means we're going to have to stay dead until we figure it out."

"That's a good idea. Are you going to let Kate and Nick know?"

"I think so. As soon as Nick gets back, we'll give Kate a call and make some plans. Jackie told me about getting the guest lists. I guess that's a good place to start."

"Yeah," I agreed. "And you might want to make a list of anyone you've pissed off here in Seattle. You did kind of take over Eddie Sullivan's shipping company. What about his associates? Would any of them want you dead?"

"I've been thinking about that." Uncle Joey rubbed his chin. "But I've been more than fair with his people. I can't think of anyone who wasn't happy with our arrangement, but then, not too many people tell me things like that, so I could be wrong."

"That's true," I said. He sent me a sharp glance. "I mean, people don't always tell you what they think...because...well, anyway... that's why you have me, right?"

"Uh-huh," he said.

I was saved from further comments by a knock at the door. Jackie jumped up to look through the peephole. She turned back and whispered, "It's Nick. What should I do?"

"Might as well let him in," Uncle Joey said.

Jackie opened the door, startling Nick with her smile. He was wondering what she was so happy about, and hated breaking her heart with the news that Manetto and Ramos were really dead.

"Come in," she said. "I have a surprise for you." She backed through the doorway and Nick stepped inside, quietly closing the door behind him.

"I don't want you to get your hopes up because it doesn't look good," he began, his head lowered with misery. "I'm really sorry to tell you this, but..."

Jackie chuckled, confusing him, then stepped out of his way and motioned inside the room. He glanced up to find Ramos and Uncle Joey smiling at him.

"Holy shit!" he blurted. "You're not dead!"

Uncle Joey smiled and hurried to greet him. "Sorry, but I had to let the Passinis think I was dead.

"I just...um..." he swallowed. "I just identified your bodies at the morgue. Sorry about that."

"That's perfect. Now everyone will think we really are dead."

Nick took a seat in the empty chair, his face white with shock. "What happened? How did you escape?" he asked. As Uncle Joey explained the story again, Nick's breathing returned to normal and soon he had completely recovered. "Someone sure went to a whole lot of trouble to kill you and make it look like it was the Passinis," he said. "How are we going to find them?"

"We can start with a list of everyone on board," Ramos said. "And go from there."

My stomach chose that moment to growl, and everyone turned their gazes to me. "Uh...I haven't had breakfast yet. Do you know what happened to my salted nut roll?"

Ramos smiled and pulled it out of his pocket. He was hoping I'd forget about it so he could eat it. "Um...yeah, it's right here."

"You were going to...um..." I let out my breath. "Geez...thanks Ramos."

He snickered and handed it over, thinking that the least I could do was give him half. I pursed my lips and tore open the package, then took a big bite. "Hmm...this is good." Unfortunately, everyone else was watching my bad manners and thinking I was being rude.

"Uh...I can go back to the machine and get another if anyone wants one," I said, wanting to redeem myself.

"I think I'll call room service," Jackie announced. "Then we can all have something to eat. What would everyone like?"

"I'll have a salted nut roll," Ramos said, his eyes glinting with challenge.

My lips twisted, but I narrowed my eyes at him. "Sure. But first I want my Diet Coke."

"Oh yeah...it's in the fridge, but I had to dump the ice," he answered.

"Fine." I found the ice bucket by the fridge and picked it up. "Anyone else? No? Okay, I'll be back." I opened the door with a shake of my head, and caught that Ramos was enjoying himself and thinking I should be glad he hadn't poured my soda in a cup with the ice I'd spilled on the floor.

I glanced back at him with venom in my eyes and he just grinned, thinking it was sure fun to tease me, and maybe he'd better come along so I didn't spill ice all over the floor again. I quickly shut the door before I said something to give our little game away, and hurried down the hall to the ice machine.

This time getting ice and a candy bar was a completely different experience from just a few short minutes ago. It amazed me how quickly everything had changed. I was still a little angry that they hadn't told me last night, leaving me to suffer with grief the whole night long. But it was water under the bridge now.

I got back to the room and knocked. Ramos let me in and I handed him his salted nut roll. "Thanks," he said. "I ordered you an omelet too. I hope that's all right?"

"Thanks, it sounds great."

As we finished up our food, my cell phone rang. "It's Kate," I said and quickly answered.

"Shelby? Why haven't you called me?" she asked. "Did they find the bodies?"

"Um...where are you?" I asked.

"At my place."

"Did you get the lists?"

"Yes."

"Great. You need to come to Jackie's hotel room. We're all here and we can go over the lists together."

"Okay," she said. "I'll be there soon."

We disconnected, and I turned to Uncle Joey. "You want Kate to know you're alive, right?"

"Yes. Of course," he answered. "But not the Passinis. I want them to suffer for a while. Maybe even be suspected of murder by the police. It would serve them right for trying to double-cross me."

I could understand his sentiments and knew I'd probably feel the same way. I hoped that didn't make me a bad person. Since the explosives didn't have anything to do with them, it was obvious they were being framed. That meant that whoever did this knew them pretty well and was probably an associate of theirs. It would sure be nice to get the lists and figure it out.

As we finished cleaning up our breakfast dishes, Kate knocked at the door. My heart pounded, knowing it was the moment of truth. I hoped she wouldn't be too mad at me for not telling her they were alive over the phone. Again Jackie pulled the door open and let Kate in. Her somber expression flooded with shock to see Uncle Joey and Ramos. She even squealed and hopped up and down on her feet...kind of like she was seeing a couple of ghosts.

Once she got over her surprise, Uncle Joey related the story of their survival and the explosion. With renewed interest, they poured over the lists. "Are you sure this is everyone who was on the boat?" Uncle Joey asked Kate.

"Yes," Kate answered, growing tired of him asking the same question over and over again.

"Even the servers?"

Kate pointed out the servers on another page. "Right here. And just below that are all the people from our company."

"I can't believe any of them would do it, but you never know." Finally Uncle Joey glanced my way with a hard expression. He was thinking this was a job for me, and probably the only way they had any hope of finding the person responsible.

"It looks like we're going to have to use our secret weapon if we want any answers," he said, looking straight at me. Everyone turned their gazes my way. I nodded to the unspoken question, and Uncle Joey smiled. "Good. This is what we'll do..."

The next evening, I was sitting in a mortuary with two caskets that held the remains of the bodies Nick had identified as Uncle Joey and Ramos. I didn't know how they did it, but the Passinis pulled some strings and got the bodies released to us for a memorial service before we took them home.

It was a little creepy, knowing there were real remains in those caskets, some of which were blown up into little pieces. Even worse was knowing the bodies were the Passini security guards. I had no idea how the Passinis got the bodies out of police custody, and since it probably involved something illegal, that was fine with me.

Earlier, Kate and I had talked to all of the servers and crew who had been on the yacht that night and eliminated them as suspects. Now we were at the funeral home where Kate had made sure all of the guests from the tragedy would come to pay their respects. Several had gathered, with more trickling in all the time.

It was my job to listen to them and find out which one had planted the explosives. At the time Uncle Joey suggested it, it seemed like a good idea, but now I wasn't so sure. Especially with thoughts of what the bodies looked like coming from most everyone. Seeing what they were thinking in their heads kind of curdled my stomach.

Jackie portrayed the grieving widow to perfection, with Kate and me standing in as her nieces. I felt kind of guilty for deceiving everyone, mostly because of how genuinely sorry they felt for us. On the other hand, I didn't feel a bit guilty for the two women who came through separately to pay their respects to Ramos. They were both beautiful and, with tears flooding their eyes, they thought a few things I'd rather not know. My face flushed red and I couldn't get my shields up fast enough.

I noticed a man come in by himself and glance around as if expecting trouble. Finding none, he quickly made his way to the casket under Uncle Joey's picture. He stood with his head bowed, but his lips were moving and I tuned into his thoughts. Again, my ears turned red, but this time it was from the rash of four letter words slipping from his mind. This guy had strong feelings for Uncle Joey, but I couldn't tell if they were good or bad. I mean...from all the swearing it seemed like they were bad, but maybe that was how bad guys talked to each other and it was really good.

I had to get close enough to find out and maybe ask him a few leading questions, so I stood just to the side and behind him and tried to piece thoughts that didn't contain swear words together. I got that he knew Uncle Joey from way back when, but something had come between them, and they hadn't spoken for years. He took a risk coming here, and he hoped no one noticed him since it wouldn't do to be seen paying his respects to his enemy, even if he was an old friend.

I quickly turned away before he noticed me staring, and fiddled with a pot of flowers on a table. His gaze wandered toward me but soon slid away, and he abruptly turned and left. It was like a breath of fresh air once he was gone, and I sighed with relief. I glanced at the casket and noticed a piece of paper that wasn't there before.

Making sure he was gone, I snatched it up, and hurried to a chair in a small corner. The writing was hard to read, but I made out most of the words and realized it was a tribute of sorts. *"From one bad SOB to another, RIP."* The signature baffled me since it was mostly a bunch of flourishes and dots. Maybe there was a D in there, or an R, but I couldn't be sure. I slipped it into my pocket, deciding to give it to Uncle Joey later. Who knew? Maybe it was a long lost friend who'd reached out one last time, and Uncle Joey would want to renew the acquaintance?

Four new people, three women and one man, arrived at the end of the line, so I made my way over to Jackie and Kate. From what I could pick up, these were some of the employees from Kate's office, and I listened with interest. For the most part, they were feeling sorry for Kate and thinking she was probably blaming herself for the whole incident, and rightly so. They certainly didn't need the Passini Shipping Company, and getting saddled with that group was going to take a lot more work than they wanted to give. They were relieved and hopeful that the merger had been called off.

The man with them was thinking the opposite and hoping the merger had gone through. It made good business sense, and now that the Passinis looked like they were responsible for the explosion, he hoped Kate would take action against them...hopefully by squeezing them out of their company altogether. If he knew Kate and Manetto's organization, the Passinis wouldn't be around very long. It was just the opportunity he needed...

"Hi Zack," Kate greeted him. "I'm so glad you came. This is Jackie, Uncle Joey's wife, and my...cousin, Shelby."

Zack's brows rose. He had no idea Manetto was married. When had this happened? He hoped it wouldn't change anything. "Nice to meet you both," he said. "I just wish it was under different circumstances."

We murmured our thanks and Kate continued. "Zack is really the one running the company," she said. "I would have been lost without him." Zack mentally agreed, and with animosity thought that it was his company no matter what she said.

"Oh yes," I said. "Kate told us about you. You're her office manager?"

The title aggravated him, just like I thought it would, and his smile didn't quite reach his eyes. "Yes, that's me."

"Well...you must do a wonderful job. Kate speaks very highly of you."

He nodded his thanks, then spoke directly to Jackie. "I'm so sorry for your loss. Mr. Manetto will be missed." He chatted for a few minutes more and then moved respectfully to the casket. His actions betrayed his satisfaction that Uncle Joey was dead, and piqued my interest. There was definitely more to him than he let on.

I stepped to his side and glanced at Uncle Joey's photo above the casket. "I can't believe he's really gone." I tried to make my voice light with sorrow. "I don't know what we'll do without him."

Zack raised one brow questioningly. "Were you close?"

"Yes. He was a really good uncle...almost like a father in a lot of ways." I tried not to snort while I said that. "He wasn't supposed to die, especially getting blown up like that. I hope we find the person responsible." I turned to pin him with a hard gaze. "Uncle Joey's death will not go unpunished."

Zack was thinking that for a sweet-looking thing, I certainly had a bloodthirsty streak. He never would have pegged me for that type, but he figured it must run in the Manetto gene pool. Good thing he had his bases covered. "I understand completely, and I'm so sorry for your loss."

"Thank you."

Zack nodded and turned away, eager to leave now that he'd made his appearance. He joined the ladies he'd come with and, after conferring together, they all left to get drinks. Between them, they were speculating about how Uncle Joey's death was going to affect the company and the merger, and Zack wanted to make sure no one thought he was any different.

Well, something was definitely up with him. I couldn't say for sure that he had planted the bomb, but he certainly had something to do with it, and I was positive I could find out with a little more questioning. I knew what bar they were headed to, but going there without backup was not a good idea. I'd just have to wait until I could discuss it with Uncle Joey and Ramos.

After he left, Kate kept giving me expectant glances and asking in her mind if I'd found the bomber yet. It made me wish that this mind thing could go two ways just so I could tell her to back off. I was ready to take her in the other room and let her know what I'd heard when the police detective from the docks came in.

He was thinking how the Passinis had a lot of friends in high places, and proving any kind of guilt where they were concerned was practically impossible. He'd found out that Manetto had ties to organized crime, and this looked like a hit by the Passinis. He hoped that by coming here, he could get someone on the Manetto side to talk, and put the Passinis away once and for all.

He caught sight of me and thought that since I'd loved my uncle so much it might be easy to get me to talk, or at least give him a hint if the Manettos were out for revenge. I didn't seem like the bloodthirsty type, so maybe I'd be willing to offer information in return for a conviction against the Passinis, rather than see more bloodshed. It was worth a shot.

"Hello, Ms. Nichols," he said. "I have some new evidence and thought you might like to hear it."

"Um...okay. Is it about the Passinis? Because I already know they didn't plant any explosives. I'm pretty sure it was either an accident or someone else."

The detective blinked and took a step back. "How do you know all that?"

"I've got my resources."

"But everything I have points to them. Maybe your resources have it wrong. Don't you want to put them away for killing your uncle?"

I shrugged. "Normally I would, but I don't think they did it."

"Then who did?"

"Beats me. But I'll let you know if I hear anything new, okay? Sorry I couldn't be any more help."

"Sure." He nodded, greatly disappointed that I'd stonewalled him so easily. I knew a lot more than I was telling but, unless I cooperated, he wasn't going to get it out of me. "Here's my card. Call me anytime."

"Okay." I took the card and wondered how he'd feel when he found out they were still alive. Probably a little upset. I watched him leave, listening carefully to his thoughts. He was pretty sure I'd never call him, but at least he'd done his job and no one could fault him for that.

Glad I'd gotten out of that rather quickly, I took a deep breath and caught Nick's gaze. He was wondering what the cop wanted, but from the way I'd handled it, decided not to worry. He glanced at his watch and, noting that the allotted time was up, quietly ushered the stragglers out.

"That was exhausting," Jackie said, slumping onto a chair. "Remind me to tell Joe that he can't die again. Going through that once was enough."

"I'll bet," I said.

"Did you find the killer?" Kate asked. That caught Jackie's attention and she straightened.

"I got some good impressions," I answered, since Jackie was right there. "Why don't we go back to the hotel and talk it over."

Kate pursed her lips, wishing I'd just let Jackie in on it so we could talk freely. Jackie was Manetto's wife for Pete's sake...what difference would it make? It wouldn't hurt her to know the truth about me. Maybe she'd let it sli...

"Don't you dare," I whispered.

Her gaze caught mine, and her lips twisted. "It would make things easier."

I narrowed my eyes and lifted a brow. "Not for me."

"Fine," she said, shrugging. Turning to Jackie she said, "Are you ready to go?"

Bewildered by our exchange and knowing she'd missed something, Jackie glanced between the two of us. "Yes." She thought about asking what was going on but, knowing my history with Kate, decided to stay out of it.

I let out my breath and smiled at her. "Good...uh...let's go then."

We arrived back at the hotel and followed Jackie into Uncle Joey's room. "I need a drink," Jackie announced. "That was hard on me." She kicked off her shoes and opened the fridge. "Joe, you'll be happy to know that a lot of people were sad to see you go. Right guys?" She turned to the rest of us expectantly.

"Yes. Definitely," Kate and Nick agreed, nodding their heads.

I nodded my head too, only I knew it wasn't true. What Jackie had taken as sorrow that Uncle Joey was dead, was mostly them feeling sorry for her as the grieving widow. Most people didn't care that much and a few had even thought "*good riddance.*" I glanced up to find Uncle Joey's gaze pinned on me, but his lips were twisted in a self-deprecating smile. I smiled back, relieved I didn't have to explain anything to him.

"That's reassuring," he said. "As much as I'd like to hear all about it, let's hear what Shelby found out first."

Everyone's gazes locked on me, so I took a deep breath and blurted it out. "I think it's Zack, but I don't know much more than that...like why he did it, or anything."

"What?!" Kate gasped. "He can't be...he's been helping me...it can't be him..."

"Interesting," Uncle Joey said. "I wonder why he'd do that."

I shrugged. "I don't know, but I'm sure we could find out if we talked to him. He was going for drinks with the girls from the office. We might be able to track him down there."

"I have a better idea," Uncle Joey said. "Let's head over to the shipping office and Kate can ask Zack to meet her there to discuss some business. Once he gets there we can find out." He was thinking about torturing him, but if I came that wouldn't be necessary. Maybe he should leave me at the hotel.

My eyes widened. I didn't want to part of any kind of torture, but I also didn't want to be left behind. I wanted to see Zack's face when Uncle Joey and Ramos showed up. He'd probably wet his pants, and it would serve him right. Damn. Did that mean I had a bloodthirsty streak? I wasn't even a real Manetto, but I was certainly starting to think like one. Maybe it was time for me to go home.

"I'll call him right now," Kate said. She'd gotten over her surprise and was eager to know why Zack had done it. Unfortunately, so was I.

Kate made the call, telling Zack she'd be there in half an hour, giving us about fifteen minutes to get set up and in our places. Uncle Joey and Ramos pocketed their guns, prompting Kate to make sure hers was in her purse. Nick patted his pocket where he kept his knife, and Jackie slipped a pair of handcuffs and brass knuckles into her purse.

I kind of felt left out since I didn't even have my stun flashlight with me.

We trekked out to the cars and I picked up that both Ramos and Uncle Joey were happy to escape their rooms. They didn't even try to disguise themselves. What was the point? Now that they knew their enemy was Zack, they were officially back from the dead.

I rode with Nick, glad to spend as little time with Kate as possible. She was starting to get on my nerves, and I had to admit that this interrogation was going to be a bit difficult with both Nick and Jackie out of the loop about my secret. That reminded me of my interrogation with Dimples a few days ago, where the guy had stabbed his wife a gazillion times. I handled that pretty well, and no one knew I was reading minds. So this should be a piece of cake. Unless Kate messed it up somehow.

We arrived at the building and Kate unlocked the doors. At nine-fifteen, it was dark and gloomy, but Kate went inside without turning on the lights. "Follow me closely," she said. "I don't want to turn on the lights in case Zack gets here before we're ready."

The rest of us followed behind and soon we were all bunched up because no one could see where to go. I was about to say something when I tripped. My momentum carried me into someone's back and he stumbled forward. I tried to pull back, but my legs got caught in his and we both went down hard.

Before I could untangle myself, a light came on in an office down the hall, and there I was, sprawled on top of Ramos. Somehow he had managed to catch me in his arms and take the brunt of the fall, or I probably would have hit my head against the wall.

"Oh crap! Are you okay?" I scrambled to get off him, planting a hand on his stomach and pushing myself up. His breath whooshed out with an involuntary groan. "Oops...sorry!" I pulled my leg up and nearly kneed him in the groin.

Ramos grabbed my upper arms and rolled me over so he was on top. Straddling me, he got to his feet and then helped pull me up. Loud snickering came from Uncle Joey, and soon Jackie and Nick joined him.

"Come on, you guys," Kate hissed, standing in the doorway of her office. "We need to hide you before Zack gets here. What are you doing?" No one bothered to answer her which was fine by me. I was embarrassed enough as it was.

Kate opened the door to the office next to hers and spoke to Uncle Joey and Ramos. "I think you two should hide in there. With the lights out, he won't see you, and I'll keep both doors open so you can hear everything he says. When the time is right, just walk in. Hurry...I'll go turn on the lights in the entrance to let him know I'm here. Shelby, you and Jackie wait in my office. Nick, you come with me."

Wow, she was certainly taking charge, but everyone rushed to take their places. No one wanted to let the cat out of the bag, and the giddy feeling of pulling a big one over on Zack kept us glued to our places in anticipation. Kate left Nick to guard the door and hurried back, taking her seat behind her desk. Jackie and I kind of stood there and blinked.

The sound of the front door opening sent my heart racing. Whoa, we'd barely made it. Zack sauntered forward, then slowed his step. He hadn't expected to see all three of us there, and a prickle of unease ran over him.

Kate stood and greeted him warmly. "Zack! Thanks for coming. I've been trying to explain things to Aunt Jackie but, as usual, I'm not doing a very good job." Both Jackie and I stared at Kate for the Aunt part, but Kate acted like she didn't see.

Zack turned his bewildered gaze to Jackie. "What can I help you with?"

Jackie had no idea what to say, so she just said the first thing that popped into her head. "Well...uh...before I go home tomorrow, I thought I should familiarize myself with things here."

"Oh...so you're leaving tomorrow?"

"Yes."

He turned to Kate. "So are you going with her? For the burial?"

"Yes...yes of course. There's a lot of things we need to do now that Uncle Joey's gone, but once they're settled I'll be back."

"To check on things, right?" he asked. At her nod, he let out a breath. "Like I've told you before, I know how to run this company. You won't be sorry you've entrusted it to me."

Kate let out a puzzled laugh, her brows drawn together. "What do you mean? Of course you'll be in charge while I'm gone, but I'll be back to run it once Aunt Jackie's got things under control. She's the one who's taking over Uncle Joey's organization."

"Jackie?" His gaze darted to her and sweat popped out on his forehead. "But...I thought you were next in line. You told me that once Manetto was gone, you'd take his place. I specifically remember you saying that as far as you were concerned, it couldn't be soon enough."

Kate's face turned red and her eyes darted from Jackie to me. "I did not," she lied.

"Oh my gosh!" I blurted. "It's all your fault. Zack tried to kill Uncle Joey so you'd leave to run his organization and Zack would get the shipping company back."

"No! You can't blame me for this," she said. "I had nothing to do with it!"

"What?" Zack asked. He hadn't missed my little slip. Did that mean Manetto wasn't dead? Fearing for his life he turned to run and yelped, jumping almost a foot off the ground. Uncle Joey and Ramos stood in the doorway. "Oh God," he said, falling to his knees. "I'm dead."

Chapter 10

All of us stared at Zack while he quivered under Uncle Joey's impassive gaze.

Kate was a little worried that Uncle Joey might put some of the blame on her, and damned my mind-reading ability to hell. I snorted after hearing that. Some people never changed, and I hoped this time Uncle Joey would see that about Kate.

Jackie wasn't too happy with Kate's involvement either. Joe had nearly died because of Kate's pride, and it angered her to the boiling point. In fact...she was angrier with Kate than she was with Zack, but maybe it was calling her "*Aunt*" that did it.

Uncle Joey was thinking that even though Kate had planted the idea in Zack's head, it was still Zack's actions that had nearly killed him and Ramos. Although he had to admit, it was a pretty brilliant plan. Planting the bomb and framing the Passinis for it took guts and initiative, and he couldn't help but admire Zack's resourcefulness. Without my mind-reading skills, he would have blamed the Passinis no matter what they'd said, so Zack might have gotten away with it.

Did he really want to kill someone who wasn't afraid to take action? He could definitely take advantage of Zack's vulnerability right now, and he had the resources to follow through. Zack's life in exchange for complete loyalty...hmm...that would benefit him more than killing him would. But he still couldn't let him get off that easily. No...some kind of punishment would be appropriate, maybe...

Uncle Joey glanced at me and his lips thinned, knowing I'd heard his thoughts. "Nick," he said, glancing over his shoulder. "I'd like you to take Shelby and Jackie back to the hotel while I settle things with Zack...and Kate."

Kate's eyes widened to be included with Zack, but she knew better than to grovel.

"Sure, boss," Nick said. He glanced at us, knowing that whatever Uncle Joey had planned, it was best if we didn't see it. "Do you need me to come back and help out?" He'd gotten good at body disposal, and wanted to offer his services, even though he knew Ramos was the real expert.

"No," Uncle Joey said.

Nick nodded solemnly, and Jackie moved toward the door to leave. I followed behind, grateful for the chance to get out of there. I didn't want to know what Uncle Joey's plans were, but at least I knew they didn't include killing anyone, so it probably wasn't too bad. Still, I cast a worried glance over my shoulder at Kate. Her face went white and she drew in a quick breath. I felt kind of guilty for that, so I smiled to make up for it. After that she tensed even more, so I shrugged and left the room.

The drive back to the hotel passed in silence. Both Nick and Jackie were thinking that Zack was a goner, and maybe Kate too, but they'd have to wait until later to find out. They also thought that I'd come through for Uncle Joey, and they would never doubt his trust in me again.

"Do you think we'll be going home tomorrow?" I asked.

"I don't know," Jackie said. "But I hope so. Even if Joe's not done here, you could probably catch a flight home." She was thinking he still had things to settle with the Passinis and probably the police, so it might take them a little longer, but there was no reason for me to stay.

"That would be great," I said.

At the hotel, I said goodnight and hurried into my room. It was good to have that confrontation over with, but the stress had gotten to me, so I filled up the tub with bath salts for a little bath therapy. After a relaxing soak, I slipped on my pajamas and settled into bed, taking my phone to give Chris an update. I'd already told him the night before that Uncle Joey and Ramos were alive. Now I could tell him who actually planted the bomb.

"Hi honey," I said. "It looks like I'm all done here." I gave him the shortened version of the night's events and he was glad it was over. He didn't quite believe that Uncle Joey wasn't going to kill Zack, but let it go since I got sent back to the hotel before I found out his plans. Then we talked about the kids and what was happening at home.

The sound of his voice soothed me and I relaxed into the pillows. By the time we said goodnight, I was feeling sleepy and calm. I turned out the lights and rolled over, falling asleep almost instantly.

I dreamed that I'd gone home and was walking down the driveway to my house. It was late at night, but I wasn't worried. Suddenly, someone appeared in front of me. It was dark, and he was in the shadows, but I knew at once it was Sean and he was holding a long knife.

I screamed and ran, only to find that my legs wouldn't move. I managed to turn and take a step, but it was too late. He grabbed my ankle and I screamed again before falling to the ground. I tried to kick him, but he sneered at my puny attempts to get away and raised his knife to cut me any place he could. As he thrust his knife toward my stomach, I screamed for all I was worth and woke, shivering with sweat and fear.

My breath heaved in and out, and I couldn't stop shaking. A couple of quick knocks on the door scared me even more, and my heart began to race.

"Shelby? Are you okay? Open the door."

I knew that voice and tried to swallow past the dryness in my throat. "I...I'm okay," I croaked, my voice still shaking. "It was just...a bad...dream."

"Open the door. Now...or I'll break it down."

"But..."

"No buts...just open the damn door."

"Okay, okay...give me a minute." I turned on the bedside lamp, then ran my fingers through my hair and wobbled to the door, dashing away the tears from my cheeks. I unlocked the deadbolt and removed the chain, then turned the knob. I pulled it open a crack, but Ramos wouldn't let me stop there and pushed it open to come inside.

As he took in my wide eyes and wet cheeks, the door clicked shut. He pulled me close and rubbed my back to warm me up. In response, I wrapped my arms around him, grateful for his comforting presence. After a moment, he half-carried me toward the bed and pushed me in, then settled beside me, wrapping the blanket and his arms around me.

His solid warmth soothed me and my shivering stopped. My breath slowed and became smooth and even. I knew it was bad to be this close to Ramos, but right now I was grateful he was there.

"What's going on?" he asked.

"Well...I think I'm in trouble," I began. "But I'm going to take care of it. When I get home, I'll tell Dimples and he can help me. So...I'll be fine. You don't need to worry about me, and I'm real sorry I woke you up."

"Huh," Ramos grunted. "In the first place, I wasn't asleep."

I blinked and, for the first time, noticed he was still in the same clothes he'd had on earlier. "Oh. What time is it?"

"Just after midnight."

"That's all? It seems later than that. Did I really scream so loud that you could hear me from your room?"

"Well, it was pretty loud, but I was just getting back and heard as I passed your door." He was thinking it had scared the hell out of him. "It sounded like someone was trying to kill you."

"Oh...well, in my dream they were. It was pretty scary..." A shudder ran through me, and Ramos tightened his hold. "I guess it's all because of a case I'm working on...a missing person's case. Even though the woman has been missing for six years, I'm pretty certain she was murdered, and I found out who did it...only he's killed like...at least four women that I know of. And after I talked to him... well... now he's after me."

"What? Did you tell him you knew he was the killer?" Ramos could hardly believe I'd do something that stupid.

"No! I'm not that stupid."

Ramos caught his breath and pursed his lips. "I know that. I didn't mean it like that... so what happened?"

"I was just talking to him about my business. That's the reason I was there, because I had a hunch he was tied to the murders. Anyway, while I was talking with him, he was thinking the person he'd been planning to kill had suddenly picked up and moved so he needed a new target, and since I fit the bill...blond hair, blue eyes...he decided I'd be next." Just saying that out loud brought out the goose bumps on my arms. "He likes to scare his victims beforehand and, since I've been gone, he hasn't been able to do that, so I think I've got some time before the actual killing takes place."

Ramos cursed a blue streak in his mind and thought it didn't matter what Manetto did to keep me safe, because trouble just seemed to follow me. It was like I had a death wish or something.

I raised my brow at him. "I do not. I can't help it if I fit the bill for this guy...I mean, just think about it...if I was a brunette with brown eyes, I'd be perfectly safe."

Ramos huffed out a breath. "Right."

"Besides," I continued. "At least I know his plans without giving myself away. Now that I know he's after me, I can be prepared."

"And what does Chris think about all this?" He couldn't believe Chris would go along with this and thought I probably hadn't told him.

I sucked in my breath. "I did so tell him. But it happened the same day I found out about you, and I left the next morning to come here. So I haven't really been around to be worried about it." I sighed. "I think I had that horrible dream because I'm going home tomorrow and I'll have to face him again."

"Who said you were going back tomorrow?"

"Well...I just thought you didn't need me anymore so I could go home. I do want to go home you know, even if there is a crazy killer after me."

Ramos' thoughts zipped through his mind like a tornado, looking for a reason for me to stay that I would accept. "We're staying one more day to sort things out with the Passinis and the police, and I'm sure we can use your help for that. Besides, we'll be taking the private jet home the next morning, and there's plenty of room for you. What's another night anyway...Friday morning as opposed to

Thursday afternoon? Not a big difference...except for one thing."

"What's that?" I asked.

"I'll be there." He didn't say *"to watch out for me"* but that's what he was thinking.

I couldn't help the smile that spread over my face and crept into that warm place in my heart. "You have a point. Maybe I will stay one more night...if it's okay with Chris."

"I'm sure once you explain everything, he'll be fine with it," he said, relieved he'd talked me into it. He rested his cheek on top of my head, liking the sensation of lying next to me. I was soft and warm. He could probably fall asleep if he just closed his eyes. "Do you need me to stay with you tonight?" He held his breath in anticipation. A big part of him wanted to stay, but he didn't think he had enough control, especially if he fell asleep, to hold me this close and keep his hands to himself.

"What? No! You'd better not...I mean...that's probably not a good idea. But thanks for talking to me...I feel lots better. In fact, I think I'll be able to sleep now...without any more bad dreams...so that's good, right? You should probably go now." I sat up straight, pulling out of his arms and adjusting the blankets on the bed to cover me up.

Ramos snorted and slid off the bed. He straightened his clothes and moved toward the door. After pulling it open, he glanced back. "Goodnight Shelby. If you change your mind you know where to find me."

The door closed softly behind him and I swallowed. My breathing was a little erratic and my pulse raced. Damn that man! I wished he didn't affect me so much. On the other hand, at least he hadn't tried anything, so I couldn't be too angry with him.

But now I was wide awake for totally different reasons. I jumped out of bed and slipped the chain through the lock across the door. Just doing that helped me feel better, and I started to calm down. Knowing I needed a distraction, I pulled my Kindle out of my purse and turned it on. I had downloaded a nice, light, little romance the other day that suited my mood perfectly, and I began to read.

At three in the morning, I was still going strong, but my eyes were starting to burn. I took that as a sign to quit and finally settled down to sleep.

I woke the next morning to my cell phone alarm. I groaned, realizing I'd forgotten to turn it off. I grabbed it and cracked open my eyes. Seven a.m. Ugh! I set it down, determined to go back to sleep for at least another hour. I'd just dozed off when it rang again, only this time it was someone calling me. With a groan of disgust, I grabbed it, pushed talk, and pulled it to my ear. "This better be good."

"Shelby?" Uncle Joey said. "I heard you wanted to stay and help me out today. Is that right?"

"Uh...yes...yes, of course." I quickly sat up and opened my bleary eyes. "I just need to take a quick shower and then I'll be ready."

"Good. We're eating breakfast in half an hour. I'll have Jackie order you something."

"Okay tha..." The line went dead before I could finish. "Geez!" Seriously annoyed, I threw my phone down on the bed and hopped out. Discarding my pajamas, I jumped in the shower, hoping the water would help wake me up and soothe my bad mood.

I probably stayed in a little longer than I should, but I decided that I could skip breakfast if I needed to. After all, there was always a salted nut roll waiting for me in the candy machine. As I turned off the water, I heard my phone ringing again. Grabbing a towel, I dashed out to the bed where I'd left it and quickly answered before it stopped.

"Hello?"

"Hi honey," Chris said. "You sound out of breath, where've you been?"

"In the shower. It was ringing when I turned off the water so I didn't know if I could get to it in time. I'm still dripping." I carried the phone back into the bathroom so I could drip in there.

"Hmm...I sure wish I was with you right now... but at least you'll be home today. That's why I'm calling, to see what time I should come to the airport to pick you up."

"Yeah...well, about that," I said, my stomach clenching with guilt. "It looks like I'm coming home tomorrow morning instead. There's a couple of things Uncle Joey needs me for today. But that's only a few more hours. I mean...I probably wouldn't make it home before later tonight anyway, so what's a few more hours, right?" I was borrowing Ramos' reasoning, but when I said it to Chris, it didn't sound near as good.

Chris sighed, and I knew he was disappointed. "I'm sorry Chris. If you'll let me, I'll be sure to make it up to you."

"Oh yeah? How are you going to do that?"

I chuckled, knowing from his tone that he was okay about it, probably because he liked it when I owed him. "I'm sure you can think of something."

"Yeah...I can definitely do that."

"Good. I hate to say this, but I'm running late, and I've got to finish getting ready. I'll call you tonight, all right?"

"Fine, but is there anything I need to take care of today since you won't be here?"

"Um...let's see, it's Thursday...so just make sure Savannah gets to dance lessons at four...she can probably get a ride with Ashley, so give her a call after school so she can arrange it. Other than that, I can't think of anything else."

"Okay...I'll try to remember to call. What time does she get home from school?"

"Call her around three-thirty," I said.

"Okay," he agreed.

"Thanks honey...I love you. I'll call you later."

We disconnected, and I counted my lucky stars that I had such an understanding husband. Chris was the best. He put up with me and all this...stuff I had to do for Uncle Joey. It made me cringe just a little that I'd spent a few minutes in Ramos' arms last night, but nothing happened, and it never would. Still, I vowed to be a better wife.

I dressed in a white knit tee and blue sweater combo with jeans and hoped that was good enough for the day. I hadn't brought much, and I was running out of different clothes to wear. In the bathroom, I turned my head upside down for a quick blow-dry, going for the wind-blown look, and added a little make-up and lip-gloss. Ready, I checked the time. Seven minutes late. That was a lot better than I thought.

I knocked on Uncle Joey's door and Jackie let me in. "Good morning, Shelby. Come on in." She was dressed smartly in a navy pantsuit, and thinking I looked pretty good for someone who'd woken up screaming during the night. That must have been one hell of a bad dream.

Crap! She'd heard me screaming? I thought Ramos said it wasn't that loud? Now Jackie wondered what she'd said to upset me since I was staring at her with my brows drawn together and my lips turned down.

I quickly cleared my expression and smiled at her. "Hi Jackie. Sorry I'm late. Has everyone already eaten?"

"Yes, but there's plenty of food."

She stepped out of the way and I hurried inside. Ramos stood from the small table, taking his plate and discarding it with the others. "Here...I'm done. You can take my place. Grab a plate and eat."

"Thanks," I said, relieved there was no awkwardness between us. I got my food and ate pretty fast, hating that I was the last one to eat. I wasn't that late, but it was obvious that the food had come earlier than Uncle Joey told me. Just as I finished up, he walked into the room.

"Oh good, we're all here," he said, glancing at me. "Let's get started." He waited until he had our undivided attention and began. "We need to meet with the Passinis today and let them know I'm not dead. I was hoping that between all of us, we could come up with something good to tell the police, since I'm sure they'll have plenty of questions." He checked his watch. "Kate's already at their office. She just texted to tell me that now's a good time to stop by, so let's head out."

I was a little disappointed that Kate was still helping Uncle Joey out, but maybe her involvement today was part of her recompense for screwing up. We dutifully followed Uncle Joey to the parking lot, and he insisted we all ride in his car. Since he insisted on driving, I ended up in the back seat sitting between Ramos and Nick. It was a little cramped, and our thighs were touching, but neither of them seemed to mind.

Nick liked the way I smelled and hoped we'd be done today so he could get home to his girlfriend. Ramos slipped his arm along the top of the seat to give me a little more room so I didn't have to sit so close to Nick. He didn't like how Nick was sniffing my hair while I wasn't looking.

I started to chuckle, drawing the attention of both of them.

"What's so funny," Nick asked.

"Uh...nothing," I said.

Nick didn't believe me, but Ramos figured it out and sent me a lopsided smile. Put off, Nick turned his head to look out the window. It was another dreary day, with gray, cloudy skies and a touch of rain, but it didn't seem as bad to me as before. Probably because I was sitting by Ramos and he wasn't dead.

We pulled into the parking lot of The Passini Shipping Company and got out of the car. Uncle Joey stood straight and tall, wanting to make a grand entrance. He fastened the button on his jacket and smoothed his hair. He looked like a movie star getting ready to play a part in the big scene. Jackie followed suit, straightening her jacket as well. I glanced at Nick and Ramos. They both had on jackets too, but it was mostly to hide their guns.

Compared to them, I looked like an outsider who didn't quite know how to belong to the group. I shrugged, maybe that wasn't so bad, and followed them inside. Since they all went in before me, I caught the tail-end of the shock and surprise coming from the office staff. After a ripple of astonishment, the whole place went quiet. Then one brave soul bolted to Jon Passini's office and barged inside shouting the news that Joe "The Knife" Manetto was alive.

Uncle Joey sauntered in on his heels, and everyone in Jon's office stood in shock. Julia Passini turned white, then flushed red. Her first thoughts that he was alive brought shock, then relief, followed by anger that he had conned them...and what did he want?

Jon's relief was more heartfelt, since he knew more than Julia. He hadn't told her that the police thought he and his family were guilty of murder and had begun building a case against them.

Alec wasn't surprised at all, although he was certainly putting on a good show. Kate had told him the whole story, even though she wasn't supposed to. I raised my brow at Kate, but she averted her face and tried to ignore me. She wasn't real happy with me since I'd claimed this whole fiasco was her fault. It wasn't, and she didn't like that I'd blamed her. Uncle Joey didn't blame her, although he had given her "the talk" about where she stood in his organization.

Uncle Joey ushered us all inside the office and closed the door. "We need to talk," he said, looking from one Passini to the other and staring them all down. By the time he got done, even Alec was starting to tremble. I couldn't help but admire the way Uncle Joey intimidated them. His presence alone commanded everyone's complete attention, and I didn't envy the Passinis.

He began his narrative, telling them how he and Ramos had survived the explosion, certain that the Passinis had orchestrated the whole thing. At this point, Julia's anger disappeared, replaced by fear of reprisal. Then her momma bear instincts kicked in and she opened her mouth to deny his accusations. Uncle Joey held up his hand, and her mouth snapped shut. After a moment of total silence, he finished by saying he'd found who it was.

"Someone in my own organization wanted me dead and set you up," he said. "Just so you know, I have taken care of the situation."

Both Julia and Jon sank into their chairs with relief, and the tension drained from the room. "The only thing to do now," Uncle Joey continued, "Is to figure out what to tell the police. I don't want them to know the truth, but I think with your help, we can come up with something they'll believe."

"Yes," Jon agreed. "That should work, but this is tough. I don't have any idea where to start."

"I have an idea," I said. Everyone glanced my way with interest. "Why don't you blame the two security guards that were killed? Maybe you could say they were conning both of you at the same time."

"Hmm...perhaps," Uncle Joey said. "But how would we make that work?"

"Maybe you could say they planted the bomb to blackmail the Passinis, but they were really telling them it was you doing the blackmailing, and you were going to set it off unless they paid you a certain amount of money. Only it would be them getting the money."

"Okay," Uncle Joey said. "I like this so far, but how were they conning me?"

"Um...I guess they were just going to kill you in the explosion? But you got away?"

"That wouldn't work," Kate argued. "If Uncle Joey was dead, then the Passinis wouldn't need to give them the money."

"Well...maybe they already gave them the money," I said in defense. "At the same time, the guards trapped Uncle Joey and Ramos in the room with the bomb and told them the Passinis wanted them dead so they wouldn't have to repay a debt." I knew that part was true, so it wouldn't hurt to put that in.

"Then Uncle Joey and Ramos ruined their plans," I continued, "by getting away and locking the guards in the room where they got blown up. Since the guards told Uncle Joey it was the Passinis who'd wanted him dead, he decided to stay dead until he knew what was going on. That should answer why you didn't come forward right away and did the whole funeral thing."

"I think that makes sense," Jackie said. But she said it like she wasn't quite sure.

Uncle Joey was thinking it a little far-fetched and made the guards look pretty stupid, but he couldn't think of anything better. "What do you think?" he asked Jon.

"It should work," Jon said. "Mostly because I never received word that those two didn't make it off the yacht. Apparently, no one knew they were missing. So as long as the case gets solved, I think the police chief will buy it. Since they were the only people killed in the explosion...that will wrap things up nicely for them." He glanced at me, thinking it was a brilliant plan so, naturally, I smiled at him.

"All right," Uncle Joey said. "Let's go over our stories and give the police chief a call."

The detective who'd come to the funeral was the one who showed up at the Passini Company. He took everyone's statements with a grain of salt, thinking that since Uncle Joey and Ramos weren't dead, he couldn't bring charges against the Passinis, so it didn't really matter. He also knew it wouldn't do a lot of good to look into it too hard since the mayor was cozy with the Passinis, and he'd be happy with whatever the police chief told him.

It still took over two hours to get everything down on paper. At least I had my Kindle, but I felt sorry for the detective. By the time he was done, he was more than glad to leave. He didn't believe that story for a minute, but what could he do? The chief wanted it wrapped up, so he'd follow his orders. The story was confusing, but in some ways that made it easier to explain. He could sum it up by saying that the cons conned the wrong people. How was that for simple?

Everyone was starving by the time we got done, so Uncle Joey took us to Pike Place Market for lunch. Just as we got out of the car, sunshine broke through the clouds, making the water sparkle in the bay and warming the air. With a lighter step, I followed the others through the market and even watched the fishmongers toss salmon to each other. Lunch in the fancy restaurant was great, and I realized it was the first time I'd had any fun since I'd gotten there.

With our stomachs full and satisfied, Uncle Joey announced that he had to go back to the office to finish up some last minute details and meet with Kate, so we headed back to the car. I slowed my step as we passed the shops, pulled like a magnet to the fabulous items along the path. There were some great tee shirts here that I could get for my kids. Some of the earrings and jewelry caught my eyes too, dazzling me with their sparkle. I lingered over them for several minutes, taking it all in, and knew I just wasn't ready to leave.

Uncle Joey didn't need me anymore, so it wouldn't hurt to stay, and I could take a taxi back to the hotel. I glanced up to catch him, but couldn't see any of them anywhere and realized they were long gone. Oops. Just then my phone rang. "Hello?"

"Where are you?" Uncle Joey asked.

"Oh, well I got distracted by all the shops, so I'm still at the market. Hey, if it's all right with you, I think I'll just stay here for a while. I'd like to pick up some things for my kids. You don't need me anymore today, right? I can probably take a taxi to the hotel, so you wouldn't have to come back. Will that work?"

I heard him take a deep breath. Then he said, "Just a minute," and covered the phone with his hand. I heard some talking going on but nothing I could make out before he came back on the line. "Where are you exactly?"

"Um..." I glanced around. "I'm real close to the guys throwing the fish."

"Good. Stay there, Jackie's coming."

"Okay," I said, and he disconnected. I realized that meant Jackie was coming to join me, and a broad smile broke over my face. Good for her. Plus, with her along, this could be a blast. She'd been through a lot these last couple of days and if anyone deserved some shopping therapy, it was her.

While waiting, I rummaged through some tee shirts on a nearby table, but didn't find anything I liked. Just then, Jackie stepped beside me. "There you are," she said, a little breathless. "When Joe told me you were stuck back here at the shops, I couldn't pass up the opportunity to join you." She glanced at the tables and shop displays, taking in all the merchandise surrounding us, and rubbed her hands together. "Let's get started."

Hours later, we pushed through the doors to the hotel, our arms laden with bags. Once we'd finished at the market, we decided to take the monorail to the Space Needle, and rode the elevator all the way to the top. Since the clouds had parted, we had a perfect view of the city below and enjoyed every minute of it. Back on the ground, we found even more shops to peruse, and dutifully looked into each one before finding a taxi to take us home.

After setting down a few bags, I managed to open my door and get everything inside. My feet were killing me, so it was a relief to kick off my shoes and set all my purchases on the bed. With enthusiasm, I dumped out the bags and began to sort through them, putting the tees I'd bought for my kids in a pile, and finding the earrings I'd bought for myself.

I slipped them on, then found my new tee shirt and tried it on. It was pink with cap sleeves and Seattle written in swirls with flowers around it, and it fit just right. At the last shop, I'd found the most adorable hat for Savannah. It was like a baseball cap, only lots cuter, and had Seattle in block letters across the front. I tried it on and liked it so well, I almost wished I'd bought it for me.

A knock sounded at the door, so I hurried to answer. Ramos smiled, taking in my new clothes and thinking I looked cute in the hat. It reminded him of the hair hat I'd bought in Orlando, and that made him smile even more. "Hey, we're having a friendly game of poker and wondered if you'd like to join us."

"What? You want to play poker with me?"

"I said it was friendly...no money involved." He was thinking of the big bag of salt water taffy he'd bought at the market to use instead.

"I love taffy...I'm in!"

I followed him into Uncle Joey's suite where they'd arranged several chairs around the table. Jackie was wearing her new tee shirt and earrings too, so we shared a high five. The evening passed quickly, with lots of laughter and joking. No one seemed to mind too much when I won most of the taffy, and I didn't always win, so it mostly worked out.

After a couple of hours, I left with my taffy to call Chris and take a bath. He seemed distracted when he answered the phone, so after I told him I'd be home about one the next afternoon, I was surprised when he said he'd pick me up.

"Are you sure?" I asked. "I'll be on Uncle Joey's private jet so I'm practically guaranteed a ride home in his limo."

"I'm sure," he said. "I can come on my lunch break. Besides, I want to see you."

My heart melted a little and I quickly agreed. "Just make certain you come to the right airport."

"Don't worry, I'll be there."

After a nice soak in the tub, I was ready for bed. As nice as today was, it was time to go home. Except for knowing a serial killer was after me, everything was great. Ramos and Uncle Joey were alive, and I'd helped solve the case. Heck, I'd even come up with the plausible story to tell the police.

I'd accomplished a lot in the last few days, so I could certainly figure out what to do about a serial killer. If I could just find a connection between Sean and one of his victims, or find one of their bodies, it would be enough to arrest him. But how to do that wasn't so simple.

At least Ramos was alive to watch out for me, and I wasn't opposed to involving Dimples either, so that would help. But to find out what I needed to know, I'd probably have to spend some time with Sean, and just thinking about it gave me the creeps. But I could be prepared and, reading his mind, I'd know before anything bad happened.

As comforting as that thought was, I also knew that even the best plans didn't always work out. Since I could end up dead, I fervently hoped this wasn't one of those times.

Chapter 11

There was nothing better than flying home in a private jet. The advantages were mind-boggling, like no getting to the airport two hours early, no worrying about missing a flight, no waiting in longs lines that dragged on forever, no passing through security and needing to take off shoes or emptying pockets, and best of all, no need to find little bottles for shampoo and toothpaste. Yup, I could certainly get used to that.

We touched down just after one in the afternoon, and a small worry that Chris knew where to pick me up tightened the muscles in my neck. As I came down the stairs, my shoulders relaxed to find his car parked behind the limo. His door opened and he stood, sending me a quick wave. The smile on his handsome face warmed me all the way to my toes.

I hurried over to greet him with a hug and kiss, grateful to be home safe and sound. As Chris loaded my luggage into the trunk, I realized I'd forgotten something so I told him I'd be right back.

I quickly made my way to Uncle Joey. "I just remembered something I needed to give you." I took a folded piece of paper from my pocket and handed it to him.

"What's this?" he asked.

"It's from your wake, at the funeral home? This guy came in and, since he looked suspicious, I kept my eye on him. He seemed kind of upset that you were dead. Anyway, he put this note on your casket, so I picked it up and read it."

Uncle Joey frowned and opened the paper. He inhaled sharply at the signature, hardly able to believe the old bastard had broken his vow and come to pay his respects. Rest in peace? Did that mean he had been forgiven?

"I couldn't read the name...it's kind of hard to make out, but I thought you should have it," I said.

"Thank you Shelby." His gaze caught mine, and his eyes glistened with sudden moisture. He blinked a few times and pursed his lips. "I trust you'll keep this to yourself."

"Of course," I agreed.

"Good." With that, he slipped inside the limo and shut the door.

I hurried back to the car. Chris held the door open for me, and I slid inside. "What was that all about?" he asked.

"Nothing," I said.

"Huh." Chris shut my door, hurried to the driver's side and started the car up, thinking that when I said it was nothing, it usually meant it was nothing I wanted to tell him about, which also meant that it was something that could get me in trouble. Why else wouldn't I tell him?

"That's not it," I said defensively. "It's something personal to Uncle Joey, and I don't even know exactly what it is, so how can it get me in trouble?"

"Um...I don't know...but you have to admit that with your track record, it's a possibility."

I sighed, not wanting to argue. Mostly because Chris had a point, and from what I'd picked up, it could definitely get me in trouble. So it was probably best to keep it to myself and hope that didn't happen.

"So, how are you?" I asked, changing the subject. "How are things going with the kids and everything?"

"Great," he answered. "How was your flight?"

"Good...I could sure get used to flying in a private jet." Chris concentrated on listening to me and kept his mind curiously blank about anything else. That wasn't like him. Usually he had several things going on in his mind at once, but not today. Now why was that? Something was off, so I continued to tell him about all the perks while trying to figure out what was wrong. He just nodded and agreed now and then to let me know he was listening, but underneath that, I could tell he was hiding something.

Sudden fear that something bad had happened to Josh or Savannah clenched my stomach. "Are the kids all right?" I blurted.

"Of course," Chris said, his brows furrowed with confusion. "Oh...and there's a folder on my desk in the den with a bunch of information about Sean Hanley. You might want to take a look at it, and we can talk about what to do tonight."

"Oh...that's great. Thanks. So...everything else is fine?"

"Yes. Everything's great." He glanced at me from the corner of his eyes like there was something wrong with me, and it kind of made me mad. I knew something was going on, but he was blocking his thoughts so well that I couldn't figure out what it was. It was unsettling to say the least, but short of calling him on it, I didn't know what else to do. I'd just have to wait until he was ready to tell me what was going on and hope it wasn't too bad.

"Wow," I said. "It's hard to believe it's Friday already. At least I'm home in time to pick up the carpool from school. Did Savannah get to dance class okay last night?"

"Yeah." He was thinking *"barely"* and that was part of the reason he'd been so distracted lately. Trying to remember what was going on with the kids, their school work, taking care of dinner, and keeping the house together, along with everything he had going on at work had worn him out. He didn't know how I did it and worried I'd be disappointed when I got home.

Picking that up sent a fresh dose of guilt over me and my stomach tightened. Yesterday, I'd had a great time shopping and playing poker, and hadn't even thought too much about how Chris was faring. Since he didn't say anything over the phone, I thought he was handling things just fine.

We pulled into the driveway and Chris pushed the garage-door opener. Now that we were home, I picked up that he was hoping I wouldn't be too upset with him. He still didn't know how it happened, but knew I'd be sad. He just hoped I wouldn't freak out. Too bad he didn't get a chance to take care of it yesterday before I got home.

Yikes! I got out of the car with trepidation, worried about what I'd find. Chris smiled and opened the door for me. I stepped inside, grateful to find the living room a little messy, but unchanged. I hurried into the kitchen. There was a lot of clutter on the table and countertops, and a few dishes in the sink, but nothing too bad.

I glanced out the sliding doors to the patio and my eyes widened with shock. "My swing!" My favorite place in the world to relax and read was completely destroyed. Only strings of charred material remained of the awning, and the cushions below were seared black with big blobs of charred padding falling to the deck. A skeleton of burned and blackened pipe stuck out on one end where the cushions had been completely destroyed.

"What happened?" I asked.

Chris put his arm around me and pulled me close. "I'm not sure. I was cooking up some burgers and the next thing I knew the awning was in flames. I grabbed the hose, but the nozzle wasn't on tight. Once I got it straightened out, the cushions were on fire too. I couldn't believe how fast it spread. Anyway, I got the fire out, but you can see it pretty much burned up the swing."

He was thinking the grill was ruined too, but at least the propane tank hadn't exploded. That would have been a disaster. "I'm glad I got it out before it spread to the house," he said. "I'm really sorry. I know how much you loved that swing, but we can get you a new one."

"Yeah, I guess so," I said, clamping my lips shut so I didn't say anything that would make him feel worse than he already did. But...still...what the freak! A fire? On the deck? And it could have spread to the house? And the propane gas tank could have exploded? I shook my head and swallowed, grateful Chris couldn't hear what I was thinking.

"I wish I could have gotten it cleaned up before you got home, but at least I've got someone coming tomorrow to haul it to the dump. Why don't we get a new swing and grill tomorrow?" He could tell by my pursed lips that I was upset, and he wanted to do something that would help me feel better.

I took a deep breath and managed a small smile. "Sure. Let's do that."

"Okay, good." He pulled me close, relieved that I hadn't freaked out and more relieved that I was home. He'd really missed me this time. "I've got to go. Will you be okay?" he asked, checking his watch. "I hate to leave, but I've got a meeting with a client in half an hour."

"Oh sure, that's fine. I'm glad you brought me home."

"Yeah...well...you can see why I wanted to be here when you saw that. Thanks for not freaking out on me." He kissed me again, and I felt the stress and tension drain from his shoulders. I realized that he did his best while I was gone, but deep down he had a hard time keeping up with everything. He hadn't told me that part, but it was because he didn't want to sound like that was the only reason he'd missed me.

"Sure," I said. "I'll see you tonight."

I waved as he backed out of the driveway. Once he was gone, my shoulders slumped and I sighed. Most of the time, I was a pretty good wife, so I tried not to get too discouraged at what I'd put my husband through. At least I had a couple of hours to get the house cleaned up and, after I picked up Savannah, I could go to the grocery store and buy something good to cook for dinner.

But before I started any of that, I wanted to take a look at everything Chris had found on Sean Hanley. Now that I was back, uneasiness filled me. I didn't know when or how, but I knew he would come after me at some point, and I needed to be prepared. In the den, a folder with Sean's name lay on top of the desk, and I thanked my lucky stars that Chris was so meticulous about his research.

Inside were copies of Sean's birth certificate, driver's license, and social security number. Holy cow, how did he get that? I turned the page and found he'd also done a criminal background check. I looked it over carefully, but Sean had never been arrested for anything and only showed traffic tickets for speeding.

The next papers in the file were property records for the house Sean lived in. It looked like he bought the house three years ago on a short sale and was the sole owner of the property. I found a notepad and jotted down the address, noting it was the same address that was on his driver's license.

Other papers in the file included tax and employment records, and it kind of made me sick to think that all kinds of records like this were available to the public. After scanning through all the information, I realized Sean looked like a regular guy, with nothing out of the ordinary that pointed him out as a serial killer.

I finished going through the folder and realized something was missing. Then it hit me...Facebook. If I wanted to know about his personal and social life, Facebook was probably where I'd find it. Most people posted all kinds of things about themselves there.

I turned on the computer and logged onto Facebook, then typed in his name. I found several Sean Hanleys, but he wasn't among them. Could that be right? A computer geek in his late twenties and no Facebook account? Did that mean he knew something the rest of us didn't?

I sighed and turned it off. At least I had his address, and I folded up the notepaper and stuffed it into my jeans pocket. The address wasn't too far from The corporate office plaza where Sean worked, and where Darcy had disappeared. That made it about ten minutes away from me. Maybe on my way to the grocery store, I could do a quick drive-by to familiarize myself with the neighborhood. That way, when I went back later to do a little spying, I'd know how to find it without a lot of trouble.

As I pulled up to the school, I was tired, but in a good way. I'd vacuumed the whole house, cleaned up the kitchen, swept the floors, and even gotten the laundry started. The bell signaling the end of school rang, and I watched for

Savannah to come out, anxious to show her the hat I'd bought.

Instead of waiting in the car, I got out and leaned against the passenger side door. I wanted to give her a hug and show off the cute hat. A few minutes later, she emerged with her friends. When she glanced up, I waved. She caught sight of me and waved back, then hurried to the car with a happy smile.

"You're home!" she said, giving me a big hug. "Did Dad tell you what he did?" I nodded, and she turned to her friend. "Dad caught the patio swing on fire last night. I got home from dance just in time to see it. The flames were shooting up so high."

She had the attention of the whole carpool now. "He got it out with the hose, but for a minute there, I thought the whole house was going to burn down." She glanced at me. "Did you see what was left of the swing? He felt really bad." She was thinking that she'd never forget the look of pure shock on his face.

"Yes he did," I said. "And to make up for it, we're going to get a new swing tomorrow."

"That's good," she agreed, and finally noticed the hat I held in my hand. "Where'd you get that?"

"It's for you," I said, smiling. "Unless you don't like it. Then I want it back." She took it from me and squealed her delight. "This is great." She put it on her head and smiled.

"Lookin' good," I said with a wink. "Come on, let's go home."

The kids piled in the car and I hurried around to the driver's side. After shutting the door and putting on my seatbelt, I turned the ignition. Just as the car came to life, a loud knock on my window startled me. I jerked and glanced up, locking gazes with Sean Hanley. I let out a surprised

yelp and pulled back from the window before I gained any
semblance of composure.

Sean's brows rose at my reaction, but he smiled
pleasantly and waited for me to roll down my window.

"Sorry about that," he said. "I guess I surprised you." He
was thinking it had made his day to see me jump like that.
"I just thought I'd say hello." He glanced inside and nodded
at Savannah. "Oh...so you're Savannah's mom? I didn't know
that. What a coincidence."

"How do you know Savannah?" I asked. My stomach
clenched, and the hairs stood up on my arms.

"I teach one of Savannah's classes...well...substitute teach.
Right Savannah?"

"What class?" I broke in before she could say anything. I
hated thoughts of her talking to him at all and didn't want
this creep anywhere near my daughter.

"Science."

"Oh. So you're a substitute teacher? How long have you
been doing that?"

"Hmm..." he said, calculating the time. "Just about six
years."

The hairs stood up on the back of my neck and a chill
ran down my spine, but I tried to keep a pleasant smile on
my face. "Really? That's nice."

"Yeah, it keeps me out of trouble." He smiled, thinking
how ironic that statement was. "Have you decided if you
want to use my company's marketing plan yet? I know I
could set up something nice for you."

"Uh...not yet. I'm still thinking about it."

"Well, let me know if you do." He smiled, thinking this
little meeting had worked out perfectly. Glancing between
me and Savannah, the similarities between us stood out.
"Wow...you two sure look a lot alike. Now that I see you
together, I can see the resemblance."

"Yeah," I said. "We get that a lot."

When I didn't continue, he decided it was time to leave. "Well...I'll let you go. It's been nice seeing you again. Bye Savannah." He gave her a quick wave, which Savannah half-heartedly acknowledged, and turned back toward his car.

I left my window down and concentrated on his thoughts, needing to pick up something useful before he got in. He was happy he'd scared me, and a rush of anticipation swept over him. Not long now, and I'd be his, then...

His door shut before I could pick up anything else, and my heart raced. I blinked and glanced at Savannah, giving her a weak smile. She was thinking that she didn't like Mr. Hanley much and was glad he was just a substitute teacher. He was too friendly, and it made her uncomfortable, especially since he seemed to pay more attention to her than anyone else in the class. He kept staring at her and it had kind of freaked her out these last few days.

Alarm prickled over my skin. "How long has he been substituting?" I asked.

"Since Wednesday."

He'd been there for three days? I'd only talked to Sean at his office on Monday, so how the hell had he managed to get a substitute teaching position at my daughter's school so fast? "What happened to your real teacher?"

She shrugged. "I think he got sick or something."

My mouth went dry, and sudden fear made it hard to swallow. This was not how I expected things to happen. Not at all.

"Can we go now?" Savannah asked, wondering why I was staring at her with a crazy look in my eyes. I was just sitting there with the car running. What was wrong with me? That thought pretty much came from everyone in the car.

"Of course," I responded, and put the car in gear. As I drove the kids home, a tide of mounting anger rose up inside of me, and I knew I'd shoot that crazy son of a bitch myself before I let him harm my daughter. Whatever he had planned for me would be nothing compared to what I had planned for him.

By the time Savannah and I entered the house, I had calmed somewhat...mostly for her sake, and showed her the other things I bought in Seattle. Josh came home soon after that and I told them both all about Pike Place Market and the other things I'd seen. Talking to them helped me feel better, especially when Josh told me his version of the swing catching on fire.

I left soon after for the grocery store, deciding to wait for another time to drive by Sean's house. For some reason, I just didn't want to leave Savannah for that long. I quickly stocked up on everything we'd run out of in the last few days, and made it to the check-out without buying anything that wasn't on my list. That had to be some kind of record.

As I waited, the candy bars tempted me and I contemplated buying a couple. Two for a dollar was a pretty good deal, and I'd been so good. Just as I reached for one, I picked up a stray thought about me and goosebumps broke out on my arms. It was Sean, and he was thinking I had certainly bought a lot of food, but I was finally done and it was time to put his plan into action. His thoughts abruptly stopped so that had to mean he'd left the store. I glanced around but couldn't see him anywhere. Did that mean he was waiting for me in the parking lot?

I chewed on my bottom lip, wishing I knew what his plans were. He wouldn't do anything stupid in the parking lot, would he? I knew he'd taken Darcy while she was getting into her car, but that was in a parking structure with no one around. This was different. Still, I was grateful I had my stun flashlight in my purse. He wasn't going to get anywhere near me without getting zapped.

My shopping cart was full, and I rolled it in front of me like a shield toward my car. Knowing something was going to happen at any moment put me on edge, and I listened to thoughts so hard that I passed up my car and had to backtrack.

Still hearing nothing, I began to unload my groceries. Where was he? What was he planning? Someone with a quiet mind walked past me and then stopped.

"Shelby?" Sean said. "Whoa, this is nuts. Twice in one day."

With my heart pounding, I turned to face him. "Wow, it really is nuts. In fact, it's so nuts, it almost looks like you planned the whole thing." That startled a laugh out of him, so I continued. "I've never seen you at this grocery store before. Do you live around here?"

"Not close, no," he answered, thinking I was quick, and he'd better tell me something I'd believe that was close to the truth. "But it's near the school, so I thought I'd grab a few things on my way home. Here, let me help you with that." He took the sack from my arms and began unloading the rest of my cart for me. With his help we got done quickly, and he closed the trunk with a smile. "I'll take your cart back for you."

"Oh, thanks."

"Sure. See you around."

As he pushed my cart away, I picked up that he was pleased he'd startled me, although my comment about him planning the meeting concerned him. Why would I say something like that? I was definitely not like the other women. I had a lot more spunk. In a way it was worrisome, but it also gave him something to look forward to.

He could take his time breaking me. I'd probably scream a lot. And all that screaming would make it even sweeter once I started to beg. Good thing he'd sound-proofed the room. He hadn't been back for a long time, so he should probably drive out there and open some windows. Maybe put out some air freshener. The smell should be gone by now, but he didn't want the odor to be a distraction. He'd go home, grab something to eat, and drive straight there. It wouldn't take long, and then he'd be back in time to get everything else ready. If it all worked out the way he'd planned, he'd have me there by tomorrow night.

My breath caught, and I jumped into my car and shut the door before he noticed me watching. I swallowed, and my fingers shook as I locked the doors. Taking a couple of deep breaths, I tried to think though the panic and calm down. I knew his plans. That was good. Now I just had to decide what to do about them.

What were my options? Since I didn't know where this 'place' was, it might be a good idea to find out. From how he thought about the smell, I could only surmise that the other bodies were there. So finding the place with the bodies would certainly be enough to get him arrested. But to find the place, I'd probably need to follow him.

There was no way I was going alone and, since he knew my car, I needed to call someone else and get them to drive. Once we found the place we could watch until he left, and then go take a look to see if the bodies were really there. Then I could call the police to get a search warrant and arrest him.

Out of Ramos, Chris, and Dimples, the person I really wanted to call was Ramos, but I was afraid he'd just shoot Sean. Then Sean wouldn't get arrested and we'd have to cover up the shooting, which probably meant not involving the police, and the cases would remain unsolved. I couldn't let that happen.

Chris would probably freak out and tell me not to go. I also didn't want to think about him bringing his gun and shooting Sean either. Dimples had a gun and was the police, so he was the logical choice, but I wasn't sure he'd go for the breaking and entering part. Still, I felt that I should at least call him first, knowing that whomever I called, they had to act fast. I pushed speed dial for Dimples' number and pulled out of the parking lot. Sean had just left, and if I was going to get to his house in time to follow him, I couldn't wait around.

I debated following him right then, but decided to go home and dump the groceries first, counting on the kids to put them away for me. Now if only Dimples would pick up. The call went to voice mail and I hit the steering wheel with my palm. Damn! I left a message to call me and put a call through to Ramos, figuring that somehow, I'd just have to make him do what I wanted. His call went to voice mail too and I swore again. Leaving a message to call me, I hung up just in time to pull into my garage, and ran into the house.

"Hey guys. I need your help...right now! Hurry! This is important." They both came running, which kind of amazed me, and I popped the trunk open. "Get the groceries inside and put them away for me. I've got an emergency!" While we ran back and forth, I put in another call to Dimples. It went straight to voice mail, so I didn't bother to leave another message. Then inspiration hit, and I called Geoff Parker. He was a retired cop...he'd be home, and he probably still carried a gun. Even better, his house was in the same direction as Sean's.

"Hello?" Geoff answered.

"Geoff! It's Shelby Nichols. I know who did it and I need your help. Can I come over right now and pick you up?"

"Uh...um...sure."

"Don't worry. I'll explain everything when I get there. We'll need to take your car...oh...and don't forget to bring your gun."

I disconnected and set the last of the groceries on the table, then turned to my kids. "Thanks for putting these away. I'll explain everything later." I ran back to jump in the car and noticed Savannah's eyes wide in alarm and Josh's mouth hanging open. They'd heard the gun part and didn't like it one bit. "I'll be back soon...don't worry."

I made it to Geoff's house in record time and pulled to a stop. To my relief, he was ready and waiting in his car. This might just work. I pulled the door open and jumped inside. "Thanks so much! Here's the address. Do you know where it is?"

"Yeah, it's not too far from here." He backed the car onto the street and we took off. "So what's going on?"

I explained everything I knew, even telling him that I was Sean's next victim. "I tried to call Dimples, but he didn't answer his phone, so I'm really grateful you're coming with me."

He nodded, thinking I was a little nuts to follow the guy in the first place, but if what I said was true, it was probably the only chance we'd get to find where he took the women. "Okay," he said. "We're almost to his house. You'd better duck while I drive by. If his car is still there, I'll pull over down the road a bit and we can wait."

As I nodded, my stomach clenched with anxiety. I hoped we hadn't missed him, but at the same time, I kind of hoped that we had.

"Okay, there it is."

I squeezed down into the foot area and held my breath. Geoff casually glanced down the drive and kept going.

"We're in luck. He's just putting some things in his car, so he hasn't left yet."

Closing my eyes, I swallowed my fear and stayed out of sight. Geoff pulled into a driveway about three houses down, and turned off the engine. "We'll just wait right here for him. As long as no one needs this driveway, I doubt Sean will notice us sitting here. You can probably get up now. Just lean over when he passes."

"Okay." I unfolded my legs and sat back on the seat. Geoff kept watch, hardly taking his gaze off the house. He was thinking he didn't want to miss this opportunity and was grateful I'd called him. He'd forgotten how exciting it was to be on the hunt and hoped this wasn't all a big mistake.

"So how did you know it was him?" he asked.

"Well...a lot of it was through my premonitions, and the rest was hard work." I sure hoped he'd buy it, since that was the most I could say. "I have to admit...I was pretty upset that he was teaching at my daughter's school. I still can't figure out how he managed that."

Geoff narrowed his eyes. "You know...that might be the link. I think one of the missing women was a school teacher. The others could have had children at the schools where he substituted, or had some other connection to them. That could be how he picked his victims and gained their trust."

"You're right," I agreed. "There's probably someone he knows in the district that's more than willing to let him substitute in any class or school available."

"I agree...wait...here he comes," Geoff said.

I ducked down and froze in my seat. Once Sean passed, I sat up and Geoff started the car. As he pulled out of the driveway, he was thinking how quick his training had kicked in, even though it had been a few years, and how much he enjoyed being back on the job. He didn't think he'd missed it until now. In some ways he hadn't, but catching this bastard was different. It was still hard to believe that I'd figured it out so fast, and he wished I would have been around before he'd left the department. But at least I'd cracked the case wide open now.

Geoff kept two to three cars between us, keeping Sean in sight. We followed his car to the freeway and I was grateful Geoff was at the wheel, expertly maneuvering between cars without following too closely for Sean to notice.

Sean exited the freeway in a poorer part of town with smaller houses and vacant lots. We exited more slowly, but the light at the end of the exit turned red and with no other cars exiting, I knew we'd end up right behind him. I quickly ducked back down, hearing Geoff swear in his mind. He hunched his shoulders and with his elbow resting on the door, held his hand to his face, covering some of his mouth and nose.

Geoff studied Sean by looking through Sean's rearview mirror, thinking something about him looked familiar. He wondered if he'd ever questioned him about Darcy's disappearance. Hopefully with his face half-covered, Sean wouldn't recognize him if he had. As Sean glanced into his rearview mirror Geoff stiffened, but couldn't tell if Sean recognized him or not.

The light changed, and Sean made the left turn through the intersection, then took a quick right at the next street. Geoff followed, but continued down the road, turning right one street further down, hoping to pick Sean up at the bottom of the street. "You can get back up now," he said. "I don't think he made us, but we'll have to be extra careful from here on out."

He slowed at the stop sign and sighed with relief to see Sean's car traveling North under the freeway before making a left on the other side. We followed under the freeway, turning left as well, but we lost sight of him. There were a few houses here, but most were in bad shape with boarded up windows and overgrown bushes and weeds.

Not seeing his car, Geoff turned right at the next street and found a lane on the left that curved toward a dilapidated house. Since the house was at the end of the curve, we couldn't see it very well, but from the way it was situated, Geoff was thinking it was the perfect place for Sean to commit murder.

Geoff pulled over to the side of the street and turned off the car. "You stay here. I'm going to take a look down that lane and see if his car is there." Before I could say a word, he was out the door and walking toward the lane.

Chapter 12

I sat tight, since it was never my intention to get out of the car until Sean was long gone. While waiting, I chewed on my fingernail for a moment, then realized what I was doing and stopped. I glanced at the other houses on the street and swallowed. I couldn't tell if anyone lived there, but if they did, I worried that they were the kind that had guns aimed at my head and could pull the trigger at any moment.

The car door opened, startling me, and Geoff jumped back in. "He's there. What do you want to do?"

I let out my breath, holding a hand to my chest. "Sheesh, you scared me to death."

"Sorry."

"That's okay," I said, shaking my head. "I'm just a little nervous. So, what's the exact address?"

Geoff glanced at the street sign. "Looks like it's four-seventy-one Ashwood Lane."

"Good. Let me write that down." I grabbed a pen from my purse and wrote it on my arm since I didn't have any paper. "This is what we'll do. From what I could pick up, he won't be there long. He was mainly just coming to open some windows and set out some air freshener. Once he leaves, we could go look in the windows for evidence or something. If we find anything that looks suspicious, we could call the cops and give them this address."

"Hmm...just look in the windows, huh?"

"Well...maybe if the windows are open, I could squeeze in and take a look around, while you stand guard. Is that okay?"

"Yeah," he said with a smile. "That should work since I'm not a cop anymore." He thought if we found any evidence it would speed things up, and the police could get a search warrant right away and arrest that no-good-son-of-a-bitch.

I smiled back, glad to know we understood each other. He really was the best choice for this job, and I was glad I'd called him.

A few minutes later, Sean pulled out of the lane and headed back to the freeway entrance. My heart rate doubled, knowing it was time to move. As soon as his car was out of sight, Geoff and I both jumped out of his car and ran down the lane.

The small house at the end looked like it was falling apart, and there were gaping spaces where the wood siding had fallen off. Half the shingles on the tall roof were missing, and the railing around the porch was broken in several places. Curtains covered the windows from the inside and a screen door hung half open and broken in front of the main door.

We hurried around back and found a few windows wide open. From Geoff's vantage point, he thought the nearest one probably opened into the kitchen, so that's the one I went for. Geoff helped hoist me up and I half-tumbled onto the floor.

"I'll keep watch," he said. "But don't take too long."

"I won't," I agreed.

My heart was pounding to beat the devil, but I swallowed my fear and took in my surroundings. Although way outdated and dusty, the kitchen was surprisingly well-kept. I noted a staircase directly in front of the backdoor that led to a basement. It was dark down there, but I figured that was the most likely place to hide a body, so with trepidation, I started down the stairs.

By the time I got to the bottom of the steps, my legs were shaking so bad I could hardly walk. I stood in front of a closed door with a bolt from this side, effectively locking up anyone inside. I swallowed, then pulled the bolt and turned the knob. A rush of cool air washed over me, but at least no smell of decay came with it. Still, I could hardly make my legs move into the room. Since it was too dark to see inside, I flipped the switch at the bottom of the stairs.

A bare light bulb illuminated two big pieces of green shag carpet that covered the cement floor. At the far end, chains with manacles dangled from the ceiling. Closer to the stairs, a longer chain was bolted into the cement just above the carpet with a similar manacle.

A roll-away bed on wheels was pushed against a wall beside an open door that led to a bathroom. Imagining the horrors of what went on in that room tightened my chest, and I couldn't seem to catch my breath. Was this enough evidence to put Sean away for good? I needed to find the bodies. They had to be here somewhere, but where?

A cold chill settled around me, and a faint breeze filled with the scent of gardenias brushed my cheek. *Upstairs.* Gah! I jumped about half a foot. Was that a woman's voice? Leaving the light on and the door opened, I ran upstairs as fast as I could, skidding through the kitchen and into the hallway. How had I heard her voice in my head? Was it Darcy? Was I going crazy?

With my chest heaving, I stopped to listen, and the scent of gardenias wrapped around me again. Two doors opening into bedrooms off the hall stood open, so I quickly glanced into each room, finding one with a bed and the other filled with boxes. Could the bodies be in the boxes?

Higher. I cringed to hear the same voice in my head, but this time it didn't scare me quite so much. "Higher where?" I whispered. There wasn't another floor...unless she meant the attic. From the high-pitched roof, I knew there had to be one, but I didn't know where to look for the stairs. I searched the hall, but besides the bathroom there wasn't another doorway, and the ceiling didn't have an opening that would lead to an attic.

Closet. "Okay, I'll check the closets." I looked through both bedroom closets, but they were empty and I couldn't find any trace of a doorway or staircase in either one of them. I groaned in frustration and a breeze whipped around me, sending my hair flying into my face. It seemed to be pushing me in the direction of the living room. I took the hint and rushed down the hall and into the room.

I scanned the room and found a closet door near the front door. "Yes!" I let out my breath with relief and opened the door. Inside, a dark staircase led upward to a closed door at the top. This was it. I hesitated, fearful of what I'd find, but time was passing and I needed to get out of that house. Plus, I didn't want another breeze to start pushing me up. That was just too freaky.

Swallowing my fear, I found enough strength in my legs to get them moving and started up the steep stairs. With each step, the wood creaked and I cringed, hardly daring to breathe, but kept going until reaching the top. I hesitated at the door, chewing on my bottom lip, then took a deep breath and grabbed the knob. It turned easily and I pushed it open.

The musty smell of decay hit me first, but I took a quick step inside and pursed my lips against a tiny scream. Shrouded in gray light, the shrunken bodies of five women sat in a semi-circle. With skin tight on skeletal remains, and blond hair still flowing from their skulls, they sat as if waiting for a play to begin. I gasped and covered my mouth in shocked horror.

My eyes watered with sudden tears at what had been done to them. I blinked them away, then swallowed and backed to the stairs. I'd seen enough. It was time to call the police. I closed the door behind me and started down the stairs. Just then, my phone rang. In the silence it startled me, and I quickly answered with a frightened whisper. "Hello?"

"Babe, I got your message. What's going on?" Ramos asked.

Relief poured over me just to hear his voice. "Ramos...thank God. I'm with a retired detective and we followed the serial killer I was telling you about. We're at his...the killer's...other house. I called you first to see if you could come, but when you didn't answer, I called the detective instead. I couldn't wait since the killer was leaving and if I didn't follow him, I wouldn't know where this place was, but we found it and we're here now. The detective's guarding the outside and I came in to find evidence to put him away. Oh, Ramos, I just found the bodies of five women...it's bad."

"You're inside? Give me the address. Now!"

"Okay..." His alarm tightened my throat and I raised my arm to recite the address, hardly managing to whisper the numbers.

"I'm on my way. Get out of there."

"I'm calling Dimples..." He hung up before I could finish, so I quickly left the closet and hurried back to the kitchen. I glanced out the windows to the back and side of the house for Geoff, but couldn't see him anywhere. A shiver of dread ran down my spine and my stomach clenched. Oh no! Where the hell was he? Why wasn't he out there?

I swallowed and glanced at my phone to push number six on my speed dial for Dimples. As it started to ring, I reached the window and began to climb out. I got both my legs out and slid to the ground, but my phone slid from my fingers. I heard Dimples answer, but before I could pick it up, I heard the same ethereal voice as before only more urgent. *Run!*

My breath caught, and I didn't know what to do. With Dimples shouting my name on the phone, I couldn't leave without picking it up. I grabbed it with shaking hands, just as the back door flew open. My eyes widened with fear to find Sean rushing toward me, his face contorted with rage.

"Four-seventy-one Ashw..."

Sean grabbed the phone from my hand and smashed it against the house. I turned to run, but he was too fast for me, grabbing my hair, and pulling it into his fist with an iron grip. I yelled but he clamped his arm around my neck and began to choke me.

"You bitch!! You've ruined everything!"

As I struggled for breath, he pulled me backwards into the house. Through the door, he dragged me down the basement stairs. My vision went dark before he released his grip and shoved me to the ground. Wheezing in deep breaths of air, I felt the cold manacle slip around my ankle and heard the snap as it locked shut.

Sean straightened and backed away, shoving his hands through his hair and breathing heavily. He was thinking how much he wanted to kill me with his bare hands, but he didn't have time. Not now that I'd called the police. He had to destroy everything or they'd arrest him and he couldn't let that happen.

A groan came from the other side of the room, and I glanced over to find Geoff, his arms manacled to the chains attached to the ceiling. Blood trickled from a gash in the side of his head. His feet barely touched the ground and his head rolled to the side. He groaned again and managed to get his feet under him, relieving some of the strain on his hands. With deep breaths, he lifted his head and glanced up, trying to figure out what had happened. Then he saw me with Sean and swore under his breath.

"You won't get away with this," Geoff said.

Sean sneered at him. "You don't know anything. You're just stupid. You're the one who interviewed me about the woman I killed and you didn't have a clue." He snorted. "And now, you thought you could follow me and I wouldn't know? That's even more stupid."

He turned his gaze on me. "What were you doing upstairs Shelby? Did you see my trophies?" He huffed out a breath. "Good thing this basement is sound-proof or you might have heard something and run off. I wouldn't have even known you were here, since your friend didn't say anything. Now that was clever. Too bad it doesn't matter since you're both going to die down here. Because of you I have to burn this place down."

Anger radiated from him, and his fists tightened. He wanted to torture me so bad it hurt. If only he could hear me screaming, maybe some of his pain would go away. He took a step toward me, then stopped. He didn't have time. Not if he wanted to get away. He had to burn this place down. No one knew it belonged to him, so there was no evidence tying him to anything. Once we were dead, and the house was gone, he could start over. He could kill as many women as he wanted, and no one would ever know it was him. He glanced at me, still burning with desire to choke me again.

I held my breath, hoping he'd turn around and walk out. Even though he meant to burn the house down, I also knew that Ramos was on his way, and hopefully Dimples had heard enough to come too.

Sean howled with frustration, then turned away and slammed the door behind him.

I sagged as relief poured over me. I'd never been so frightened in my life, and it wasn't over yet. I sat up and glanced at Geoff, hot remorse tightening my stomach. "I'm so sorry I involved you in all this. Are you hurt bad?"

"Nah, just a bump on the head...and don't be sorry. This is my fault. I let him get the drop on me. I feel like an idiot. The worst part is, he looks vaguely familiar, but I don't really remember that guy, and he's the killer."

"Don't worry. We'll be out of here in no time."

"How's that possible?"

"I told a friend where I was and he's on his way." I quickly explained Ramos' phone call on the staircase, and in the process, happened to mention his name.

"Ramos?" Geoff asked. His brows drew together. "You don't mean the guy who works for Joey "The Knife" Manetto do you?"

"Uh...yeah," I said. "I think that's the same one." I tried to play dumb, but that only went so far.

"How the hell do you know him?" Geoff couldn't believe a nice woman like me could be involved with someone like Ramos. He was a hit-man. I couldn't possibly know that...unless...

"Um...well...it's a long story."

Geoff's eyes widened and he choked back another curse before shaking his head and sighing with resignation. "It's all right. Don't tell me about it. Not a thing. I don't want to know."

"That's probably best," I agreed.

Geoff closed his mouth on a snort. In his position, he could hardly complain if the famous hit-man came to his rescue. Good thing he wasn't a detective anymore. But how did I know him? That was quite the puzzle. Maybe it had something to do with my premonitions? Hmm...if we got out of this alive, maybe he'd have to check it out, just for the hell of it.

"I'm afraid Sean's out there setting fire to the house," I said.

Geoff nodded. "Yeah. Let's just hope your friend gets here first." He panted a little and closed his eyes against the pain in his head. He was hurt worse than he'd said, but he didn't want me to worry. The pain in his side from a couple of broken ribs hurt the worst, and he didn't know how much longer he could hold up without passing out.

My stomach knotted with worry. "Just hold on Geoff. He should be here soon."

Geoff tried to nod, but couldn't move his head very well. He was thinking that even if Ramos got here in time, there was the big problem of the locked door, as well as getting us out of our manacles without a key.

"Ramos is good with locks," I said. "And I'm not sure Sean bolted the door."

Geoff's eyes widened and he swore in his mind, thinking that I'd just answered his thoughts, almost like he'd said them out loud. That was a little freaky.

I ignored Geoff and stood, hoping the long chain would let me reach the door. Sean had left so fast that I didn't think he'd taken the time to lock it from the other side. I prayed I was right, but got to the end of the chain before I could grasp the handle.

Stretching as far as I could, I managed to touch the knob with my fingers. Straining harder, I finally got my thumb around it and gave a short twist. The door opened, and I fell back, heaving in deep breaths. From the twinge in my leg, I knew I'd probably pulled a muscle, but at least the door was open.

It also let me hear a little of what was going on upstairs, and I flinched. The sound of breaking glass and a faint smell of smoke tightened my chest with fear.

"Did you hear that?" I asked Geoff.

"Not really, but I can smell the smoke. At least we're in the basement. The fire shouldn't reach us for a while. That should give your friend enough time to get here."

Overwhelmed with fear, I could hardly nod my head to agree with him. I sat back down on the carpet and could barely see the bottom of the back door for the smoke gathering around it.

"So what did you see in the attic? What did he mean by trophies?" He hoped I'd found something, but more than that, wanted to take my mind off our impending doom.

"It was bad," I began. "There were five bodies in the attic, one more than we thought. And they were sitting in chairs...with what was left of their mouths gaping open. I don't know if they were still alive when he put them there, but it kind of looked like it."

Geoff cursed a blue streak in his mind. "That son-of-a-bitch! If he succeeds in burning this place down, all that evidence will go up in smoke."

As if on cue, the scent of smoke got stronger, and I felt the blood drain from my head. "Oh no! It's getting worse."

Geoff swore out loud this time, and I heard the desperation behind it. Something inside me snapped, and I jumped to my feet, frantic to find anything that would get us out of there. The chain reached to the bathroom, so I hurried inside to search for any kind of tool I could find.

Of course there was nothing useful, but I did find some towels, and wet them down in the sink. We could wrap them around our heads to help us breathe, right? At least it was better than nothing. A loud boom shook the house, and dust rained down over my head, making me cough. Dread tightened my throat and my heart raced. The fire was spreading quickly now, and I didn't know if anyone could get inside to rescue us. What if the fire blocked the stairs?

The smell of smoke got worse, causing my eyes to burn. Taking the wet towels with me, I moved as close to the staircase as I could get, hoping to see if the way was clear. There was still light coming down from above, but I couldn't get a clear view of the back door. Another crash sounded on the ceiling right above my head, and the light bulb popped, leaving us in darkness. I cringed back toward the wall and held a towel to my face. The fire was getting worse. It wouldn't be long before the ceiling gave way and buried us.

I glanced at Geoff, but could barely make out his shape in the dark. He could see me though, and regret poured from his mind. "It's been nice to know you Shelby. I'm real sorry..."

"Shelby!" Ramos shouted. "Shelby! Where are you?"

Hope blossomed in my chest. "Down here!" I yelled. "Down in the basement."

The glow of a flashlight illuminated the stairs then came to rest on me. A rush of footsteps sounded, and then he was there, striding toward me. He held a fireman's jacket over his head, and dropped the flashlight as he knelt beside me. "Thank God you're alive. Are you tied up?"

"It's worse...I'm chained to the wall. We both are."

Ramos froze, glancing between us, his face distorted with dismay. I'd never seen him look like that, and all at once, I knew I was going to die. "You'd better get out while you can," I said.

"No. I can get you out. I know I can, just give me a minute." He pushed a button and talked into the radio. "I found them in the basement, they're alive, but they're chained to the wall. I need help getting them out."

"Who is this?"

"Get Detective Harris," Ramos growled. "He'll tell you who I am. In the meantime, get someone down here."

The smoke was starting to get thick, and hurt my throat. "I've got some wet towels ready. Can you give this to Geoff?"

Ramos took a towel and hurried to Geoff's side. After a quick perusal of the chains, he found a catch on the wall and undid it. The chains loosened from the ceiling, and Geoff slumped to the ground. Moving quickly, Ramos pulled the chains through the pulley and Geoff was free.

A fireman appeared out of the smoke at the bottom of the steps in full gear and raised his visor. "There's no time," he shouted. "We've got to go now. The whole place is coming down."

"Here," Ramos said, helping Geoff up. "Take him out. We'll be right behind you."

The fireman took the weight of the chains over his shoulder while Geoff held the wet towel over his head and face, and they quickly disappeared up the steps. Ramos grabbed the other wet towel and wrapped it around his face, then handed me the flashlight. "Shine it at the lock."

As Ramos took a pouch out of his jeans pocket, I held the light steady. He was thinking he'd never picked this kind of lock before, but it couldn't be too hard. He got out the tools he'd need and got to work, trying to find the catch.

Suddenly, the ceiling where Geoff had been standing cracked and part of it gave way, sending pieces of burning rubble to the ground beside us. It filled the space with smoke and cinders.

I lurched back and dropped the flashlight, choking on the smoky air. "Ramos...it's okay. There's no time. You have to go...I don't want you to die."

His gaze caught mine. "I'm not leaving you." He coughed, and shook his head. "I'm getting you out." He was thinking he'd rather die with me here than leave me behind, so I'd better not ask him again.

Tears streamed from my eyes and I found it hard to breathe. Ramos bent to his task, and I picked up the flashlight. I tried to hold it steady, but I was shaking and coughing so bad, it was moving all over the place. I closed my eyes against the burn, and held the towel tight, but the smoke was so bad I thought I might pass out.

All at once the lock clicked open and my breath caught with relief. Ramos quickly threw the fireman jacket over my head and spoke into the radio.

"I've got her. We're coming up." He secured the towel around his head and glanced at me, knowing that running up those stairs into a hail of burning debris might still kill us, but it was the only way out. "You ready?"

"Yes."

With his arm around my waist, we ran to the stairs and started up. Water sprayed all around us, and I slipped on the steps, but Ramos held me firmly to his side. Within seconds we'd made it up and out the door, black smoke spewing behind us. After running several feet, both of us doubled over with coughing from the smoke. Taking deep breaths, I turned to look back at the house.

Orange-red flames engulfed the entire structure, then suddenly, parts of the building started to collapse. The ground shook, and a fireman came beside us, quickly ushering us back even further. As I stepped back, I couldn't pull my gaze away from the roaring inferno, and realized that we'd barely made it out in time. Just another minute or two and the whole thing would have come down on top of us.

My throat burned and I couldn't seem to catch my breath. Then my legs went weak, and darkness clouded my vision. As I slipped to the ground, Ramos caught me. He said something, but it sounded like he was speaking from far away and I couldn't make out the words.

Chapter 13

Something cool pressed over my nose and mouth, and I struggled to open my eyes. Taking a breath, fresh air poured into my lungs and I finally felt like I could breathe again. I opened my eyes to find Ramos holding the oxygen mask to my face, and realized I must have fainted.

"Better?" he asked.

I nodded, grateful I wasn't out long. On one knee beside Ramos, Dimples hovered over me, his eyes anxious and worried. After a few more breaths, I pulled the mask away and gave them both a feeble smile. Dimples sighed with relief and smiled back. Someone tapped his arm and motioned toward the ambulance. "I'll just be over there if you need me," he said.

A paramedic held my wrist to check my pulse. "We should get her on a gurney and take her to the hospital," he said to Ramos.

"Where's Geoff?" I asked, my throat raspy. "Is he all right?"

"He's fine," the paramedic answered. "He's in the ambulance...where you should be."

I glanced at Ramos. He didn't seem to have a problem breathing. "What about him? Does he need to go too?"

The paramedic frowned. "He didn't faint."

I sniffed and that made me cough. Ramos put the oxygen mask back over my face and I gratefully took a few deep breaths. Feeling better, I thought I should stand up and walk over to the ambulance. "Help me up," I asked Ramos.

"Are you going to faint again?"

"I sure hope not."

"Let's give you a few more minutes, and then if you're feeling up to it, I'll help you up." He was thinking that by then the gurney would be here and he wouldn't have to worry about me fainting.

"Chicken," I said. He smiled, and even with a soot-covered face, he still looked good enough to melt my heart and warm my toes. Maybe that's why I'd fainted. I decided I might as well relax and enjoy being held in his arms while I could.

"So what happened?" I asked. "Did you get Sean?"

Ramos' eyes darkened. "No. He got away. I could have gone after him, but with you inside that burning house...it was a no-brainer. I had to break the door down, and by then the firemen and Harris had arrived. They were taking too long, so I grabbed a jacket and flashlight off the truck and came in to find you myself. Harris saw me do it but didn't try to stop me."

"I wonder how the firemen got here."

"Apparently a neighbor saw Sean light it and called nine-one-one."

"Wow...that was lucky," I said. After a moment I tilted my head so I could catch his gaze. "Ramos...thanks for not leaving me...I thought I was going to die down there. I would have if not for you." Tears blurred my vision and a lump caught in my throat.

Ramos' lips turned up in a half-smile, but he was thinking he'd never been so scared in his life. "Yeah. That was close. I think you owe me. So...maybe I deserve that kiss now?"

I smiled at his teasing, grateful he wasn't getting all mushy and sentimental. "If you'll take it on the cheek... then yeah... maybe."

He snorted, thinking that when I got close he'd just turn his head. Then what would I do? That startled a laugh out of me, but it turned into a cough, and I had to hold the oxygen over my face to get my breath back.

Dimples came back to check on me. He was thinking about the phone call I'd made to him, and how it had taken two years off his life. Good thing Ramos and the firemen showed up when they did, or I'd be dead for sure. He wanted to yell at me for scaring him so bad, but he also felt guilty that he hadn't been able to answer his phone the first time I'd called. Next time I called, he'd answer no matter what, even if he was in a meeting with the police chief and the mayor.

Watching me right now, holding an oxygen mask over my face, with my skin all blackened and streaked with tears was one of the best sights he'd seen all day. Somehow I'd made it out alive, which counted as some sort of miracle in his book.

"How are you doing?" he asked.

"Good," I answered. "Thanks to you and Ramos. I guess I'll have to make you some cookies or something." Dimples smiled, and I grinned to get a peek at his cheeks with their whirling indentations. "How's Geoff holding up?"

"He'll be fine. They'll take you both to the hospital as soon as you can make it over there."

I was enjoying myself right where I was, so I asked him a question instead. "What can you tell me about Sean?"

"We've got an APB out on him. We'll find him Shelby, don't worry."

I sighed and then coughed. My throat still felt raw and burned. "I found five bodies up there in the attic. Now they're gone."

"It won't matter. We can still get him on attempted murder."

"But it does matter. The families of those women need to know what happened to them."

Dimples' lips tightened. "We're going to do everything we can to find whatever's left of them. I've got my best forensics team coming in on it. That's about the best we can hope for."

"Okay."

The paramedic came to my side wheeling a gurney over the grass. "The ambulance is ready to go. Let's get you on the gurney."

"Fine," I agreed, a little sad to leave the comfort of Ramos' arms. He helped me stand, then quickly maneuvered me onto the gurney. A touch light-headed, I gratefully laid my head on the pillow, while the paramedic lifted my feet onto the gurney. He strapped me in and rolled me over to the ambulance with Ramos walking by my side.

Before lifting me in, Ramos squeezed my hand. "I'll be going now."

"You sure you're all right?" I asked.

"Yes, I'm fine. I wasn't down there as long as you."

"Oh...okay. I'll see you later?" I asked.

"Sure," he agreed. He was already thinking about how he was going to find Sean. He didn't want me to worry that Sean could ever hurt me again, so he had to find him first.

Before I could tell him not to kill Sean, he strode away. I opened my mouth to call him back, but with my throat so sore I shut it instead and watched him go. Something settled in me to know Ramos wasn't going to let Sean hurt me again, and in some ways, I wanted Sean dead. That probably made me a bad person, but right now, I didn't care.

Dimples had turned away to answer his phone. He hurried back to my side, holding the phone out to me. "Shelby...it's Chris. He wants to talk to you."

Surprised, I took the phone and tried to make my voice sound normal. "Hi honey. Did Dimples tell you what happened?"

"Yes," he said. "Are you okay? He said they were taking you to the hospital."

"Yeah. It's no big deal, just a little smoke inhalation. Will you meet me there?"

"Of course. I'll leave right now." He disconnected, and I handed the phone back to Dimples.

"Thanks for telling him what happened," I said. "He didn't sound too shook up, so that's good."

Dimples smiled, but it didn't reach his eyes. He felt sorry for Chris. What I put that man through...what I put all of them through...was enough to make a person go crazy. "Yeah," he agreed. "I think he's taking it pretty well." He doubted that, but lied since he didn't want to make me feel bad.

They lifted me into the ambulance, and I smiled to find Geoff on the gurney beside me. "Hey Geoff. Can you believe we made it out of there?"

"Well..." he said, his brows lifting, "to be honest, I didn't think we would, but then your friend came barreling down those stairs. Now that was a sight to behold. One look at him, and I changed my mind." His eyes held speculation, and he thought there was a lot more to my friendship with Ramos than I let on. But...he didn't want to pry, glad that whatever it was, he'd always be grateful I had a friend like him.

"Yeah," I agreed. "He saved us."

"Too bad Sean got away," Geoff said. "But it's good to be alive, so I guess it's okay...as long as they catch him." He worried Sean would come after me. The guy might think he was smart, but his kind hated to get bested, and he was afraid Sean wouldn't be able to resist his impulse to kill me just for spite.

"Uh...I'm sure they'll find him," I said, hoping it was true. I knew between the police and Ramos there was a pretty good chance he'd get caught. Still, I couldn't help the knot of worry that settled in my stomach like a dead weight, and I had to agree with Geoff that Sean didn't seem like the type to rest until I was good and dead.

We arrived at the hospital and whisked into the emergency room. I'd only been there a few minutes when Chris came in. He took in my blackened face and oxygen mask with shock, but then quickly recovered and rushed to my side. Pulling me into his arms, he held me close.

"Shelby..." he moaned. "You nearly gave me a heart attack. The kids called after you left saying something about a phone call to a detective. I thought it was Harris, so I tried not to worry too much. Then I just got this bad feeling so I called him. That's when he told me you'd been locked up in the basement of Sean's house. He said the house was on fire and you barely made it out alive. What the hell happened?"

I grimaced and swallowed, sorry for what I'd put Chris through. I cleared my throat to talk and ended up coughing. "I'm sorry," I croaked.

"It's okay," he said, instantly contrite. "Just rest...do you need a drink of water?"

I nodded and Chris left to find a nurse. A moment later he came back with the nurse, and I gratefully sipped from the cup of ice water she handed me. The cold water felt amazing on my parched throat, and I closed my eyes in relief.

The doctor came in and pulled the curtains closed around us. He introduced himself and then proceeded to listen to my lungs and heart. He prescribed a lung treatment that would take about half an hour and told me I could go home after that, but needed to take it easy for a few days. He was a little puzzled that my throat was so sore until I remembered that Sean had nearly choked me to death. After I explained that, he was thinking I was lucky to be alive, and glanced at Chris with sympathy.

Dimples showed up to get my statement and I explained what had happened, relieved Chris could hear it at the same time so I wouldn't have to go over the whole thing again with him. Dimples assured us both that they would do everything in their power to catch Sean and that he'd keep me posted.

Before leaving, I wanted to say goodbye to Geoff and introduce him to Chris.

"Hey. I'm so sorry I put Shelby in danger," Geoff said, swamped with guilt. "I never would have agreed if I thought we might die."

"I understand," Chris said. "Shelby is..." he glanced at me with narrowed eyes. "Well, let's just say she gets into trouble a lot, so it kind of goes with the territory."

"I'll have to remember that," Geoff said, chuckling. "Next time, I'll be better prepared."

Chris nodded and smiled, but raised his brows, thinking there had better not be a 'next time' like that for me. He couldn't imagine anything worse than being locked up in a basement with a house burning down around me.

"Yeah...it was pretty bad," I admitted. "I think I might need some bath therapy tonight." Geoff glanced at me like I had lost my mind, but Chris understood what I meant. "Anyways...I'll keep in touch. Thanks again for coming with me. I hope you get better soon and that you wife isn't too mad at you." I knew he was worried about that, and I couldn't help commiserating with him since I knew how it felt.

Geoff's lips thinned in a tight smile, but he nodded and waved us out, thinking it was my premonitions that had to make me say stuff like that. But then it hit him that if I had premonitions, why didn't I know what was going to happen at the house? How had Sean taken me by surprise? He opened his mouth to ask about that, but I ducked out of the room before he could, pulling Chris behind me.

Just that tiny bit of exertion made me a little light-headed, and I sagged beside Chris. He quickly put his arm around my waist and held me to his side. "Are you okay?"

"Yeah...I'm just exhausted. I can't tell you how upset I was to find that Sean was teaching Savannah's class. He'd even singled her out, and I think I went a little crazy. That's one of the reasons why I had to follow him. I couldn't stand the thought of him being around her. I hope you're not too mad at me."

Chris held me close, trying to imagine how he'd feel if he'd been there and how he would have reacted. "I would have done the same thing."

I smiled up at him, my eyes filling with tears. "Thanks honey...that means a lot."

He helped me inside the car, taking extra care to make sure I was comfortable, and it warmed my heart. As we pulled into traffic, he asked me to tell him how I got out of the burning building since I'd left that part out of my narrative. I explained how Ramos got Geoff out, then stayed behind to pick the lock on the manacle around my ankle, telling him it was a close thing and we'd both nearly died.

Chris took it all in, thinking he owed Ramos and how much he didn't like it. What could he say to a man who had saved his wife, especially since this wasn't the first time? It was enough to give him a complex.

"It's not that big a deal," I said, not wanting him to feel bad. "You don't even have to say anything. Just do that little chin lift you do to each other. That should work."

Chris snorted and then shook his head, but he was smiling, and I knew he felt better.

A few minutes later he took a deep breath and blew the air slowly out of his mouth. He was thinking about Sean and what would happen next. "Sean's still out there," he said. "Do you think he'll come after you?"

"No," I said quickly. Chris raised his brow and gave me that look that said he knew I was lying. I sighed. "Okay...maybe. But with both Ramos and Dimples after him, I should be fine."

Now Chris sighed and was thinking he couldn't rest until Sean was caught. In fact, if he could, he'd like to call Ramos and offer his help, so that when Ramos caught the SOB he could be there to shoot him in the kneecaps and then, while he was screaming, set him on fire. That might help him feel better, because right now he was angry enough that he could probably do it.

"Hey...do you think we could get take-out tonight?" I asked. "I'd love some Café Rio. And then tomorrow, you promised me a new swing, remember? I'm really looking forward to that. We could cook up some burgers on the new grill too. Sound good?"

Chris took a deep breath and let his frustration go. He knew what I was doing, and had to admit that it worked. He also had to remember that he had me. I was safe and I was alive, but even better, I was his. I grounded him and, as crazy as it sounded, I kept him sane. It wasn't always easy being married to me, but he couldn't imagine the pain and agony he'd feel if I wasn't there. Having me in his life made everything else he went through worth it. He glanced at me, and understanding beyond words passed between us.

"Did I tell you I loved you today?" I asked, taking his hand in mine.

"Nope," he said.

"I love you."

"I love you too," he answered.

The next morning my throat didn't hurt as much. Even the croak was gone, and I took a deep breath to test my lungs. When I didn't cough, I relaxed, pleased and happy to feel better. It was Saturday, and I could hardly believe how fast the week had passed.

Chris was already up and outside mowing the lawn. It was another beautiful October day, and I wanted to soak it all in and just enjoy being alive. In the kitchen, I found the newspaper on the table with a photo of a blazing house fire on the front page.

I recognized it immediately, and just seeing it tightened my stomach, sending a dark cloud to hover over me. It reminded me that I hadn't told anyone about the voice I'd heard, or the smell of gardenias. I could almost convince myself that it hadn't really happened. I mean...if it did...what did that mean about me?

Since I could read minds, was that the reason I'd heard Darcy's voice? It was enough to give me the creeps. It was bad enough to hear people that were alive, but dead people?

No way. Since it hadn't happened before, maybe it wouldn't happen again. I could always hope.

I glanced at the article and checked the byline, but Billie hadn't written it. The article was short and precise, only saying that the authorities were investigating, and everything so far pointed to arson. It also indicated that two people were rescued from the basement. No mention of my name was given, but I knew it was enough for Sean to know I didn't die, and a wave of dread washed over me.

As much as I'd tried to convince myself that I didn't need to worry about him, I still did. With a sigh, I went straight to the ads, hoping for a good deal to take my mind off my troubles. To my delight, I found a full page ad with all the patio furniture and outdoor grills on sale. Even better, it featured the perfect patio swing and, I had to admit, it was nicer than the one that burned up.

With new purpose, I got the kids up for their Saturday chores so we could leave for the store and buy one before they were all gone. Chris borrowed a truck from our neighbor, and it wasn't long before our whole family arrived at the store. We picked out the swing and grill we wanted and got the boxes out to the truck.

As the boxes were getting loaded, I caught a thought about me from someone in the parking lot. My heart raced, and my knees went a little weak. It was Sean, and he was thinking what a nice little family I had, and if he couldn't get me alone, he might just have to kill all of us, but he'd save me for last. I glanced around the parking lot to find him, but his thoughts cut off, and I knew he'd retreated inside his car.

Trying not to panic, I pulled myself together, knowing I had to do something before it went any further. After getting over the initial shock, hot anger flooded over me. No way could I let Sean hurt my family. I had to do something about it today, before it was too late. Probably something that would involve drawing him away. But if I could get the right help, it could work out, and a plan started to form.

We got home, and Chris and Josh carried the boxes to the deck to put the swing and grill together. I waited until everyone was right in the middle of things before I made my announcement.

"Hey, I'm going to run to the store real quick. I need to pick up some hamburger buns and a few other things. I'll be right back."

"Wait," Chris said. "Don't you want someone to go with you?" He was thinking I shouldn't be alone if Sean was still out there.

"Oh no...I'll be fine. It's the middle of the day with plenty of people around. Nothing's going to happen. You guys just keep working and I'll bring you all a treat."

Chris opened his mouth to protest, but I slid the door shut and hurried into the garage before he could stop me. I snagged Chris' cell phone, since mine was smashed to bits, and jumped into the car. I took my time backing out, making sure that if Sean was watching, he'd see me leave.

Slowly driving up the street, I caught sight of a car pulling out from a few houses down. I didn't know if it was Sean, but I couldn't take any chances. I pushed the numbers for Ramos' phone and waited for him to pick up.

"Babe, what are you doing?"

"I just left to go to the grocery store and I think Sean is following me."

"Yeah," he said. "I see him."

"What? You're following him?"

"Yes."

"Okay. Then what should I do?" I asked.

"Just go to the grocery store and do your shopping. I'll take care of Sean."

I let out a breath of relief. "Okay. If you need..."

"I won't." He disconnected before I could thank him. It kind of bothered me, but just knowing he was watching my back gave me the boost I needed to pull into the parking lot and get out of my car. The lot was full and I had to park far away which made me nervous but, with Ramos watching, I had to believe everything would be all right.

Halfway to the doors, I heard Sean's thoughts, and my step faltered. He was thinking about stalking me in the store, just to scare me, but knew the risk was too great if I spotted him. He decided to wait in his car until I came back. While I was putting my groceries in the trunk, he'd sneak up and stab me through the heart a few times. He wanted to make sure the last thing I saw before I died was his face. He could do it quick and be out of there before anyone suspected....

His thoughts abruptly stopped. Did that mean he was back in his car, or did Ramos have him? I made it inside the store, feeling like I'd just run a marathon. My heart raced and my mouth was dry. I grabbed a cart and hurried over to the deli section. Pulling a cup from the dispenser, I filled it up with ice and diet soda, then took a big gulp before paying the clerk.

Feeling better, I settled down enough to think about what I was doing there. Oh yeah...hamburger buns...and treats. As I browsed through the aisles, my mind was only half on what I was doing. The other half was imagining what was going on with Sean. If Ramos had caught him, what would he do to him? Would he just kill him in the parking lot, or take him somewhere else?

I made it to the other end of the store with practically nothing in my cart. At least I had the buns, and a box of chocolate donuts, as well as some Cheetos and chips. I should probably make cookies for Dimples and Ramos, so I got those ingredients too. Finally calming down, I let out a deep sigh, and my head cleared a little. Ramos had promised he would take care of Sean, so I had nothing to worry about. I could check-out, go home, and everything would be all right.

Another swallow of soda wet my dry mouth and, with a deep breath, I headed to the check-out stand. For so many people, the line went fast and in no time, I was pushing my cart out the doors. Was it just yesterday Sean had followed me? I listened for all I was worth and slowly made my way back to the car. This was the moment of truth.

With my heart pounding, I made it to my car unscathed. Hearing nothing from Sean, I popped open the trunk and began to set the bags inside. I mostly turned to face the cart so he couldn't sneak up on me. Anyone watching would probably think I was a nutcase, but right now, I didn't care. Done, I closed the trunk and pushed the cart into the nearest stand. I glanced around, searching for any sign of him, but again heard and saw nothing.

Could it be true? Was he really gone? I unlocked my car and opened the door, then checked the back seat to make sure it was empty before getting in. Swallowing, I turned on the ignition and backed out of the space. I kept checking my rearview mirror for the car Sean was driving to see if he'd followed, but he wasn't there. At last, turning into my driveway, the knot of fear loosened. I'd made it home and, with any luck, Sean would never bother me again.

I hurried inside and out onto the patio. Chris glanced up, relieved to see me. He couldn't understand what had possessed me to leave like that, and he'd been sick with worry. Sorry I'd put him through that, I rushed over and gave him a hug, noticing the swing was all put together. "Wow, you did it. It looks wonderful."

"Try it out," he said.

I sat down beside Savannah and clapped my hands. "This is great you guys. It's perfect, and for all your hard work, I bought some chocolate donuts."

"Sweet," Josh said. "I'll bring them out." He rushed inside.

"Don't forget the milk," Savannah called.

"You could go help," I suggested. She frowned, but got up and left Chris and me alone. I grabbed his arm and pulled him down beside me, hugging him tightly. "I don't think we have to worry about Sean anymore."

Chris caught his breath and pulled away, catching my gaze. "Why is that?"

"Um...well...I don't know for sure, but I think Ramos might have something to do with it." Chris raised his brows. "Anyways...could we get me a new phone today? Mine's busted and unless you want to give me yours, I could certainly use a new one."

"Are you going to tell me what Ramos did?" he asked.

"Nope," I answered. "But only because I don't know, and if you want to know the truth...I don't think I want to know."

"All right," he said. "So he's really out of the picture?"

"Uh-huh," I said.

A wall of relief rolled over Chris, and he let out a breath, thinking this was one of those times he was grateful and relieved I knew Ramos.

"Wow...I never thought I'd hear you thinking that."

"Shelby..."

"Well, you have to admit it's pretty crazy that you're thinking you're actually grateful that I know a hit-man...whoa! What are you doing?" In a quick move, Chris grabbed me around the waist and started tickling me. "Okay...okay," I laughed. "That's enough." He wouldn't stop, so I grabbed a pillow and began hitting him in the face. We wrestled and laughed, but quickly pulled apart when the kids came out with the milk and donuts.

"Yay...treats!" I said, hoping to shift the focus to the donuts instead of what Chris and I were doing.

Of course the kids noticed, but they took it in stride. Chris chuckled, and quickly stood to get the chairs situated around the table. We took our places and dove in. With my first bite of chocolaty goodness, the stress of the last few days melted away.

I glanced around the table and my heart swelled. I was alive and here with the people I loved most in the world. Even better, my mouth was filled with the flavor of pure decadence. Chris' gaze let me know he adored me, even if I was sometimes a pain in the butt, and I sighed with happiness just to be alive to enjoy it.

Chapter 14

The next morning I got a phone call from Dimples. "Hi Shelby, I've got some good news."

"Great. What?"

"We found Sean."

I gasped. "Really? Where?"

"Well, that's the interesting part. A janitor found him this morning in his office at Marketing Solutions. He's dead and it looks like suicide, but aside from that, he left a signed confession. He wrote down five names and admitted to killing them all. Four of them are the cases you were looking at. The other one is from a long time ago. We looked her up and it turns out she went to high school with him, and she's been missing from clear back then."

"Was she his girlfriend or something?" I asked.

"I don't know, but I'm hoping his brother might be able to help us sort it out. Anyway, I just wanted to let you know that you don't have to worry about him anymore."

"Thanks, I really appreciate it."

"Sure," he said. I heard him take a breath and let it out. "There's just one thing that's been bothering me. I'm a little puzzled that he left a note naming his victims before he committed suicide. Usually suicide is the last thing a serial killer will do. They normally think they're too smart to get caught."

"Oh...really? Well, maybe his conscience got the best of him."

"Hmm...maybe, but usually people like that don't have much of a conscience, so I'm thinking it might be something else."

"Like what?" I asked, my stomach tensing with sudden nervousness.

"Well...I guess we'll never know, since he's dead." Was he thinking Ramos had something to do with this? "Anyway," he continued, "I can't complain...with his confession it certainly wraps up this case, and I can't be sorry the guy's dead either."

"You're right about that," I agreed to reassure him. "But if it makes you feel any better...I think Sean knew he was going to get caught, so he probably killed himself because he's a control freak and wanted things to happen on his own terms, rather than yours. I also think that confessing to his crimes and giving you their names was because of his pride. I mean...just think about it...when he talked to me, he called the women in the attic his 'trophies,' so claiming them makes sense in a sick sort of way."

"Hmm...I guess when you put it that way it makes sense," Dimples agreed.

"Have you told the families yet?"

"No, but we'll probably contact them today."

"I want to tell Tiffany Shaw," I said. "She's the reason I got involved with this whole thing in the first place."

"Sure," he agreed. "Without you we never would have solved it."

"Thanks. I'll see if I can meet with her today."

"Good idea. The media's been hounding us all day for news about the fire. Once they get wind of this, we'll have to release a statement."

"By media, do you mean Billie?" I asked.

He chuckled. "That's right. In fact, she's waiting just outside to talk to me."

"If it will help, tell her once I've had a chance to talk to my client, I'd be glad to give her an exclusive interview."

"Of course that would help," Dimples snorted. "But are you sure you want to do that? She can be a real pain in..."

"You mean she's tenacious?" I interrupted.

"Yeah...that's a good word for her...it's better than what I was thinking."

"I can imagine," I said with a laugh. We said our goodbyes and disconnected.

I took a minute to collect my thoughts. I knew Ramos had something to do with Sean's death, and it boggled my mind to think he had gotten a signed confession out of him. I also had to believe Dimples knew what he was talking about, especially the part about serial killers not having much of a conscience. So how did Ramos manage it? Was it really suicide? Probably not, but did I even want to know? Nope. Not ever. Still, it made me realize that as well as I knew Ramos, there was a lot about him I didn't know.

I found Tiffany's number and gave her a call. I told her I had news about her mother and wanted to meet with her.

"So you know where she is?" she asked.

"In a way...yes, but I'm afraid it's not good news. I'd like to tell you what happened to her, and I'd like to meet with you today. Will that work?"

"Oh...okay." There was silence on her end while that sank in. Then she took a breath and spoke. "How about we meet at the same place we met the first time...near the library. I can be there in half an hour."

"Sounds good."

⁂

I got to our spot on campus only a few minutes late, but Tiffany was already there. With her blond hair so much like mine blowing in the wind, I felt a bond with her that hadn't been there before. I hated to give her bad news, but it had to be better than thinking her mother had deserted her. She caught sight of me and smiled, waving me over with surprising resilience.

I picked up that while she was disappointed after talking to me, she wasn't afraid to know the truth. It was the reason she'd hired me, and she wanted to know what had happened. I smiled and sat beside her, grateful to know she could handle what I had to say.

"My mother's dead isn't she?" she asked.

"Yes. She never would have left you otherwise." I began my story, deciding to tell her everything, including how I'd felt Darcy's presence in the dead files room, and in the plaza where she'd worked, pointing me toward Marketing Solutions. "It was there that I found her killer, and since I had blond hair and blue eyes like her, he turned his focus on me."

Tiffany's eyes rounded with shock. "You mean he came after you?"

"Yes." I explained his link to my daughter's school as a substitute teacher and how I thought that may have been how he found his victims. "I don't know for sure, but it seems right."

She was mortified to think he had been one of her substitute teachers and that's how he'd lured her mother away, but shook it off and asked me to continue. I told her about Geoff Parker and his investigation when Darcy first disappeared, then sped forward to his part in helping me track Sean down to the house he'd used to kill them.

"We decided to look for evidence, but it kind of backfired, since Sean recognized Geoff and came back. But I did find the bodies of your mother and the other victims in the attic first. I think she led me there."

I didn't tell her I'd heard Darcy's voice, but I did tell her about the smell of gardenias. "Every time I got close to something important, I'd get a whiff of them. It kind of freaked me out a little. Anyway, Sean caught us and left us chained up in the basement while he proceeded to burn the house down, so I'm afraid her body's gone with the house."

"What? You were chained up in the basement? How did you get out?"

"I was able to call a friend and the police. They got Geoff and me out in time, but Sean got away."

"He's still out there?" she gasped.

"No...they found him this morning. He committed suicide, but left a confession with all of the names of his victims. It will be in the news tomorrow. That's why I wanted to tell you what happened first."

"Wow." She glanced at me with admiration. "You were nearly killed over this. I don't know how to thank you. I have more money..."

"Please...that's not what I want. I feel like your mother did most of the work anyway."

She let out a startled laugh. "It's so funny that you should tell me that because...all these years, I have to tell you...I've felt like she was with me at times. Every once in a while I've gotten a whiff of gardenias too. In fact, just before you came here today, I smelled them again, but I thought it was just my imagination since there aren't any flowers here."

"You don't know how relieved that makes me feel," I said. "I thought I was going crazy, smelling those flowers all the time. I'm so glad you told me."

"Thank you Shelby," she said. "I feel like a huge weight has been lifted from my shoulders." She finally felt closure, but couldn't let go of the grief yet.

"You bet. Would you like me to tell your dad? I can do that for you."

"No. I want to tell him myself. I'll go over there when we're done. But thanks." She chewed her bottom lip, suddenly nervous, before glancing at me with a shy smile. "You might think this is strange but, ever since I met you, I've felt a connection between us. I didn't tell you this before, but when I first saw you walking toward me, for just a tiny second, I thought you were my mom. I mean...a lot younger version, but still her."

She clasped her hands together and glanced at her fingers. "I know it's asking a lot, but would you consider coming to my wedding? I know it sounds crazy, but I just feel like you have a connection to my mom and it would mean the world to me to have you there. What do you think?"

"Oh Tiffany! I would be honored to come." I smiled and put my hand over hers. Her breath hitched and she gave me a tight hug.

"It's this Friday, I hope that won't be a problem."

"Um...I don't think so," I said.

"Great. And you can bring your husband with you."

"Oh...well then, that settles it. We'll be there for sure," I agreed.

"There's one more thing," she said. This time her face went pink with embarrassment. "I know it sounds crazy, but I was out shopping Friday and I found this gorgeous dress. It was something that I just knew my mom would love...so I got it. I don't know why exactly, but I couldn't leave the store without buying it. It's the perfect dress for my wedding, so maybe I thought that if you found her, she could wear it. Now that I know she's gone, do you think you could wear it? Unless it will freak you out...then you don't have to."

"Tiffany...as long as it fits, I'd be happy to wear it. What size did you get?"

"Well, it's kind of funny because after I met you I figured we were about the same size and so that's the size I got. Kind of weird, huh? Anyway...it's a size eight. Will it fit you?"

"Yes," I said, raising my brows. "That's my size."

"Awesome!" She clapped her hands together, then gave me another hug. "I left it in my car. Let's go get it. Oh...and I have invitations so I can give you one of those too."

As we walked to her car, we talked about her wedding and how excited she was to get married. She popped open the trunk and pulled out a large box. She touched the box with reverence and I couldn't wait to see the dress inside. Removing the lid, she pushed aside the tissue and pulled it out to show me.

"Oh my, it's beautiful!" I exclaimed. The gauzy folds of all-over tiered ruffles hung in perfect symmetry over a V-neckline and cap sleeves. The pin-tucked empire waist with a cascade-detail skirt in a light violet color gave it an ethereal feel. I couldn't wait to try it on.

Tiffany held it up to me and smiled. "The color's perfect on you." With a happy sigh, she folded it gently into the box and replaced the lid, then handed it to me. "It's yours. I want you to keep it."

I felt a little guilty taking the dress until I heard her thinking that it hardly made up for the horrible experience I'd been through, but she hoped it helped. I smiled, knowing she had a point, and took the box. "Thanks Tiffany."

"Let me grab an invitation. The wedding's at four o'clock with a dinner and reception to follow." She opened the car door and took out an envelope. "Here you go."

I took it, surprised to find my name already written on the outside. I glanced at her, but she just shrugged, thinking that with my premonitions, she hoped I wasn't too surprised. "And please don't bring a gift," she said. "Just having you there will be enough." Now she was thinking she probably owed me a couple hundred dollars or more, and maybe I wouldn't ask for it if I didn't have to bring a gift.

"Okay," I said with a chuckle. "That should make us even."

Her face flamed with embarrassment, but she laughed to cover it up. "Thanks Shelby, I hope you know how much this means to me."

"You're welcome," I said. "I'll see you in a few days."

I drove home, happy and pleased that I'd helped Tiffany find the closure she needed. I was also a little bit nervous about popping in at her wedding like I was taking her mother's place, but it was her day and I wanted her to be happy. I just hoped everyone else could accept my presence there with a good attitude.

That afternoon, I got the call from Billie I'd been expecting. She begged me to let her come over and do an interview, so I gave in, deciding we could go out on the deck and sit on my new swing to talk. That way, reliving the horror of those moments might not turn me into a blubbering idiot since just thinking about it still gave me the shivers.

She arrived with a two-liter bottle of diet soda which, I had to admit, was a nice surprise. I got some glasses with crushed ice and she raised hers in a toast.

"To Shelby, the best PI I know."

I laughed and we touched our glasses together. "Thanks Billie, but it was close. I almost died." I told her the whole story, except the parts where I heard Darcy's voice and smelled the flowers. I even told her that Ramos rescued Geoff and me, but told her not to put that in the paper. "He'd have to kill you if you did." I was only half-joking. "You can say it was one of the firefighters. That would almost be the truth."

Billie shook her head. "Fine," she agreed. "But someday you're going to have to tell me the story of how you met Manetto and Ramos."

She set her glass down, thinking I certainly had my share of adventures. Then she was suddenly struck with the brilliant idea that she could write a book about me from all of them. Then if I wouldn't tell her any more details, she could make some up, and maybe add a few characters to make it juicy...although she had a sneaking suspicion that the real details were probably better than anything she could come up with. Once she got it in book form, it would probably become a best-seller. If she ever got laid off her job, or decided she needed a change, that's just what she'd do, and she sincerely hoped I'd go along with it.

Yikes! I didn't like hearing that, and I didn't want anyone writing about me. I was in enough trouble already. "So...how's the investigation going with the Attorney General?"

"Haven't you heard?" she asked. "My article ran on Friday, and it caused quite a stir. The city council is asking for a complete investigation into the allegations. Even a few councilmembers have called for his resignation."

"Wow, that's huge. Way to go."

"Thanks. I appreciate your help on that." She was thinking how grateful she was for my help, and hoped I'd help her again.

"So, are you and Dimples still dating? How's that going?"

She blushed a little, transforming from a jaded journalist into a lovelorn puppy. Wow. She had it bad. I sure hoped Dimples felt the same.

"It's good," she said. "Except when I'm on the job I think I probably get on his nerves a little, but otherwise, we're doing great."

"Nice," I said, happy for her. Taking a deep breath, I relaxed back on the swing and closed my eyes. Reliving that horrible night had brought all the fear back and, for some reason, made me a little shaky.

"Hey...are you all right? After everything you've been through...I just can't imagine it."

My chest tightened that she noticed, and sudden tears came to my eyes. I sniffed, but couldn't hold them back. "Wow...I guess I am struggling a little. You know, with my family, I've been trying to make light of it and be strong, but now that you ask...I have to tell you, I really thought I was going to die. It was pretty bad."

Billie handed me a tissue and listened while I poured out my soul. By the time I got done, I felt more like myself. "Thanks. I feel so much better now."

"Sure...that's what friends are for. And don't worry...I won't print a thing about it."

"You'd better not," I said, laughing. Billie said goodbye and I watched her leave. Sharing all of those emotions had drained me, and with the gentle swaying motion of the swing, it wasn't long before I took a nice little nap.

The next day I made a big batch of chocolate chip cookies and divided them onto three plates: one for Dimples, one for Geoff, and the other for Ramos. I took the first plate to Geoff, happy to find him doing well, and even better, his wife wasn't mad at me. After visiting for a few minutes, he handed me a small box with a blue ribbon tied around it. "Here it is. Just like you wanted."

"Thanks Geoff." I'd had a nice chat with him the day after the fire, and tucked this special gift into my purse.

Everyone was jealous of Dimples at the police station, but he was nice enough to share his cookies. It also earned me some extra points with the police chief, so it all worked out well. Even Bates took a cookie and thanked me. Who would have thought that could happen? Best of all, I'd dropped in at a time when no one needed my help, so I could actually leave when I wanted to.

Hoping my luck would hold, I drove to my last stop at Thrasher Development. As I entered the elevator, my stomach clenched with a sudden fit of nerves. I took a deep breath and tried to relax, wondering what was wrong with me. I didn't have anything to be nervous about.

The elevator doors opened and my nerves turned into excitement. I sure hoped Ramos was there so I could get this over with. Jackie sat at her desk and jumped up to give me a hug.

"Shelby! It's so good to see you. Are you all right? We heard about the fire." She was thinking that Joe wasn't happy with me for that, but he'd just have to get over it.

"Yes...I'm fine, just a little smoke inhalation. I brought something for Ramos. Is he around?"

"Yeah, he's with Joe in his office. Why don't you go on back?"

"Okay, thanks."

I hurried down the hall and found the door open, so I knocked as I entered. Uncle Joey sat at his desk, and Ramos stood next to him, holding some papers in his hand. They both glanced up and smiled to see me.

"Shelby! What a pleasant surprise," Uncle Joey said. "Come on in. I'm glad to see you're all right. Come sit down." He motioned to the chair in front of his desk, thinking I looked pretty good for someone who'd nearly died. The way Ramos had taken off like that, only telling him I was in deep trouble, had given him quite a scare. And this time, it didn't even have anything to do with him. What was up with that?

"I just brought you some cookies," I said.

Ramos chuckled, his brows lifting with surprise. He'd forgotten that I'd said I'd make some cookies for him, and was secretly pleased. He couldn't remember the last time anyone had done that. "Nice. What kind are they?"

"Chocolate chip," I said. I set the plate down on Uncle Joey's desk and took off the plastic wrap. Both of them grabbed a cookie and started eating.

"These are great," Ramos said. "Thanks."

"You're welcome," I said. "So...how are things going around here?"

"Pretty well," Uncle Joey said. He was wondering if it was too soon to ask for my help with something. I raised my brow at him and he shrugged. "All right...there is something I need your help with, but it can wait. Right Ramos?"

"Yes," Ramos agreed. He was thinking he might have to fly back to Seattle for a few days. If he found what Manetto was looking for, the job would go smoother if I could help out. But that was something for another day. Right now he just wanted to enjoy his cookie.

I smiled and stood, ready to go home before I got roped into something I wasn't sure I wanted to do. I needed a break for Pete's sake. "Well...guess I'll be going. Enjoy the cookies." I glanced at Ramos, wishing there was a way I could tell him I needed a moment alone with him.

"I'll walk you out," he said, reading the need in my eyes.

"Thanks." Relieved, I smiled up at him and turned to leave. I caught a hint of curiosity from Uncle Joey, but only smiled and waved at him before sauntering out of the room. As we walked down the hall, I glanced at Ramos and whispered. "I have something else for you."

Puzzled, his brows drew together. "Like what?"

"Here...I'll show you." I took the blue-ribboned box out of my purse and handed it to him.

"What's this?" he asked.

"Open it and see," I said.

He glanced down the hall to find Jackie watching us and scratched his brow. "Let's go in the conference room."

I nodded and followed him inside, grateful to have some privacy. He sat on the edge of the table and pulled the ribbon. It came apart and he stuffed it in his pocket. Next, he took off the lid and peered inside, then pulled out a shiny golden wristwatch and studied it.

"It's handmade," I said, excited. "Geoff...the guy with me in the basement...he makes them as a hobby and I got this one for you."

Ramos didn't know what to say. He hadn't expected anything so nice, and it took him by surprise.

"Look at the back."

He turned it over to find the inscription I had Geoff put there for me. *To Ramos, My hero, From Shelby.* "I know you probably think it's corny, but I didn't know what else to say. I mean...I don't know how to thank you for always being there, and I just needed you to know how much it means to me...and to thank you for saving my life...and..."

He reached out and clasped my upper arms in his firm grip. "Babe...it's perfect. Thank you." He caught me up in a tight hug before pulling back to glance at me. His gaze caught mine then traveled to my lips. "I don't know if this is better than a kiss," he growled, "but I'll take it." He smiled that sexy half-smile of his and let me go, then pulled his gaze away as he fastened the watch around his wrist.

Breathless, I took a step back and swallowed. "Well then...good. I'm glad you like it. I guess I'll be going now. See ya." I didn't wait for a response, but hurried out of there, passing Jackie with a little wave. It wasn't until I got in my car that I relaxed. A few minutes later, I shook my head and berated myself for being so nervous. That was just silly. It was Ramos. I didn't have to act that way around him. From now on, I was miss-cool-chick; no more swooning for me.

Still, I needed some friend therapy real bad after all I'd been through, and I couldn't wait to talk to Holly. Even though I'd had a nice chat with Billie, Holly was the only person with whom I could share all the juicy details. I called her on the way to the car and set it up for the next day. Just doing that relieved some of the tension in my shoulders, and I looked forward to spilling my guts.

Friday dawned bright and clear, making it the perfect day for a wedding. I'd only had a few bouts of anxiety since I'd talked to Holly, but the shadow of death still haunted me. It was hard not to think about being locked up in the basement with no way out, but I knew it had to stop, so I pushed it from my mind and decided to enjoy this gorgeous day.

I put on that lovely dress, and it was so fun that I had to twirl around in it a few times. The material floated around me, making me feel beautiful and feminine. Chris donned his black suit, and my heart raced to find him looking so good. He smiled, thinking how good it felt to escort such a beautiful woman.

"That's just what I was thinking...only the other way around...about you I mean."

Tiffany's wedding was held in a beautiful little chapel with stained-glass windows, and decorated with all kinds of flowers and draped material. Chris and I got there early and sat down in the back. A few minutes later, Tiffany's dad approached us and I introduced him to Chris.

"Thank you for coming," he said. "It really means a lot to Tiffany. In fact, she asked if I would come out and find you. Could you go talk to her for a minute?"

"Of course," I said, and followed him to the bride's room. He knocked and opened the door to let me inside.

Tiffany turned, her eyes alight to see me. "Oh Shelby, thanks for coming."

"Tiffany! You are stunning," I said, taking her hands and giving them a squeeze. The silky folds of her dress hung perfectly from her waist with delicate lace overlaying the pin-tucked bodice.

"Thanks. Do you think my mom would have liked it?"

"I'm sure she would." I gave her a careful hug. "Are you ready?"

"Yes."

Just then a slight breeze from the open window touched my skin, bringing with it the scent of gardenias. Tiffany caught her breath and we glanced at each other in wonder.

"Your mom," I said. She nodded, her eyes glistening with tears. I didn't hear any words this time, but got a strong impression that I needed to tell Tiffany something. "I think your mom wants you to know that she's okay where she is and that she loves you."

"Thanks Shelby," she said. "I think you're right."

Her maid of honor came in, so I squeezed her hands and left the room. As Tiffany came down the aisle a few minutes later, I could tell something about her had changed. The dark shadow of sorrow and pain had lifted, leaving her vibrant and happy.

A feeling of peace came over me, banishing the shadow of the last few days, and I realized that even though I'd put on a brave face, nearly dying because of a crazy killer had taken its toll. It had worn me down more than I'd thought. But now that fear was gone, and being here was just what I needed. There were a lot of bad things that happened in this world, but there was also a lot of good, and I needed to remember that.

Thanks Darcy. A hint of gardenias touched my senses and I smiled, knowing I would never smell that flower again without thinking of her.

After the ceremony, we enjoyed a delicious dinner, and Tiffany's family and friends treated us like royalty. It was a relief to be accepted and looked after by virtual strangers. Once the dancing got started, Chris took my hand and led me to the dance floor. He held me close and I enjoyed being in his arms. It was also fun to hear people thinking what a handsome couple we made...and how much in love we looked.

"What are you smiling about?" Chris asked.

"Well...I just heard that we make a great couple. What do you think? Is it true?"

Chris smiled. "Of course." Then his gaze turned pensive, and he couldn't hold the thoughts he'd been trying to shield from me any longer. "Shelby...I know I've haven't always been happy about your whole mind-reading thing. I've had a difficult time of it, and this case...It was bad, and I wished you'd never taken it. But being here with you...I just want you to know how proud I am. These people had a horrible thing happen to them, but look around you. They're celebrating. It's all because of you and I couldn't be prouder."

"Oh Chris...thanks. I know I put you through a lot..."

"Yes you do," he interrupted. "But you're an amazing woman Shelby...and right now, I wouldn't have it any other way." His lips met mine in a gentle kiss, and I was afraid my heart would burst with love for this man. We had come such a long way from the day I started reading minds. It had been so hard on both of us, but now I realized we were closer because of it.

He pulled back and our gazes met, his eyes full of promise and love. "Shall we...

"Go home?" I finished. "You bet."

He took my hand, and I heard my favorite words in his mind... and laughed.

Thank you for reading **Deep in Death: A Shelby Nichols Adventure.** Ready for the next book in the series? **Crossing Danger: A Shelby Nichols Adventure** is now available in print, ebook and on audible. Get your copy today!

If you enjoyed this book, please consider leaving a review on Amazon. It's a great way to thank an author and keep her writing!

NEWSLETTER SIGNUP For news, updates, and special offers, please sign up for my newsletter on my website at www.colleenhelme.com. To thank you for subscribing you will receive a FREE ebook.

ABOUT THE AUTHOR

USA TODAY & WALL STREET JOURNAL
BESTSELLING AUTHOR

As the author of the Shelby Nichols Adventure Series, Colleen is often asked if Shelby Nichols is her alter-ego. "Definitely," she says. "Shelby is the epitome of everything I wish I dared to be." Known for her laugh since she was a kid, Colleen has always tried to find the humor in every situation and continues to enjoy writing about Shelby's adventures. "I love getting Shelby into trouble...I just don't always know how to get her out of it!" Besides writing, she loves a good book, biking, hiking, and playing board and card games with family and friends.

Connect with Colleen at www.colleenhelme.com

Made in the USA
Middletown, DE
07 August 2020